FROSTBORN

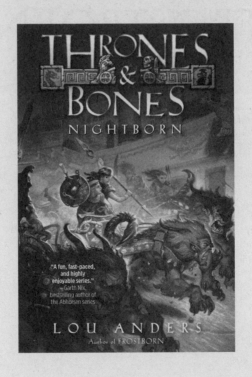

THRONES & BONES

FROSTBORN

LOU ANDERS

illustrations by JUSTIN GERARD

A YEARLING BOOK

Text copyright © 2014 by Lou Anders
Cover art and interior illustrations copyright © 2014 by Justin Gerard
Maps by Robert Lazzaretti; map copyright © 2014 by Lou Anders
Rules of Thrones and Bones Board Game™ copyright © 2014 by Lou Anders

All rights reserved. Published in the United States by Yearling, an imprint of Random House Children's Books, a division of Penguin Random House LLC, New York. Originally published in hardcover in the United States by Crown Books for Young Readers, New York, in 2014.

Yearling and the jumping horse design are registered trademarks of Penguin Random House LLC.

Visit us on the Web! randomhousekids.com

Educators and librarians, for a variety of teaching tools, visit us at RHTeachersLibrarians.com

The Library of Congress has cataloged the hardcover edition of this work as follows:
Anders, Lou.
Frostborn / Lou Anders.
pages cm. — (Thrones and Bones)
Summary: Destined to take over his family farm in Norrøngard, Karn would rather play the board game Thrones and Bones, until half human, half frost giantess Thianna appears and they set out on an adventure, chased by a dragon, undead warriors, an evil uncle, and more.
ISBN 978-0-385-38778-1 (trade) — ISBN 978-0-385-38779-8 (lib. bdg.) — ISBN 978-0-385-38780-4 (ebook)
[1. Adventure and adventurers—Fiction. 2. Dragons—Fiction. 3. Animals, Mythical—Fiction. 4. Mythology, Norse—Fiction. 5. Board games—Fiction. 6. Fantasy.] I. Title.
PZ7.A518855Fro 2014 [Fic]—dc23 2013046709

ISBN 978-0-385-38781-1 (pbk.)

Printed in the United States of America
10 9 8 7 6 5 4 3 2 1
First Yearling Edition 2015

FOR ARTHUR AND ALEX

NORRØNGARD

Wendholm ●

Korjengard ★

THE COLD
SEA

N

W   E

S

0   100   200

Miles

YMIRIA

Trollheim

Gunnlod's Plateau

Ruins of Sardeth

Dragon's Dance
Helltoppr's Barrow

Korlundr's Farm

Bense

Plains of the
Mastodons

SERPENT'S
GULF

Dvergrian
Mountains

ARALAND

CONTENTS

FROSTBORN

The Girl Who Fell from the Sky

Escape was all that mattered. Escape at any cost.

In the skies between one place and another, Talaria gripped the reins of a strange beast so fiercely her knuckles were white. She dug her heels hard into its scaly flanks as the creature banked and turned in the cold night air.

She was a long, long way from home. Talaria had flown for nearly a week. Each time she had landed, to rest or scavenge food, they had found her. Then the chase had resumed.

They had found her again this morning. So she had taken back to the skies and flown to the northeastern-most corner of the world. Here the breath froze in the air, and the land was covered in an unfamiliar whiteness the natives called "snow," and only the hardest of hard peoples lived. Here was nowhere she had ever meant to be.

A bolt of searing heat narrowly missed her. It blew past her head like a spear of white flame. Talaria jerked the reins hard. Her mount veered sharply to the left, snarling at her angrily. It was surly and temperamental and very hard to control, but it knew the danger they were in. It had flown full speed for days and still flew hard. How much longer it could fly, Talaria didn't want to consider.

You'll be the death of me, her mount spoke into her mind.

"I'm sorry," she answered. It was a weak reply, but she meant it.

Another flash of heat. This time she felt the tips of her long black hair singed.

"We might lose them in those forests," she said, glancing down at the trees racing by underneath her.

Not with them right on my tail. We'll never shake them this close.

Her mount was right. It was a reptile. It didn't pretend everything would be okay when it wasn't. It didn't lie or soften its words for the sake of feelings. It had a cold view of things.

A cold view. Talaria felt an idea forming.

Farther ahead she saw the jagged peaks of the Ymirian mountain range—the mountains at the top of the world, or nearly so. There were heavy clouds amid the white peaks.

"We go there," she said, and dug her heels in.

The wyvern growled, but it beat its wings in a mighty burst. They surged forward, just as instinct made Talaria duck. Another burst of flame shot over her head.

Talaria risked a glance behind her. There were three of them. All rode wyverns just as she did. Black-scaled beasts with great, batlike wings and mean, snakelike faces at the ends of long necks. The riders were armored in gleaming brass and black leather. They carried the traditional fire lances of their order. Talaria wore merely her traveling clothes and cloak. She was armed only with her determination. But she carried something else.

It was that something else they were after. It wouldn't do her much good here, but back home it could change her world. For good or for ill. Mostly for ill, which was why she had taken it, and why they had followed her.

It was a straight race now to the mountains. Without armor, she weighed less than her pursuers. It made her mount just that much faster. Below them, the forests of alpine trees were thinning out and giving way to scrub and frozen tundra. The ground was sloping upward as they crossed the border into Ymiria.

Her pursuers refrained from firing their lances now. They wouldn't waste charges when she hovered at the limit of their range. They bent low over the necks of their wyverns to reduce the drag from the wind. Talaria did the same. As cold as she had been, she felt the air grow even colder.

She looked behind her again. She had gained some

distance on her pursuers. The clouds were just ahead. She just might make it. But what was the middle rider—the leader—doing? Talaria saw the woman's hair whipped up in the wind as she lifted off her heavy bronze helmet. She tossed the helmet into the air and it was snatched away, spinning off into the sky. Then she began to unbuckle her bronze chest plate. That too was tossed into the wind. With a sinking feeling, Talaria realized the woman was lightening her load. Saddlebags were cut loose next. Free of the extra weight, her wyvern began to pull ahead of the others.

The woman came into range just as they hit the cloud bank.

Talaria's mount screamed as fire rolled across its left wing. Then they were plunging down and tumbling over and over in the air. All Talaria could do was fight to stay on.

Her wyvern pulled out of the roll. They had lost altitude. Their pursuers were high above, hard to see in the dense cloud. The mount winced. Its wing still beat against the air, but Talaria saw that it was badly injured. Wind whistled through ragged holes burnt in its leathery membrane.

We are going down, her mount spoke. Rather uncharacteristically, it added, *I'm sorry.*

"You can't take my weight anymore," Talaria said. It was a statement, not a question. "Without me, you might have a chance." The mount did not answer. It did not

4

have to answer. Talaria reached a hand to feel the stolen object tucked inside her shirt. Good. It was still there.

"There's no point in us both dying." Talaria stood up in the saddle. The cloud cover just might hide her next action.

What are you doing? the wyvern asked.

"Lead them away from the mountains. With any luck, the snows will have covered me before they realize their mistake and come searching for my body."

You can't be serious.

"They can't be allowed to find it. You know that." Talaria pulled the reins hard, causing the mount to tip sharply to one side, shielding her momentarily from her pursuers' line of sight. Letting go, she tumbled from the saddle. As she fell, she heard her mount's final words in her mind. They carried a note of cold approval.

Die well.

CHAPTER ONE

Thirteen Years Later

"Pay attention, Karn. Today's a big day."

Karn blinked his eyes and mumbled, hoping he'd be left alone. He was focused on the game board balanced on his lap. It was hard enough to keep it level because of all the rocks in the road. Plus, he was concentrating. Karn was playing himself, playing both attackers and defenders. So far, this had led to a succession of stalemates. He was hoping one side or the other would win.

"Karn!"

He looked up from the board. The scenery hadn't changed any since the morning. Or any morning of the last week. Unending forest on the right. The cold waters of Serpent's Gulf on the left. Carts, one of which he rode in. Barrels of cheese and milk and grain. The smelly back ends of the oxen before him. Pofnir glaring at him expectantly from the bench opposite. Nothing worth looking up for.

Pofnir cleared his throat. Out of all the employees and family members who worked the Korlundr farm, right now the former slave turned freeman was Karn's least favorite.

"What?" said Karn.

"Your father expects you to know this, so you will know it," Pofnir replied. "Now pay attention. Six arctic fox pelts equals how many ounces of silver?"

"I don't know," Karn said. "Three?"

"Three?" Pofnir glared. "That's a bit generous. You could get eighteen fox pelts for three ounces!"

Karn shrugged and risked another glance at the board. He moved one of his shield maidens into position beside an attacker, then switched his thinking and immediately started looking for a countermove.

"Karn!" chided Pofnir.

"Two, then," Karn replied without looking up.

"Two? If three get you eighteen, then how do two get you six? Who taught you math?"

"I don't know. You. Um, four?" said Karn. He brought another one of his attackers into position, capturing the shield maiden between the two undead pieces. He took it from the board, pleased with at least one half of his gameplay.

"You'd better listen to him, nephew," said Karn's uncle

Ori, looking up from the book he'd been reading. "Your father expects you to know this. We'll be in Bense tomorrow, and he wants your help with the trading."

At the mention of his father, Karn looked toward the head of their procession. Korlundr rode on his horse at the front, his broad back ramrod straight in the saddle, just as he'd been all week. His blond hair was braided into a long ponytail. His great sword, Whitestorm, hung at his side. He looked like he should be out slaying dragons and fighting trolls, not worrying about fox pelts and cheese.

"My father has a hundred people to do this stuff for him," Karn said. "Can't one of them handle it?"

"It isn't proper," said Ori. "Bartering needs to be conducted by a family member. You'll be expected to do it for yourself when you're the hauld of the farm."

Karn didn't like to think about that. His father was hauld and always would be. The title referred to a farmer whose family owned a farm for six generations or more. Apart from being a Jarl, or High King, it was just about the only rank one could claim in Norrøngard. But there was more to life than farming. There was a whole world out there he longed to see. As it was, Thrones and Bones was his only escape from the sameness of farming life. He looked down longingly at his game board. Then an idea occurred to him.

"Uncle Ori, you can do it!"

Ori smiled. It wasn't a warm smile.

"That's not my lot in life, I'm afraid." He glanced toward where his brother rode up front.

"Ori will have to start his own farm soon, I expect," said Pofnir.

"What do you mean?" Karn asked.

"This is something you would know if you ever looked up from that board game," sighed Pofnir. "Korlundr's Farm has grown as big as it can get. Ori will be given a handful of servants, a portion of the sheep and cattle, and some silver, and be sent off to build his own farm. Probably sometime in the spring."

Ori could be surly, but he had a dry sense of humor that often made Karn laugh. Karn would miss it.

"So, Uncle Ori, you'll really be leaving?"

"It does sound like a dreadful amount of work, doesn't it? All because my twin brother appeared a few measly minutes before I did."

"When you put it that way," said Karn, "it doesn't seem fair."

"My thoughts exactly. Of course, I could have inherited the farm from my brother. But now there's you. You have four older sisters, but even so, you'll have to be the one to bear the burden of leadership. Norrøngard is such an enlightened place."

"Exactly," said Pofnir, oblivious to the sarcasm. "Father to eldest son down through the generations, as pleases the gods. So, pay attention. If you do well tomorrow, I'm sure Korlundr will take you with us to trade with the giants later this season."

Karn sat up at the mention of giants. Meeting actual frost giants would be something different, even if it was intimidating. But Pofnir was still droning on about more mundane matters.

"Now, six ewes, two being two years old and four older, all thick-haired and without any visible bald spots, with their lambs, equals how many cows?"

Karn sighed. He shuffled on the hard wooden bench of the cart.

"I don't know. Three?"

"Three!" screeched Pofnir. "No! Not three. One." Pofnir saw that Karn had turned his attention back to his game. "Oh, for Neth's sake," he swore. Neth was the goddess of the underworld, but her name was often invoked in frustration. "Look, you know I think you spend too much time bent over that unhealthy obsession, but if I agree to play you one game of Thrones and Bones, will you give me thirty minutes of concentration?"

Karn thought about it.

"That's no good," he said. "I beat you too easily."

Pofnir turned expectantly to Ori, who had returned to his book.

"You play him, then," Pofnir told Karn's uncle. Ori shook his head but Pofnir's gaze was insistent.

"Must I?" said Ori. Pofnir nodded.

"Please, uncle," said Karn. "There's only so much I can learn playing myself."

"Oh, very well," said Ori, putting aside his book and leaning forward. "But I have to warn you, Karn, I play to win."

"Isn't that the only way?" said Karn.

"Yes," replied his uncle. "But you'll find that I'm a very poor loser."

A few hundred miles nearer to the frozen crown of the world, another game was playing out.

"You are going to lose, and lose hard, little half-breed," growled one of the nastier players. Thianna glared up at the giant, trying to outstare him. The giant glowered down at her over a large bulbous nose and bushy blond beard. Her eyes were darker than his, just as her hair and skin were darker. It was just one way among many that she stood out from the crowd of giants on the field.

Her fierce determination also set her apart. In principle, Thianna had always hated losing. But even more, she hated the thought of losing to Thrudgelmir. The big oaf was her constant nemesis. He went out of his way to make life in the village miserable for her, every chance he got.

Today the best payback would be beating him fair and square on the playing field. She crunched her feet in the hard snow and waited for the starting signal. She clenched the wooden bat in her hand and steadied her breath.

"Lace my shoes while you're down there." Thrudgelmir snickered. He never tired of making jokes about her height. True, Thianna was only seven feet tall. It was the fault of her mixed blood. Thrudgelmir, however, was a healthy, full-blooded young frost giant. He was easily fifteen feet tall. This meant that her head was level with his belt buckle. Odds were high that she was going to be squished when the game started. None of the giants, least of all Thrudgelmir, could be expected to go easy on her because of her smaller size. If she had half a brain, she wouldn't be playing at all. Frost giants were a tough breed, and so they played tough games. But that was just it. *Frost giants* played tough. If Thianna really was one of them, then she would play tough too. And while the game of Knattleikr might be dangerous, it was also a lot of fun.

"Go!" cried the giantess Gunnlod as she tossed the heavy stone ball high into the air over the field. Thianna didn't wait to see where it landed. She ducked her head and threw herself forward, tucking into a roll. While Thrudgelmir cursed loudly above her, she somersaulted between his legs.

Coming out of her roll, Thianna flipped onto her back. Kicking with her two feet, she struck Thrudgelmir behind both of his knees. The oaf was bent down with his head between his legs looking for her. When his knees buckled, he tumbled right over in a heap.

"Why, Thrudgelmir," she laughed, "I didn't know you could somersault too."

Before the giant could untangle his limbs, she sprang up and leapt back over him, landing just as the ball came down. She whacked it hard with the bat, sending it down the field toward her teammate Bork. He knocked it the rest of the way over the line. First point to her side.

Thianna broke into a quick victory dance.

Thrudgelmir's bat whacked her hard in her calves. Her feet shot out from under her, and she went down in the snow. On instinct, she rolled quickly aside. The bat pounded the snow where she had been. She scrambled to her feet.

"What was that for?" she demanded. Thrudgelmir shook his bat at her as he rose up onto his knees.

"For your cheating!" he roared.

"Cheating?" Thianna was dumbfounded. Knattleikr wasn't a sport with a lot of rules to break. It was pretty much an "anything goes" sort of game. "How was that cheating?"

"No frost giant could have tumbled like that. And this is a frost giant game. So it must be cheating."

Thianna was incensed.

"Just because you're too clumsy to do something doesn't make it illegal!"

"Clumsy?" roared Thrudgelmir, getting to his feet.

"I'll show you clumsy." He swung his bat at her again, but Thianna leapt right over it. Then, as Thrudgelmir's swing was carrying him around, she kicked him hard in the back of the leg and he went down again.

"You're right, Thrudgey," she laughed. "You did show me clumsy."

"Squash you flat," Thrudgelmir spat through a mouthful of snow. Before he could make good on his threat, Gunnlod again yelled, "Go!" The village chieftain tossed the ball onto the field, and Thrudgelmir and Thianna joined the crowd chasing after it.

The Knattleikr match went on in this manner for much of the day. In the end, Thianna's team won with a score of forty-five to thirty-three. She had been involved in at least twenty of the goals. Furthermore, when the injuries were tallied, it was found that there were four broken arms, three busted noses (one of them Thrudgey's), a dozen black eyes, and several missing teeth. This was judged by all to have been a good game.

Karn was nervous. The enormous man staring sternly at him from across the market-stall table wasn't helping. The man stank of the sea. Even though they stood amid a bustling fish market, with dozens of tables piled with the carcasses of sea creatures of every kind, and the salt air from the harbor at their backs, most of the smell seemed to be coming off of him. Not that the smell was the most intimidating thing about him. The man had dirty, wild hair escaping from an imposing helmet of hide and steel. With his bushy black beard, his enormous spear strapped to his back, the ax strapped to his belt, he looked like one of the Norrønir raiders that used to sail across the seas to burn villages in Araland and Ungland. In reality, however, Bandulfr was a longship captain. This meant he was a fisherman, working the waters of Serpent's Gulf. But the notches in the head of his spear, the dents in his helmet, and the chips in the blade of his ax were suspicious.

"Well?" said the big man in a gruff voice.

"I don't know, three?" said Karn.

"Three?" repeated Bandulfr. Karn wondered how he could talk so loudly through clenched teeth. Maybe the words escaped through the black gaps where teeth had been knocked out. "Are you sure?"

Karn looked around at the other stalls on the busy docks of the seaside town of Bense, hoping to find inspiration. He found none. He absolutely was not sure. "Uh, yes," said Karn hesitantly.

Bandulfr smiled.

"Three oxen it is," he said, pounding down a meaty fist on his table.

Beside him, Karn heard the sound of his father slapping a palm to his forehead. His heart sank. He realized he'd gotten it wrong. Korlundr sighed and shook his head, his long blond ponytail swinging like a skittish horse's mane.

Bandulfr chuckled.

"You are right, my friend," he said. "Letting your son conduct the bartering was a great idea. A single barrel of fish for three oxen is the best price I've ever had." Bandulfr slapped Korlundr on the shoulder. Korlundr nodded grimly, then gave his son a crestfallen look.

"Three, son?" Korlundr said softly. "Really?"

Three oxen was obviously a very bad trade. It had been hard enough keeping straight just how many fox pelts equaled what amount of silver. It wasn't fair that he was expected to remember oxen, and fish, and cheese, and barrels of milk. He'd no idea haggling in the markets of Bense could be so complicated.

"Oh well," said Bandulfr, trying to stifle a chuckle. "You can't learn to climb a mountain without falling down a few hills, right?" He reached out to punch Karn playfully in the sternum. Karn winced at the force of the blow, but he gritted his teeth and tried to smile.

"I suppose so," Karn's father said. "We'll get the better of you next season, perhaps."

"Perhaps," said Bandulfr, who had lifted a barrel of assorted fish—mostly haddock, salmon, and coalfish—up onto the table and was now hammering the lid shut to seal it for shipping. "I do hope your brilliant boy will do the negotiating then too."

Karn winced at this. So did Korlundr. Karn realized how much his failure must sting his father's pride.

"If only Karn thought as much about bartering as he does about his board games," Korlundr said.

Bandulfr stopped hammering on the barrel and looked up.

"Board games, you say?"

"Yes," said Korlundr. "Karn is obsessed with them. He's always playing."

Bandulfr peered at Karn again.

"What's your game, son?"

"Thrones and Bones," Karn replied.

"Any good?"

Karn looked up into the big man's eyes. He thought he recognized a familiar glint in them that hadn't been there before. He stifled the urge to grin. The ground suddenly felt a little surer under his feet.

"I think so," he said.

"Sure you do," Bandulfr said dismissively. "What do you know? You play with other children."

"I play with anyone," said Karn, who recognized Bandulfr's bluster. The big man might look like a fierce raider, but he was just another gamer. Karn knew how to handle those. "Anyone man enough."

Bandulfr looked skeptical. Karn dipped a hand in his satchel and withdrew two of his "bones."

Bandulfr whistled. He extended a tentative hand for the playing pieces.

"May I?" This was the first time Bandulfr had bothered to sound polite.

Karn nodded and passed the game pieces to the man. Bandulfr brought them up to his bloodshot eyes to inspect them.

"These are whalebone," he said appreciatively. Karn nodded. The rounded game pieces were carved to resemble little skulls. They were pieces from the attackers' side. The skulls were meant to represent draug, the nasty undead warriors that dwelt in cursed grave mounds and preyed upon the living. Karn was exceptionally proud of his set. Playing pieces would normally be carved from stone or wood or cow bone. Whalebone pieces were much rarer, and therefore highly prized.

Karn dipped another hand in and brought out one of the defenders' game pieces, a gleaming shield maiden. This one was polished marble, but with actual silver inlay. Bandulfr whistled. He studied it a moment, then handed both the pieces back carefully.

Bandulfr lowered the big barrel of fish onto the ground in front of them; then he slapped two stools down on either side. He came out from behind his market stall, producing a checkered game board from somewhere as he did so. He placed the board atop the barrel as he sat and gestured for Karn to take the stool opposite.

"Do you play attackers or defenders?" asked Bandulfr.

"I'll beat you at either," Karn said. "But I prefer the Jarl's side."

Bandulfr grinned, impressed that Karn preferred the defenders. Playing the Jarl's side was generally considered to be the harder position.

"You must really think Kvir's fortune smiles on you, huh, boy?" he said, invoking the god of luck and games of chance.

"Wait, wait, wait," said Korlundr, waving his hands. "Karn and I still have quite a few markets to visit today, if I stand any chance of making back my loss."

Bandulfr grunted. He pointed a thick finger at the board.

"This is serious business, Korlundr. No boy can grow to be a true son of Norrøngard unless he can swing a sword, hurl an insult, or play a good board game."

Karn's father crossed his arms, unconvinced.

"It's okay," Karn said. "Trust me on this. This is my territory." Before his father could object, he looked across the game at Bandulfr. "My father and I will bet you two oxen versus my playing pieces. If I lose, you get my Thrones and Bones set. My expensive whalebone and marble set. If I win, then you agree to give us the barrel of fish for the price of only one of our oxen. And if I win in less than ten turns, then you'll make it two barrels of fish for one ox."

Bandulfr's eyes went wide; then he grinned. He spat a gob of saliva into his hand and held it out for Karn to shake. Karn spat into his own palm and took the big man's hand, sealing the wager with a squishy handshake.

"Well, Korlundr," laughed the fisherman, "I do think there's hope for your boy after all."

Thianna was heading home when she was suddenly lifted high off her feet. Thrudgelmir had found her.

"Let go of me!" she yelled, her feet dangling in the air.

"Shut it, half-breed," he growled back at her. "You think you are so clever, jumping around like a little fox in the snow? Just shows what a freak you are. Giants don't move like that."

"I am a giant."

Thrudgelmir guffawed. He shook her so that her feet swung back and forth.

"Your feet don't exactly touch the ground now, do they?"

Thianna grimaced, glaring into his beady eyes.

"Do they?" Thrudgelmir shook her.

"No," she admitted, teeth rattling.

"So what does that tell you?"

"That you are dumber than you look, Thrudgey," she said, grinning wickedly. Thrudgelmir frowned. He knew that he had the advantage, and therefore he should be the one grinning. If Thianna was grinning, that meant something. But before he could work out what, she kicked him hard. As she was up in the air, her toes were level with a very uncomfortable place.

Thrudgelmir howled. He dropped Thianna, cupping himself and falling to his knees. Thianna didn't wait for him to recover. She turned and bolted.

Thrudgelmir struggled up, hobbling after her.

She risked a glance back. He was having trouble walking, but his face was so red he looked like he could melt snow with it.

"You want to know what real frost giants do for fun, little half-breed?" he roared. "We throw things." He scooped up a boulder the size of her head and hurled it her way. It struck a rock outcropping and shattered. Thianna flinched away from the shards. Realizing she'd seriously angered him this time, she ran faster.

"I'd like to see you lift that rock," he called after her. "Maybe when I catch you, I'll lift you. And toss you right off the plateau."

Thianna's feet slipped on the icy ground. Behind her, Thrudgelmir lobbed another boulder. She was heading for a boulder too, but not to throw it. She'd stashed something there.

Thrudgelmir was gaining. After all, he had the longer legs.

Thianna slid to a halt in the snow. Leaning behind the boulder was her prized possession. Two long, slender shafts of rare wood. Her snow skis. She snapped them on, tightening the laces right up until the moment that Thrudgelmir's shadow loomed over her. As his long arms reached down for her, she kicked off. Thianna shot away. Her furious poling and a slight decline were carrying her off faster than the lumbering giant could run.

"Don't think you're clever!" he hollered at her rapidly retreating back. "Just because you can ski and I can't. It just proves you don't belong here. You'll never belong here. Do you hear me? If you were smart, you'd head downhill and just keep going."

Thianna bit back a response, choking down her emotions. She could beat them at Knattleikr every time, and she could always get the better of Thrudgelmir, but the giants would never accept her as one of their own. It wasn't her fault, her mixed blood. She didn't ask to be a half-breed. She'd cut her human half out in an instant if she could find a way to do it. As she hurtled down the icy slope, she told herself it was just the wind in her eyes making her blink.

"I won, didn't I?" said Karn. He was feeling rather good about himself, his Jarl having broken the siege of draug and escaped the board in less than ten turns. Bandulfr was now obliged to pay them two barrels for just one ox. It had truly been a great game. Across from him Uncle Ori grinned, but his father shook his head.

"He did win, brother," Ori said. "Isn't that the important thing?"

The three of them were squeezed onto benches at

a long table that ran down the center of Stolki's Hall. Korlundr's broad shoulders rubbed people on either side. Everyone was talking and singing and trading clever insults. A few Norrønir were engaged in the time-honored tradition of flinging leftover bones and other table scraps at each other with the intent to wound. Karn and his father and uncle all had to raise their voices to be heard over the din, and the smoke from a large fire pit stung Karn's eyes. For those coming in from isolated farms or smaller towns, he could see how the nonstop nature of Bense's noisy, violent nightlife might prove overwhelming. Not so for Karn, who yearned for a life beyond the family farm. He was loving every minute of it.

Korlundr, however, glared at his younger brother.

"That's not the point," Karn's father said. "There's a good deal more to life than playing games."

"That's right," said Karn, grinning at his uncle. "There's swinging swords and hurling insults."

Ori snickered.

"He's got at least one of those down," his uncle said. "Tell us again what it was that you called Bandulfr right before you beat him."

"A bugger-nosed bulge bottom," said Karn proudly.

"Good one, that," said Ori. He turned to Korlundr. "See? Find your boy a sword and call him a man already."

"For Neth's sake, don't encourage him, Ori," snapped Korlundr. "Karn will be hauld of the farm one day. He needs to grow up."

Ori glared for a moment, then nodded.

"So be it," he said, staring down into his drinking horn. "I will leave you two haulds to it." He got up from the table and walked away. Korlundr watched him go. Karn wondered how his father and uncle could be twins and yet stumble around each other so. Korlundr took a long swig of his mead and then cast the horn aside.

"Walk with me, son."

Karn followed his father. He had to step quickly to catch up with Korlundr, who was shouldering his way out of the crowded room. Generally, Norrønir rose with the sun and went to bed with its setting. They might be the descendants of sea raiders, but they lived a farmer's existence. Trading season saw a break in this routine, but the streets were still unlit at night.

Karn glanced up at the stars in the sky. He dipped his head respectfully to the goddess Manna when he spotted her moon, though its own smaller sister was hidden behind the shining sphere.

Karn trailed his father through the night, their footsteps loud on the planks of wood that lined the larger streets. He felt a knot in his stomach, more complicated than just what the spicy mutton Stolki served could account for. Karn really did love his father. But he wasn't like him. Korlundr was a larger-than-life figure. For him, commanding a hundred people to work a farm came naturally. But it didn't come naturally to Karn. Whatever his father said, a time when Karn was the hauld felt as remote now as Manna and her distant moon.

"Don't listen to Bandulfr," his father suddenly said. "Or Ori. Or any of these fools." Korlundr jerked his chin to take in the boisterous mead halls lining the street. "Few of them have farms as large as ours or the discipline to run them if they had. Don't get me wrong. I'm proud that you beat old Bandulfr at his own game, but not every fisherman and farmer will be a gambler. Life isn't a game of Thrones and Bones. It's responsibility. Commitment. You need to know more than just how to call someone a bugger-nosed bulge bottom if you're to be hauld one day."

"That's just it, Father," said Karn, who found that his mouth was running ahead of his brain. Before he could stop it, he heard himself say, "What if I don't want to be hauld?"

And there it was. The words hung in the air between them under the silent stars.

Korlundr stared at his son then, hard. Then he turned his face away.

"Then pray to the High Father I live long. Because you will be hauld one day whether you like it or not."

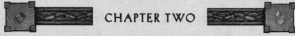

CHAPTER TWO

The Summons

It was late when Karn found his way back to the lodgings where they had rented bunks. He sat down on his bench and bent to unlace his boots.

"Karn?" said his father.

"Hello, Father," he whispered back. He heard his father sit up on his own bench. Even in the near pitch-dark, Korlundr was such a solid, imposing presence.

"I'm sorry we had words," his father began. "Karn, Korlundr's Farm isn't just any farm. I'm not even the Korlundr it's named for. Being a hauld means that we possess a farm that's been in the family for six or more generations."

"I know," said Karn.

"I don't think that you do. Oh, you understand the words. But you don't really think about what they mean."

Karn thought he knew what they meant well enough. Korlundr's Farm had been founded by his great-great-great-great-grandfather, who was also named Korlundr.

"When we die, son, we go into the earth, down to the great cavern to be with our foster mother, Neth. We give up our earthly attachments then. It isn't right to do otherwise."

Karn knew exactly what his father left unsaid. Those dead who clung too tightly to their worldly treasures often refused to go down to Neth's caves. Instead, they became draug—"After Walkers"—horribly rotting corpses that dwelt in barrows jealously guarding their wealth. Karn nearly jumped when Korlundr placed a hand on his shoulder.

"But that doesn't mean that we give up our love for our families, Karn." His father's warm hand was reassuring. "My father waits down there, son, as does his father, and his father's father. They're all watching me now, seeing what sort of man I've become. One day, I'll join them, and I'll have to account for how I've managed Korlundr's Farm, and all who depend on it for their livelihood, to say nothing of the animals. Being a hauld is a great responsibility. Sometimes I think you want the opposite, a way out of responsibility, not a way into it."

Karn shifted uncomfortably. From imagining draug in

the dark, he'd gone to imagining a host of dead relatives all peering up at him and sticking their noses into his business. He wondered how far from Korlundr's Farm you had to go to get away from their scrutiny.

"When I go into the earth, Karn, I want to know that I'll be able to look up and be proud of you."

"That's a long time away," said Karn, finally shaking off his father's hand altogether. He didn't want to think about a time when his father wouldn't be around.

"Fortune and fate don't always go hand in hand, Karn. You know that it's said that the gods' end may be written in the runes, but not even they know the path to get there."

Karn had heard the death-and-destiny talk before. He yawned loudly, hoping his father would get the point.

"I'll see you in the morning, Father," he said, lying down heavily on his bench and making a show of rolling over. Maybe tomorrow he could find someone in Bense who could give him a good game of Thrones and Bones. It was all well and good to talk about destiny and responsibility, but board games were serious business.

Thianna didn't come home until well past sunset. She slid open the ornately carved stone door in the cliff wall as carefully as she could. Softly, she tiptoed down the hallway to her bedroom cavern. Her caution only made her feel worse. Being able to tiptoe at all was just another trait that marked her as different. No giant could ever step this softly. Only a sneaky little human could.

Thianna wanted to slip into the pile of furs atop her block of ice as fast as possible. She had had enough of this day and wanted to put it behind her quickly. Sadly, that was not to be.

"Is that you, Thianna?" a deep, rumbly, but pleasant sort of voice called. Thianna sighed. "I suppose you could answer, 'Who else could it be?'" the voice went on. "And while it could be any number of persons, I confess that it is extremely unlikely that it is anybody else but you. So I'll amend my words to 'Hello, Thianna,' if you'll permit me."

"Hi, Dad," Thianna called out. Some people might find it annoying, but she found her father's rambling way of talking endearing.

"Hello, Thianna," her father replied. "It would please me if you could come talk to me before you knock off for the night."

So much for ending the day quickly. She continued past her bedroom to a cavern farther on, where Magnilmir kept his workshop. Thianna stopped in the archway, taking in the familiar sight of her father in the flickering candlelight.

Magnilmir was sitting on a stool at his workbench, but he turned toward her as he saw her approach. Thianna saw his carving tools and several pieces of ivory spread out before him on the ice tabletop. She was sad to see that the ivory was untouched. Magnilmir's elbows were propped on the table and he was rubbing his great knuckles over and over in his palms. He did this when he was distracted or concerned.

Magnilmir opened his arms, beckoning her to him. She came forward and let him embrace her in a great bear hug, disappearing in his bushy red beard.

Magnilmir stayed seated so that he could look his daughter in the eye. Large even for a giant, Magnilmir was eighteen feet tall, a good eleven feet taller than she was, so even seated, his face was a little above hers.

"I understand, er, I mean, it's come to my attention . . . that is, I was told . . . that you got into another scrape with Thrudgelmir today."

"Who told you that? Was it Eggthoda?" asked Thianna, naming an older giant that was on friendly terms with her father. "She's not telling the truth. Not all of it."

Magnilmir shook his head.

"Everyone is talking." He chuckled softly. "Apparently the stupid lad still can't walk straight." Magnilmir swallowed his laugh and tried to look stern.

"It wasn't a fight exactly," said Thianna. "Anyway, it wasn't my fault. It just set him off that I beat him at Knattleikr."

"He has been beaten at Knattleikr before," said her father. "He's really a rather unexceptional player, if you ask me. Actually, he's a poor player even if you don't ask me. Just the same. Anyway, losing a ball game hardly seems cause for a fight."

Thianna wasn't sure she agreed with that. She didn't like to lose at anything. But she hadn't lost.

"I'm so much faster than he is. I can jump around in ways that he can't. He's just a big, clumsy—"

"Giant?" her father suggested.

Thianna dipped her eyes for a moment. She picked up a piece of ivory, then set it down again.

"He hates me because I'm not a giant."

Magnilmir turned his daughter to face him.

"You *are* a giant, Thianna. You absolutely are a giant. It is simply not all that you are."

Thianna turned away from her father's gaze. She looked up at a ventilation shaft tunneled through the roof. In the daytime, its angle would allow sunlight to fall on her father's workbench. Looking through it now, she could glimpse a handful of gleaming stars in the night sky.

"I wish that it were. I wish I was all giant and nothing else."

She didn't turn toward her father, but she could hear the shifting of leather and furs as he sank into himself, as if he were sighing with his whole body.

"Come with me," he said after a time. He didn't wait for her, but rose and walked out into the hallway leading deeper into the mountain. He unbarred their rear door and led her into the larger network of natural caverns inside the mountain.

They walked along an icy ledge in silence. The plateau was the outer face of the village, but the bulk of the settlement was inside the rock and ice. To their right, Thianna could hear the rush of water in the river that flowed through a small canyon inside the cave, though it was too dark to see down into its depths. The subterranean river gave the village a constant source of fresh water, as well as blind cave fish. The river, though, was also treacherous, and spilled into tunnels too small for a frost giant to move in. Once, a giant had fallen in and the current had carried him inside one, only to wedge him against a low roof, where he drowned. They found his hat far away on the other side of the mountain, where the river emerged.

They crossed a bridge of ice to a ledge on the opposite side and Thianna frowned. She knew where they were going. The Hall of the Fallen.

At the great vaulted entrance to the cavern, Thianna squared her shoulders and stepped inside.

The hall was brightly lit at all hours by magical fires that gave a cold blue light but no ice-melting heat. They walked past scores of shadowy figures glimpsed beneath sheets of ice. After a time, they stopped at one.

Magnilmir waved his hand through the air and the frost on the ice wall faded. The wall became transparent, as clear as crystal. They both looked at the figure entombed inside.

"Hi, Mom," Thianna said.

Her father said nothing. Just closed his eyes and bent to lay his forehead against the wall. A foot beneath the ice, Thianna saw her mother, as beautiful as the day she died. The Hall of the Fallen was where all the deceased members of the village were interred. It was an honor, Thianna supposed, for a human to be placed there.

"Once upon a time," Magnilmir began, speaking in a deep, soft voice, "a giant looked up into the sky to see a human woman falling from the clouds. And he caught her."

Thianna bit down on her lip. She knew this story by heart, by all of her heart, but she wouldn't dream of interrupting.

"Her name was Talaria, and that was all of her background she would ever tell him. The woman pleaded with the giant to shelter her in his village. He did this despite the objections of several other giants. It wasn't long before his combination of strength and honor won her over. Or maybe it was just his sense of humor. I'd like to think it was his good looks, but I'd like to think a lot of things. At any rate, they fell in love. They had a child they named Thianna, after her mother's people, whoever they were. For a time, the giant was the happiest giant in the world. But even the ice atop the world will melt one day. . . ."

Magnilmir turned to his daughter and knelt down. He placed a hand on her shoulder.

"There is a human woman under that ice, Thianna. A tiny, little human woman, smaller even than you. And that human woman means more to me than all the giants of Gunnlod's Plateau and all the giants of the world, frost and fire and earth. And I won't have you disrespect her or her kind."

"Father, I—"

"Quiet," he said in a rare stern voice. When Magnilmir stopped rambling, it meant he was serious. Then he reached inside the furs of his vest and fumbled around. When he withdrew his hand, he clutched something small within his fist. At first, Thianna thought it might be one of his carved ivory pieces, but its craftsmanship was more delicate than he could work, and it was made of metal, not ivory or stone.

"Take it," he said, holding the object out to her.

"What is it?"

"It was hers," he said by way of answer. "Something of her culture, of your culture."

"I—"

"Take it!"

Thianna did so.

"I believe it is a drinking horn," Magnilmir said. "The tip was cut off, so I mended it. I plugged it with ice."

"I don't know how good a cup this will make," she said.

"It doesn't matter," said her father. "You will carry it with you."

"I don't want—"

"You will carry it. Perhaps having something of hers will awaken you to your full self."

Thianna saw the pain in her father's eyes. As much

as she hated her human half, she hated the pain she was causing him more.

"I will carry it," she agreed.

Sunrise found Thianna sitting on the very edge of the plateau, dangling her feet over the cliff. The light of the new day set wind howling through the mountains. She paid the wind no mind. Instead, she stared at Talaria's horn in her hands.

"Oh, troll dung," she spat. Her body heat, hatefully so much hotter than a pure frost giant's, had melted the ice plug in the end of the drinking horn.

She wished she had the guts to toss it off the plateau. What good was a broken drinking horn except to remind her that she didn't fit in?

Thianna ran her fingertip around the hole in the narrow end. It didn't look damaged. The hole was smooth, with a slight lip. The details were probably too fine for Magnilmir's eyes. Maybe it wasn't a drinking horn at all? Maybe it was a horn, just not one meant for holding liquid.

Thianna drew in a great breath, filling her lungs with the mountain air. She gazed around at the peaks of Ymiria, then stared due south to the world of humans beyond.

She placed the horn to her lips. She blew long and hard and strong.

There was no sound. *Nothing*. Not even a squeak. She blew several more quick blasts. Nothing.

"Stupid thing," she said. "What good is a horn that doesn't work?" Thianna raised her arm to toss it off the cliff, but then she hesitated, remembering her father's face. She put it back into a satchel at her waist and stared down the mountain at the clouds below. "Stupid, useless thing," she said again.

Thousands of miles away, far beyond the borders of Ymiria or any of its neighbors, a noise not meant for human—or giant—ears rang out. And thousands of miles away, countless hordes of scaly creatures howled.

CHAPTER THREE

The Woman in Bronze and Black

Karn was back in Stolki's Hall, killing time. Though the city of Bense held its share of excitement, Karn found bartering to be a tedious affair. So while his father's hirelings loaded the carts with their newly acquired goods and harnessed the few remaining oxen, Karn busied himself with his favorite pastime. He was playing Thrones and Bones with a dwarf named Gindri.

Gindri was a traveler from the Dvergrian Mountains who visited their farm once or twice a year, selling his services as a healer, metalsmith, and general handyman. He was always good company, though this was the first time Karn had ever played him in a board game. Unfortunately, Gindri was proving disappointingly easy to beat.

"Check," said Karn with smug satisfaction. He had

spied an exit from the board for his Jarl and could win in the next turn if Gindri wasn't careful. There was one move the dwarf could make to block him, but he didn't seem to see it. Gindri had been playing poorly the entire game, taking the obvious moves and missing the subtler ones.

"Do you concede?" Karn asked, grinning. The dwarf held his eyes for a moment, then broke out into his own smile.

"Only that you are about to get your butt well and truly kicked," Gindri said. He laughed, which shook his broad frame and made all the bits and bobs of metal he had woven into his clothing jangle like wind chimes.

"I don't think you see the situation you're in," said Karn, but Gindri reached across the table quick as lightning. His large hand came to rest on a draug on the far side of the board, which he brought into play now for the first time. Gindri placed the piece alongside Karn's Jarl, sandwiching him between the draug and a hostile square. Karn was captured. Grinning, the dwarf plucked Karn's Jarl from the game.

"I win," he said.

Karn stared at the board. He was impressed. He was also a bit miffed. He rarely lost. "Well done," he said sincerely. At least they hadn't been betting anything.

"Oh, it was, if I do say so myself," said the dwarf.

"But—how did you . . . ?"

Gindri hopped to his feet.

"Come with me," he said, and led Karn across the room to the bar where Stolki served his customers. Gindri was little more than half Karn's height, but he was almost as wide as he was tall, so he still cut an imposing figure even amid all the Norrønir crowded into the room. Plus, Gindri wore antlers shoved into his hat.

Gindri reached up over his head to the bar and rapped on it loudly until he had Stolki's attention.

"What'll it be?" said Stolki, leaning forward and then rearing away just as quickly, avoiding an antler poke in the eye in the nick of time.

"Water. Two bowls of it, please," said the dwarf.

"Water? That's it?" asked Stolki.

"Yes, and quickly," barked the dwarf. "I have a lesson to impart."

Stolki shrugged and set two bowls on the tabletop, pouring water from a jug into each.

Gindri rummaged around inside his heavy fur cloak. Then he brought both hands out, closed into fists. Karn wondered what he was grasping.

"Place your palms under my hands, Karn," he said.

"What for?" Karn asked.

"Just do it. Don't they teach you to listen to your elders?"

Karn placed his palms under Gindri's fists. Gindri winked and opened his own hands, dropping two identical stones into Karn's open palms. Or nearly identical. One stone felt warm, while the other was icy cold.

"One is giant-cooled," said the dwarf. "The other is dwarf-heated." Spells like this were often used to help preserve or heat food. The people of the mountains were capable of such useful magics, which humans couldn't master. "Squeeze them both tight for a moment," Gindri said, and Karn did as he was told.

"Now put the stones down," said Gindri, "and place your hands in the water."

"In the water?" Karn asked.

"Yes," said Gindri. He grabbed Karn's wrists and plunged them into the bowls. One bowl of water felt hot, almost painfully so, while the other bowl was chilly.

Karn frowned. He had seen water from the same pitcher being poured into both bowls, and yet their temperatures were very different. Or were they? It was his hand that had held the hot stone that now felt cold while his hand that had clutched the cold stone felt hot. Had the dwarf somehow magicked the bowls as well? Karn looked up and saw Gindri smiling at him.

"The water hasn't changed temperature, has it?" Karn asked. "I just think it has because of what my hands each felt before?"

"Never trust appearances," said Gindri with a smile. "You bring false assumptions with you. You see a dwarf play a poor game of Thrones and Bones and you let your guard down. You should have considered that I was leading you into a trap. As old as I am, don't you think I've played my share of board games?"

Karn nodded. The Stone Folk were long-lived and Gindri was rumored to be older than most. He should have watched the board, not the absurd antler hat bobbing across from him. Next time, he'd pay more attention to his opponent, not just to their moves.

"Little wisdom from a little man," said a new voice. Karn and Gindri both looked up.

A woman stood above them. She was tall, dark-haired, dark-eyed, and olive-skinned. She elongated her vowels in an odd way, a strange accent that Karn had never heard. She was clearly not a Norrønur. She wore a bronze breastplate that was more finely sculpted than any armor Karn had ever seen. It was cast to look like the body underneath it. Karn could see every muscle in its metal abdomen. It even had a navel engraved on the stomach. Below this metal torso, straps of black leather hung down over a black tunic. The woman's knees were bare despite the cold northern temperatures, though she had made a concession to the weather by wearing fur boots and a fur cloak. Under one arm, she clasped a bronze helmet with a black mane. There was a sword at her side and also a long lance slung on her back.

Karn was sure he'd never seen anything like her before. Her clothing and weapons were intriguing. They hinted at faraway places and grand adventures more interesting than life on a northern farm, but there was something haughty and dangerous about her too. Karn didn't like the way she had dismissed Gindri because of his height.

He had misjudged Gindri himself, but he hadn't been quite so rude about it. Perhaps that was why Karn surprised himself by speaking up.

"A little wisdom is better than none at all," he said. "My father taught me truth is where you find it." The woman's eyes narrowed. She gave him a cold look. Then she smiled, but it didn't reach her eyes.

"But of course." She took a step back and raised her voice, speaking to the whole room. "I am Sydia," she said. It was an odd name. Karn thought that it sounded like the ancient names of the old Gordion Empire. "I'm looking for some truth now," Sydia continued. "I'd be willing to reward any who could help me find it."

"What truth is that?" called Stolki.

"Something that was lost years ago," she told him before turning again to Karn. "Perhaps as long ago as this boy is old. Perhaps near the mountain range to the north."

"Ymiria," said Karn. "No one lives there." Gindri coughed at this, and Karn dipped his head apologetically. The dwarves were originally of Ymiria, before they had been driven from their mountain halls. "Humans don't live there anyway."

The woman raised an eyebrow.

"Trolls, giants, a few goblins, but no humans."

"Trolls, goblins," she said, still drawing out her vowels. "And giants. Boy, tell me about these giants."

Like a bird of prey, she leaned into Karn, but he squared his shoulders and stood his ground.

"Are they deceitful?"

"Deceitful?" repeated Karn.

"I've never trusted them," said a voice. He spun around and saw his uncle Ori. What was with everyone sneaking up on him today? "They look dumb as rocks, but they are far too shrewd when it comes to bartering."

"You trade with them, then?" asked Sydia.

Uncle Ori nodded. "From time to time. My brother is weird that way."

"There's nothing weird about trading with the giants," said Karn defensively. "Father says any good trade makes a good trader."

Uncle Ori glanced at his nephew.

"Speaking of your father, Karn, it's more than time to go."

Karn turned to say goodbye to Gindri, but found the dwarf studying Sydia appraisingly. There was something cold and dangerous in Gindri's look as well, but when the dwarf felt Karn looking at him, he gave the boy a wink. Karn said a quick goodbye as the mysterious woman began speaking quietly with Stolki.

As they were leaving the mead hall, Uncle Ori stopped at the door.

"Hold up, Karn. I think Stolki has given me the wrong change for my meal. You head on, and I'll catch you up."

Karn suppressed a sigh. Uncle Ori was known to be a bit cheap, and Karn didn't want to watch him haggling shamelessly with Stolki over next to nothing. Karn left the mead hall, but glancing behind him saw his uncle approaching the woman Sydia. Karn was wondering what that could be about when the door to the hall closed.

He debated going in after his uncle when something hissed loudly behind him. Karn jumped and spun around. The monster that reared in his face made him jump again. A black leathery head on a serpentine neck, like a giant snake, loomed at him. He scrambled backward until he hit a wall.

Karn didn't normally carry a sword, but he wished he had one today. Trying to keep at least one eye on the hideous face, he looked around for a stone or a stick.

The creature's black beady eyes darted to where Karn was looking, then to his face. Karn felt a trickle of cold sweat.

Cruel laughter broke out around him. A woman's voice called something in a language Karn didn't speak. The creature hissed once more; then the long neck withdrew, pulling the head back.

The creature's neck connected to a body slightly larger than that of a horse. It was some sort of reptile, with two wings and two legs, and Karn saw that opposite the long neck it had an equally long, very vicious-looking barbed tail. The creature also wasn't alone.

There were three of them, all hissing and bobbing their heads threateningly, and two of them had women riders. It was the riders that had laughed at him. The women were dressed identically to Sydia, with sculpted bronze breastplates and black tunics. They wore their bronze helmets on their heads, their black manes fluttering in the slight wind coming in off the sea. Each bore a long lance. The shafts were entirely metal, rather than wood, and instead of a spearpoint, the end had a small opening. They were black in color but decorated with strange red runes that suggested flames.

"Sorry if our mounts frightened you, boy," said one of the riders with the same strange accent as Sydia's. Karn didn't like her tone any better either.

"I'm not afraid," he said, hoping he sounded like that was true. He jerked his chin toward the creatures where they snarled and pawed at the mud. "What are they?"

"Wyverns," said the other rider. "Do you know what they are?"

Karn shook his head.

"I've heard . . . I don't know."

"Maybe you just call them 'monsters,' boy," said the first woman. Karn could see the sneering curl to her lip. He realized they were with Sydia, and the fact that they were waiting out here with the animals while she went inside probably meant that they were her juniors. Just bored lackeys, left outside to mind the beasts, trying to frighten someone for fun. They had backed him up against a wall. It wasn't a strong position, like having one of his shield maidens backed against a hostile square in Thrones and Bones. It was time to take control of the game.

"Really, I think they're too small to be called

'monsters,'" he said, deliberately stepping away from the wall. "I doubt either of you have ever seen a real monster."

"We've seen monsters," said the second rider, her voice strangely flat.

"Not like we have here," said Karn, noticing for the first time the chill bumps on both women's exposed arms and legs. Wherever they were from, they weren't used to this climate. "We know that you southerners are soft. You must be, coddled in your nice, warm world. These 'wyverns,' as you call them, aren't half the size of a proper linnorm. Just shrunken little worms, dried up in the sun. Like those grapes I've heard you grow."

One of the beasts hissed at him then. Did it understand the insult? Karn wondered if maybe the mounts were more intelligent than they seemed. But he refused to let up.

"Why, here we have serpents the size of sailing ships. Or haven't you ever heard of Orm Hinn Langi, Orm in the Blasted City?"

"Orm?" said the first woman. "There was some legend about—"

"About Orm," said Karn, smiling. "Orm the Great Dragon. Orm the Largest of All Linnorms. The king of all serpents. Orm who swept in and ate an entire city and claimed its ruins for his den." They were all watching him now, riders and mounts.

"How big is this Orm?" asked the second woman, her swagger gone.

"Orm is bigger than any ship. Bigger than a small village. Orm would eat all three of your wyverns for breakfast and still be hungry for their riders."

"Where is Orm now?" asked the first woman. She was clearly nervous.

"He sleeps," said Karn. "In the ruins of his last meal. But he doesn't like to share the skies with anyone. If I were you, I'd keep an eye out. Next time you fly, I mean. If Orm sees you, he just might decide you would make a nice snack."

"Enough," said a voice behind him. Sydia had left the mead hall. "Stop harassing the locals. Some of them are actually proving useful."

Sydia marched passed Karn and mounted her wyvern. She took up the reins and turned to her two underlings. They threw Karn nasty looks as their mounts began to extend their wings. Karn forced himself to match their stares.

"Watch your backs when you fly," he said. "Orm is always hungry."

Sydia cast a scornful look at Karn. "We fly."

The wyverns beat their wings, kicking up a cloud of dust. All three riders took to the skies.

"She doesn't like me," said Thianna.

"She likes you just fine," Magnilmir replied.

"I don't like her, then. She's cold."

"She is a frost giant. We are all cold."

"You know what I mean."

Thianna stood with her father outside a modestly carved stone door that opened onto Gunnlod's Plateau. Her father had brought her here under protest. Loud and constant protest.

"Eggthoda will teach you important things," he said.

Thianna wasn't so sure. Thianna thought Eggthoda was as gruff as giants come, though it was true that the giantess had never been unkind to her. Quite the opposite, in fact. The giantess had never married. And Thianna's father had never remarried. But there were things in life that were made easier if you had a partner, so Eggthoda and Magnilmir helped each other with domestic duties.

Magnilmir stared over the mountains. He seemed to look past the snows to the lands beyond. Thianna thought he might be imagining the mysterious land of her mother's birth. Finally, he turned to her and knelt.

"Eggthoda will teach you lessons that will assist you in finding your place in the world," Magnilmir said. Thianna thrust her chin up.

"My place is here," she replied.

"Yes, of course. But don't you think you might want to see the rest of the world someday?"

"I can see the top of it from here," said Thianna, deliberately putting her back to the cliffside and facing the mountain. "Everything else is just downhill."

Magnilmir shrugged. He rose and knocked upon

Eggthoda's door. It opened after a moment, and there she was. Big, bulky, and brusque.

"Hello, Thianna," said Eggthoda. Thianna grumbled something in reply. If the giantess took offense, she didn't show it. "I'm just applying a frost charm to a batch of mugs," Eggthoda continued, "but if you give me a minute, I'll be right with you."

"Magic?" Thianna said, brightening. The entire village of frost giants knew only a few spells between them, and Eggthoda was the one who knew most of them. As a result, Thianna regarded even small magics as mysterious and intriguing. Eggthoda beamed. "Perhaps you would like to help me with them?"

"Could I?" said Thianna, her earlier resentment forgotten.

Eggthoda nodded and held her door open. Thianna rushed inside. Her house was modest compared to Thianna's home. Where Magnilmir's walls were finely worked, Eggthoda's were crudely tunneled. Rough shelves carved out of the stone walls held a dizzying array of cooking pots, drinking mugs, boxes, and storage chests. Eggthoda bought the containers from the humans down south, then enchanted them. Her magical hoarfrost would keep cold whatever food or drink was placed inside and preserve food through the summer months.

Eggthoda put her hands to either side of a small metal cup and closed her eyes. She began to mumble, and Thianna strained forward to hear her.

"Skapa kaldr skapa kaldr skapa kaldr skapa kaldr," she murmured.

Thianna started as twin puffs of whiteness traveled from Eggthoda's palms to the mug. The inside of the mug frosted over. Eggthoda sat back and opened her eyes.

"Amazing," said Thianna.

"You like?" asked Eggthoda.

Thianna nodded. "And that will keep it cold forever?"

"What?" said the giantess. "Oh no. Just for a year, that's all."

"What happens then?"

"It wears off."

"Oh," said Thianna.

"I'll let you in on a secret," said Eggthoda, bending her neck down to the girl. "The longer I chant, the longer it lasts. It could last forever if I held the chant long enough, but I cut it off after a year's worth."

"Why?" Thianna couldn't imagine putting a time limit on such useful magic.

"Repeat business," explained the giantess. "Why sell someone the last ice chest they'll ever need? I want to make sure they come back to trade next year."

"Ah," said Thianna. Perhaps she could learn more from Eggthoda than she originally suspected.

"Can you teach me to do the cantrip?" Thianna asked.

The giantess smiled. "That and more," she said. As they set to it, Thianna was so absorbed that she didn't even notice her father had left.

After that, Thianna visited Eggthoda every afternoon. She practiced summoning the hoarfrost, and Eggthoda taught her about the other peoples who called Ymiria home besides the giants at Gunnlod's Plateau. The mountain range was also home to trolls, a small remnant of goblins, and other, stranger creatures. Thianna learned which were inclined to be friendly and which were inclined to be dangerous, and what to say to shift that inclination one way or the other.

One such day Eggthoda took Thianna with her higher up the mountain than Thianna had ever been. The air was so thin here that even as someone born and raised on Gunnlod's Plateau, she felt her breathing grow shallow and her head go light. As they picked their way over sharp rocks and scaled steep inclines, Eggthoda made Thianna practice a strange, high-pitched warbling whistle. The giantess would not tell Thianna what the whistling was for, but she insisted that she get it right. Thianna was growing irritated with both the whistling and the climbing when they came to a cave, little more than a small tunnel in the snow.

"Whistle now," Eggthoda said, "as loud and long as you can."

Thianna let out a long blast in the high mountain air.

"Well?" she said.

"Wait for it," Eggthoda replied.

"Nothing's happening. What's supposed to happen?"

"Shhh."

Suddenly the wind picked up around them. Flurries of snow were caught up into the air, but instead of blowing in a single direction, they circled around and around in tight little whirls. Thianna stared at the snow flurries. There seemed to be several separate little vortices spinning and dancing around the girl and the giantess, almost as if they were alive.

"Whistle again," Eggthoda said.

Thianna whistled, and more snow was suddenly swept up into the air. The vortices grew thicker with the white powder, and as they did, they seemed to take definite shapes.

Thianna gasped. Three long-tailed creatures spun in the air around her. They were like the eels that her father very occasionally brought back from trading with the peoples down the mountain. But these creatures had no flesh. Their bodies were defined entirely by the flurries of snow.

"What are they?" Thianna asked, her voice full of wonder.

"Frost sprites," said Eggthoda. "Elemental creatures of pure cold. They are always here, invisible, but hoarfrost lets us see their shape." The giantess smiled and spread her large hands. She lowered her eyelids and chanted, "Skapa kaldr skapa kaldr skapa kaldr skapa kaldr." As the hoarfrost spread from her open palms, the frost sprites grew more substantial.

"They're wonderful," said Thianna, laughing as one of the sprites coiled around and through her legs.

"Yes," said Eggthoda, "but they can be very dangerous too. Call to them in the manner that they respect, and they will appreciate and respond to you."

"Skapa kaldr skapa kaldr skapa kaldr skapa kaldr," said Thianna, thrilling as more hoarfrost flew from her hands. The sprite that wrapped around her legs coiled up to her arm and twisted in obvious pleasure.

"All creatures behave according to their nature," said Eggthoda. "Find out what their nature is, and you can deal safely with them."

Thianna nodded. She thought of Thrudgelmir and Eggthoda, their natures so clearly defined. Spiteful bully. Patient teacher. Then she thought of her own nature, child of two cultures. Undefined. "Skapa kaldr skapa kaldr skapa kaldr," she said, turning her palms inward and pressing them into her chest. She hoped to freeze away her human half, though she feared it was impossible.

CHAPTER FOUR

The Unwelcome Intruder

"Wake up, Karn. Time to get up."

Karn blinked his eyes and stared into the grinning face of his elder sister Nyra.

"Go 'way," he muttered, rolling over to face the wall. He grabbed a fistful of the fur pelt he slept on and shoved it against his ears, trying to shut out the sound of shuffling and scuffling that was the Korlundr household starting to awaken.

"Mother says you've slept enough," said Nyra, pounding him on the back. Karn grumbled at her.

"Come on, Karn," she teased, prodding him again. "No lamb for the lazy wolf."

"I don't want any lamb," Karn moaned.

"You know what I mean."

Karn shut his eyes and gave a loud pretend snore.

"You're not fooling anyone," Nyra said.

Karn let loose a second snore, louder than the first.

"Have it your way," his sister said. He heard her skirts swishing as she stood. Was she going to leave him alone?

Suddenly, Karn was tumbling into the air as Nyra yanked the fur pelt off the bench. He fell to the ground, landing awkwardly on the dirt floor, then stumbled to his feet to the sound of Nyra's giggles. He started to scowl but saw that she was rolling his sleeping furs and stowing them in the basket under the bench. All around Karn, servants and family members were doing the same.

At the far end of the longhouse, the goats had begun bleating in their pen, adding to the growing din. He saw Pofnir stoking the fire pit in the center of the room, brightening the house and sending a fresh coil of smoke wafting to the hole in the roof.

"No lamb for the lazy wolf," the freeman admonished him.

"I'm up, I'm up," he muttered. "Why is everybody obsessed with wolves?" Karn staggered over to a row of rock slabs that ran across the floor from one wall to the other. He lifted one of the slabs, exposing a small channel of running water. Karn rubbed his hands in the cold water, then splashed some on his face. The sharp chill made him wince and shake his head. "That did it," he said. As his senses roused, his nose suddenly took in the jumbled smells of animal musk, human sweat, and woodsmoke that defined life on Korlundr's Farm. "I'm really up."

"Good," said Nyra. "Mother says it's your turn to slop the pigs."

Karn grumbled at that—he hated slopping pigs—but he went to the fire pit and gathered up the buckets where the scraps of last night's meal had been placed. Several servants called to him as he made his way to the front door, and he greeted them in return. Stepping outside, he blinked in the new morning light. Farmhands were already busy spreading manure on the homefield—not a job Karn envied—and tending to the longhorn cattle.

"On pig duty again, are you?"

Karn started as his uncle drew alongside him.

"Yes," he muttered. He gave Uncle Ori a sideways glance. "You aren't going to start in on me about lazy wolves, are you?"

Uncle Ori's eyebrows rose.

"The wolves are lazy now?"

"Not the ones with lambs, I'm told."

"Oh, those wolves," said his uncle. "No, I'm sure there are more ways to get a lamb than being the most bright-eyed and bushy-tailed."

He looked down at the buckets of slop in Karn's hands, wrinkling his nose at the stink.

"I tell you what, my nephew, why don't I do that for you, and you can feed the chickens for me."

"You'd do that?" said Karn, who couldn't believe his luck.

"You'll owe me," said Uncle Ori. "And I always collect my debts. But I'm happy to help you this once. What do you say?"

"Don't have to ask me twice," said Karn, eagerly handing over the smelly slop. Uncle Ori took the buckets, handling them gingerly. Karn wondered what his uncle was getting from this deal, but he was too relieved to ponder it for long.

"Well, run along, little lamb," said Uncle Ori. "The chickens won't feed themselves, you know."

Karn nodded his thanks and hurried around to the granary. Inside, he grabbed a sack of grain and slung it over his shoulder, then made his way to the chicken shed.

It was strangely quiet. None of the birds were in the pen yet. He unlatched the door to the shed and his eyes took in the torn feathers scattered across the ground. He saw a hole punched through the wooden staves of the back wall. Only something strong could have snapped the thick wood so easily.

Karn ran out the door to look at the hole from the other side. Then he noticed a footprint in a patch of softer mud. The print was large, deep, six-toed, and clawed. Karn's eyes widened. He knew what had made that print.

"Troll!" he yelled.

"He may catch you one day, you know," said Eggthoda. They were in a room in Eggthoda's home, one of her storage chambers.

"He'll never catch me." Thianna had been fighting with Thrudgelmir again. It didn't matter how the fight started. She knew it was really about her size.

"If he could catch me," she went on, "it would be because I was big and clumsy like he was. Then it wouldn't matter."

Eggthoda nodded sagely. Then she rubbed her considerable chin with her large hand.

"Hold on a minute," she said. She rummaged inside a chest and pulled out something.

Thianna looked at the object uncertainly. "It's a wooden sword?"

"There's a book that goes with it. A manual of sword fighting." Turning to the chest again, Eggthoda removed a tattered leather volume. "You read, yes?"

"A little," said Thianna, who had only seen a few books in her life.

"A useful skill, reading. Or I think it is. The print is too small for me, but there are pictures. The book will teach you to sword fight."

Thianna objected immediately.

"But giants fight with clubs and axes," she protested.

Eggthoda stood up straight, unclipping her club from where it swung at her belt. It was a huge stone thing, like a boulder with a handle.

"Here is my club," she said, holding it out to Thianna. "Can you lift it?"

"No," said Thianna, scowling.

"Then take the sword. Practice swinging it, and practice reading too."

"It doesn't seem a very gianty thing to do," said Thianna. Still, she liked the grip of the hilt in her hand, and she couldn't resist a few practice swings. She lunged at Eggthoda playfully.

Unfazed, the giantess grinned. "It may not be gianty, but it does seem to be Thianna-y."

Swinging the wooden sword back and forth now, Thianna couldn't help agreeing.

Karn spun around, prepared to race back to the house and get help. The only problem was the eight-foot-tall monstrosity blocking his way. Karn's mouth dropped open at the expanse of green and gray flesh before him, all warted, mottled, and lumpy. The creature wore only a skirt of dirty fur bound around its waist with a bit of rope. It grasped a huge tree limb in one of its hands. It also had two heads. A few leftover chicken feathers were sticking out of one of its mouths, the one on Karn's left.

"Um, hello," said Karn. It was a silly thing to say, but it beat screaming.

The mouth with the feathers in it chewed slowly and screwed up its beady eyes, peering at him.

"Hello," said the mouth on the other head. Ugly yellow-brown teeth protruded upward from behind the lower lips of both mouths. Some of the teeth in the right-side mouth were broken off. Both heads were bald, though one of them had a bristly brown beard that started around its neck and reached almost to its waist. The other, the one with the chicken feathers still crunching in its teeth, had a long, bushy mustache.

"Chicken good?" asked Karn, who was at a loss for words. Mountain trolls were rare this far south of Ymiria, though Karn had been brought up on stories of how they would occasionally venture from the woods to raid farms. They were said to be dangerous and nasty, but no one thought they were particularly smart.

"Mmmmph," said the head that had been eating, nodding in agreement. It puffed out a chicken feather. Then it cast a sideways glance at the other head. "But, well, they are crunchy, a bit hard on the teeth really. Also, chickens are a little scrawny."

"Yes," agreed the right-side head, patting their shared belly. "Perhaps we want something a little more filling."

"More filling?" said Karn, who wasn't sure he liked where the conversation was going.

"Yes," said the mountain troll's mustached head. It smacked its lips and leaned forward. Karn stepped back to avoid being poked in the face by the troll's big, bulbous nose. This close, its breath was horrendous.

"Like maybe this man-kid?" said the other head. "They do come bigger, but he's got at least a few chickens' worth of meat on him."

Now Karn was *sure* he didn't like the direction of the conversation. Ending up as a mountain troll's breakfast before he'd even swung a sword or traveled farther than Bense didn't sound like the sort of life that the skalds wrote songs about.

The mountain troll shifted its grip on the tree limb. Karn was out of time.

Something clicked inside Karn. He assessed the mountain troll the way he would size up an opponent in a Thrones and Bones game. The bearded head had black metal hoops in both its ears, whereas the mustached head sported some sort of crude facial tattoo on the cheeks and forehead. Did these suggest differences in personality? And why did only the mustached head have chicken feathers on its lips?

"How come only *he* ate chicken?" asked Karn.

"What?" said the mountain troll's right-side head.

"Only one of you had any chicken." Karn plucked a feather from where it was glued to the thick, gray lips. "Weren't you both hungry?"

"Only one stomach," said chicken-feather mouth. "It all goes to the same place."

Karn nodded nonchalantly.

"But don't you like the taste too?" he said, directing his question at the other head.

"What?" asked the right-side head. The mountain troll shifted its grip on the tree limb.

"The taste. The taste of the chicken."

"Um—" began the head being addressed.

"Chickens are crunchy," interrupted the left-side head. "Hard on the teeth." The right-side head frowned at this but nodded.

"Hard on the teeth?" asked Karn. "They aren't hard on my teeth. How can they be hard on such big, fierce teeth as you have?"

"Well," said the left-side head, "they aren't usually, but he's broken a few." He nodded at his other head. "The fool tried to munch on some boulders."

"That will do it," said Karn, though he obviously had no experience eating rocks.

"Anyway," said Broken Teeth, "it doesn't really matter. Whatever he eats goes to the stomach. I don't feel hungry after." The mountain troll again shifted his grip on the tree limb and lifted it up off the ground. "So, bearing that in mind, let's get on with it."

Karn glanced around hurriedly. Where was everyone?

"Of course," said Karn. "But you don't just eat for hunger. You eat for pleasure too. Don't you miss that?"

"No sense crying once the milk is spilt," said the left-side head. "Now, if you don't mind, we'll be moving to the clubbing-and-eating-you part of this conversation. You know what they say: No lamb for the lazy wolf."

What was it with lambs and wolves today? Karn wondered. Then he tried not to flinch as the troll hefted the tree limb high overhead.

"Speaking of milk," said Karn, "what if I told you I have something you could both eat that was soft and sweet and very, very filling?"

The troll hesitated at the start of its downward swing.

"Soft and sweet, you say," said Broken Teeth. "What is that?"

"Our farm makes the best cheese in all of Norrøn-gard," said Karn.

"Cheese is salty," said the left-side head.

"Also, my ma's skyr is the freshest, creamiest skyr you've ever tasted." Karn was speaking of the unique Norrønir yogurt. "You could eat barrels of it, and you wouldn't even have to chew."

"No chewing?" said the right-side head.

"None," said Karn. "You could practically drink it. You just suck it down."

"I don't see any skyr here," said the left-side head. "Just pound this boy into a puddle and drink him."

"We eat the skyr with honey," added Karn. "Best thing you ever tasted. Way better than puddled boy."

"Mmmmm, honey," said the right-side head.

"And sometimes lingonberries," added Karn.

The broken-toothed head frowned at this. "These lingonberries, they aren't crunchy, are they?"

"Not that you'd notice," said Karn. "Anyway, you could just have the honey."

"And the skyr? I could have the skyr too?"

"Yes, honey and skyr. And cheese as well, if you want."

The mountain troll lowered the tree limb to the ground. "Hey!" said the head that was in favor of eating Karn. "What are you doing? Just puddle him and let's get on with it. No lamb for the lazy wolf, remember."

"I can't eat lamb," lamented Broken Teeth. "But I'd like me some skyr and honey."

Left-side head blew out a breath in aggravation.

"Give me that," it said, and reached across with its other hand for the club.

"No," said the other head, jerking the club back. "I think I want to try me some lingonberries." Karn watched in amazement as the two hands fought for control of the tree limb.

"I want my lingonberries!" hollered Broken Teeth. He ripped the club out of the opposing hand and shook it angrily at himself. The troll's left hand then grabbed one of the broken teeth, yanking it savagely.

The right-side head howled in pain, then swung the tree limb around and brought it down heavily on its other head.

The left-side head's eyes rolled up and the head collapsed, its neck going limp. The troll had knocked its other head out.

"That will teach him," the right-side head said proudly.

Then the troll's left leg buckled, and the monster fell heavily to the ground.

"Hey!" hollered the troll, struggling in the dirt. The remaining head tried to get back on its feet, but its bulk was too great to move without all of its limbs working together.

"Gotta run," said Karn.

"But what about the skyr?" complained the troll.

Karn hightailed it to the longhouse, where his father was outside, in conversation with several freemen.

"Troll!" Karn proclaimed.

"Troll?" said his father, his hand instantly on the hilt of his famous sword, Whitestorm.

"Behind the chicken shed," said Karn. "It ate a few of the birds."

"Karn, get in the house. We'll deal with it," said Korlundr.

"Oh, it's okay," said Karn. "I've taken care of it already." Korlundr looked puzzled. "Here," said Karn, "I'll show you."

Kolundr whistled appreciatively when he saw the monster still struggling on the ground, trying unsuccessfully to rise and blubbering about skyr. He sent Karn to the house while he dealt with the troll properly. Afterward, he called for the day meal early, so that Karn could tell his tale over and over again. Karn's shoulders were soon sore from all the manly claps he had to endure, but that and a swelled head were far better than being in a troll's belly, and he enjoyed being a hero. His uncle was strangely silent, no doubt from guilt over switching duties with him. Karn didn't worry about it, but he did feel slightly sad for the troll when he poured lingonberries over his skyr.

"Seriously. I don't see why I have to go."

Thianna sat on a stool in her father's workroom, hunched over.

"If you burn any hotter, daughter of mine," said Magnilmir, "you will surely start to melt the walls in here. Then where will we live?"

Magnilmir was packing various objects into a large backpack. Thianna watched as he selected a bowl made from hand-carved mammoth ivory, several cleverly wrought stone mugs, and a belt made of linnorm scales. All were small in her father's great hands. Thianna frowned at the little human-sized objects, knowing who they were intended for.

"I'm just as cold as you are," she said.

"It will be your first time off the mountain." Magnilmir looked at his daughter. She rewarded him with a scowl. "It is something giants do."

"Not all giants," said Thianna. "Thrudgelmir isn't going. Neither is Elma or Marbor." The latter two were young giants who often ran with Thrudgelmir. Neither of them was particularly fond of humans. Nor were they fond of half-humans.

"Since when do you let Thrudgelmir, Elma, or Marbor dictate your behavior?" said her father. "If you don't mind my saying, and really, even if you do, you don't get along with any of them. Why should you care what they think?"

"I don't," said Thianna. "I'm just pointing out that not every giant goes."

"Well, the smart ones do," said Magnilmir, stuffing a final few items into the pack and then lacing it shut. "As much as I enjoy the colder weather, the humans have supplies we'll all be glad of once winter gets here. Thrudgelmir's stubbornness only means that he'll have to trade with me later for what he needs rather than with a human now, and he won't get nearly as good a deal. Besides, it's a tradition."

They were speaking of the giants' biannual trip down the mountain to the border of Ymiria and Norrøngard. Ordinarily, giants didn't venture that far south, where the warmer weather made them uncomfortable. Nor did humans regularly travel very far north into the icy Ymirian mountain range. But as the weather was turning from warm to cold or cold to warm, the giants of Gunnlod's Plateau and the humans of Korlundr's Farm met at a place known as Dragon's Dance for a week of feasting, storytelling, and trading.

"You two packed and ready to go?" asked Eggthoda, barging into the workshop and setting down several large packs that she handled as lightly as if they were stuffed with feathers.

"That is a difficult question," explained Magnilmir. "We are physically ready, but perhaps not emotionally. My daughter does not wish to go."

"Nonsense," said Eggthoda, placing her great palm

across Thianna's back. "You want to go, don't you, Thi?" Thianna wasn't sure what to say, so she shrugged. She didn't want to disappoint Eggthoda, who she had become quite fond of, but she wasn't ready to alter her position.

"It seems that my daughter's great friend Thrudgelmir isn't going," explained Magnilmir.

"Thrudgelmir? Who cares what he does? He'd go to the goat house to get wool, if you know what I mean. Besides, Thianna has been helping me cast hoarfrost cantrips for weeks now. Of course she'll want to help me sell them, won't you, Thi?"

"Maybe," said Thianna, who hadn't considered that her work might be good enough to be sold alongside Eggthoda's.

"Besides," continued the giantess, "I'll need this clever little giant's help if I'm really to get the better of the humans in a trade, won't I?"

"My help?" said Thianna, brightening.

"Of course. You helped me with the cantrips. That's only half the job. Now we have to sell them. You don't get off until the work is done. We giants stick together, don't we?"

"I guess we do," said Thianna, glad that somebody considered her a giant.

"Then grab your skis, Thi. We're going downhill."

"That," said Thianna, "I can do."

CHAPTER FIVE

Dragon's Dance

The first thing that Karn noticed was all the dragons. His party had been following the course of a wide river for a week, traveling due north through mostly alpine forests. After hours of staring at his own feet, he looked up into the bright light and blinked. As his vision adjusted, he saw them—dozens and dozens of dragons.

"Amazing," said Karn.

"I suppose that it is an impressive sight the first time you see it," said Pofnir with a superior grin.

Karn nodded. One glance and it didn't take a genius to see how Dragon's Dance had gotten its name. Like many Norrøngard settlements, the camp was constructed on a hill for added visibility and security, but unlike others, this hill was covered with stone dragons. Or rather, it was covered with dragon heads. The hill was dotted with roughly twelve-foot-tall stone poles topped with ornately carved dragon heads. The poles were paired, crossing right below the dragons' necks, so that it looked like they were partnered in a dance. Horizontal stone poles ran between every two cross-frame constructions.

"They're tent frames."

Pofnir nodded. "That's why we didn't bring any wood poles, just the tent clothes. You need to be quick and grab your spot." Then he pushed past Karn and hurried up the hill. Others in Karn's party were doing the same.

Karn saw that the crossed stone poles served as gables, while the horizontal poles were the ridgepoles. These were permanent structures built to supply the scaffolding for tents. As he watched, several people unfolded linen sheets. They tossed these over the ridgepoles and then affixed them to the ground. The prime spots were being taken.

Realizing he was wasting time, Karn hopped the low stone wall that encircled the hill and raced up the incline.

As he reached the summit, Karn noticed three standing stones nearby, but not exactly centered on the crest. Each bore a dragon carving etched into its surface. There were also a few wattle-and-daub cabins clustered together, though no one seemed to be claiming them. Karn guessed they must be for other purposes, storage or food preparation, something relating to the upcoming trading festival but not for sleeping in. Then Karn noticed some frames of enormous size, easily eighteen feet tall or more.

"For the giants," said his father, stepping up beside him. Of course, giants would need giant-sized tents.

"We're really going to see them?" asked Karn. Until this moment, he hadn't actually believed it.

"More than that," said Korlundr, clapping his son on the back. "You're going to spend several days bartering with them." As if on cue, up rose a thunderous, pounding noise like a herd of elk stamping their feet. Karn could see a wave of treetops shaking.

He was speechless as the frost giants came trudging out of the woods. They were immense. Colossal. Fifteen to twenty feet tall. With great beards that fell to their waists in cascades of hair that were larger than the pelts of bears or elk.

"They're like giant people," Karn said, and immediately realized what a stupid statement that was. They *were* people, just giant-sized.

Unlike regular Norrønir, however, the frost giants wore mostly furs, from their boots to their hats. They shouldered massive packs, and they carried enormous axes, clubs, and hammers. He saw one giant casually swinging a club that was bigger than Karn was tall. He imagined being on the receiving end of that club. It wasn't a pretty thought.

"You are sure they're friendly, right, Father?" he asked.

Korlundr laughed. "They're friendly. This lot are, at least. We've been trading with this village for years now. Don't worry. You'll like them. Particularly Magnilmir. He's a gentle sort, if a bit long-winded. Come, I'll introduce you."

"Do I have to?"

"Do you have to what?" asked Magnilmir, who was busy tossing a large mammoth hide over the top of a ridgepole set higher than Thianna could reach. "Whatever it is, I'd appreciate it enormously if you could help me tie this down while you tell me why you don't want to do it."

Thianna tugged the bottom of the dusty hide taut.

"Tie it down well," said her father. "We'll be here for a week, you know."

"I know," said Thianna, who wasn't relishing the idea. "Don't worry, I'm tying it fine."

"Yes, yes, you are," said Magnilmir, bending low to inspect her knots. "Now, what is it you don't want to do?"

Thianna was thinking about whether to answer "Speak to the hot bloods" or "Set foot out of my tent at all" when someone shouted.

"Magnilmir, be healthy!"

Thianna was shocked for a moment. Even kneeling, the voice wasn't coming from much above her head height. The speaker, she saw, was like a giant in miniature. To learn the humans were just like everyone else, only tiny, was odd and unsettling. It felt wrong, made humans seem too close to her own kind. There was another, slightly smaller human next to the speaker, gaping stupidly at them with wide eyes.

"Be healthy, Korlundr hauld Kolason," said her father, smiling at the diminutive newcomers. He was obviously thrilled to see them. He bent down to Thianna's ear and whispered, for her benefit, "'Be healthy' is how the Norrønir say hello. Careful, though—it's also how they say 'Drink up.' They're a cheerful bunch, these Norrønir, even when they're knocking each other's teeth out."

Thianna stood up. She watched the eyes of the smaller of the two little Norrønir follow her up as she rose. She had a foot or more on him. Almost as much on the speaker. Despite herself, she felt a grin pulling hard at the corners of her mouth. She had never been taller than anyone before.

"Magnilmir," said Korlundr, "I'd like you to meet my son, Karn." He put his arm around the smaller Norrønur. "It's his first visit to Dragon's Dance."

Well, obviously, thought Thianna. Studying the two humans, Thianna thought she could see a family resemblance. They shared blond hair and the same steely look in their eyes.

"It is a pleasure to meet you," said Magnilmir. "Be healthy, Karn Korlundsson." He held out his hand. After a moment, the boy nervously placed his small hand in

Magnilmir's great one. She never thought it would take nerve to shake her father's hand, but she realized Karn was being brave.

"And may I present my daughter, Thianna," said Magnilmir, pushing her slightly forward.

Korlundr's eyes widened at "daughter," but he was gracious enough to smile and take her hand. Thianna didn't want to touch a human, but she couldn't help being fascinated by a hand that wasn't that much smaller than her own. When she took it, she ran her fingers over it, looking at the little digits. If this shocked Korlundr further, he did a good job of hiding it.

"A pleasure to meet you as well, Thianna Magnilmisdóttir." Thianna blinked at the odd string of syllables appended to her name. Her father coughed.

"Er, we don't use last names, patronymics and matronymics and such, the way you do in Norrøngard," Magnilmir explained. "Maybe something to do with giants being long-lived, if you'll excuse me pointing that out." He coughed again. "Anyway, it's just Thianna. I mean, er, it isn't *just* Thianna; she's rather special. But her name is Thianna. Very pretty sounding, don't you think? One word. *Thi-anna.* There you go."

"Delightful," said Korlundr, obviously wondering where this foreign-named, tiny giant came from, but too polite to ask. He reached into a pack slung at his side. "Before we get into the thick of haggling tomorrow, I brought an extra wheel of cheese. I thought you might like to share it and trade news."

Magnilmir beamed at this. There wasn't much he liked in the wide world more than the cheese from Korlundr's Farm. He always bartered for a great deal of it each trip, but disconcertingly little of it ever made it back to Gunnlod's Plateau.

"Do come in," he said. "The tent's only just gone up. We can try it out. The tent, I mean. And the cheese, of course. Thank you. And I've still got a few bottles of Dvergrian Stout that I scored off a passing dwarf six months ago. I recalled you liked that last time—the stout, not dwarves, er . . . not that I mean to imply that you have anything against them—anyway, so I saved us two bottles."

Korlundr smiled.

The two men, Ymirian and Norrønur, disappeared into the tent, leaving Karn and Thianna standing outside. They peered at each other uneasily. Then Magnilmir poked his huge head through the flap.

"Why don't you two youngsters run off and get to know each other while we talk over our boring old grown-up business."

"I can see you salivating, Dad," said Thianna. Magnilmir smiled sheepishly and smacked his lips. "Go have fun," she said.

Magnilmir smiled gratefully. "Be healthy," her father said, ducking back through the tent flap.

"So," said Karn, looking at the frost giant's daughter.

"So," said Thianna, not looking at Karn so much as gazing at the top of his head and smirking.

"You've never been here before?"

"Nope."

"Neither have I. You want to wander around?"

Thianna thought about this. Actually, she did.

"Okay."

Karn glanced to either side.

"Let's go down the hill and walk the stone-wall border."

"Sure," said Thianna.

As they walked, Karn stole sidelong glances at this strange girl. Even apart from her size, Karn had never seen anyone quite like her. Her hair, skin, and eyes were darker than most northerners', and there was something in her features that hinted at faraway places. Instead of wearing a woolen dress like other girls, she was outfitted in a woolen shirt, long trousers, and a three-quarter coat, fastened with a belt like those worn by Norrønir men. It was hard to think of her as a giant when she was half their size. But she was certainly bigger than any human girl he'd ever seen, and he thought that she wasn't done growing either. Despite her size, she didn't stoop like other tall girls he'd known. If anything, she seemed to be walking on her tiptoes a lot.

"What are you staring at?" she asked. Karn felt his cheeks redden in embarrassment. He hadn't realized he'd been so obvious.

"Nothing," he said.

Thianna scowled at him.

"It's only that . . ."

"What?" she said, her voice dropping into a low growl.

"Don't take this the wrong way," he said, "but you are so . . ."

"So what?" she said. Karn was keenly aware of the wooden sword she had bound to her belt with a leather thong. The width of her shoulders suggested that she could raise quite a welt with it, wooden or not. Nervous, Karn's mouth ran away from his brain.

"You're so tall," he blurted out.

"What?" said Thianna.

"I'm sorry. I didn't mean . . ." Karn stopped. He felt stupid. He rarely got to talk with girls around his own age other than his sisters, but he knew enough to know that telling a woman she was as big as an ox wasn't the kind of thing they liked to hear. He winced, readying himself for an outburst. It didn't come. Instead, the strange girl was smiling at him.

"Thanks," she said.

"For what?"

"What you said. No one has ever called me tall before."

"I can't imagine why," said Karn, whose mouth was happily running away from him again. "You're enormous."

Thianna grinned wider.

"Now you're just flattering me."

Karn shook his head.

"Anyway, here's the wall," said Thianna, making a show of lifting her leg and stepping easily over it. Karn paused to ready himself, then clambered across as well. Not waiting for him, Thianna began to follow it around. She called over her shoulder. "See if you can keep up, Short Stuff."

"Hey," said Karn, who wasn't sure what he thought about this odd girl, but he wasn't going to let her leave him behind. After they'd gone around twice, she dropped to a slower pace and turned to him.

"I've had enough of this. You do anything else for fun down south besides walk in circles?"

Karn had never considered where he lived "south" before. Norrøngard was just about as far north as it was possible to go. But as for "fun," he'd wanted a life beyond the farm for a while now.

"Not much," he said after some deliberation. "Feeding chickens and pigs isn't exactly high entertainment."

"Oh," said the girl, clearly let down. Karn was surprised to find that he didn't want to disappoint her.

"I do play games," said Karn.

"Oh," she said again, but with an entirely different intonation. "Games. Games are good. Let's play one."

Thianna began scanning their immediate surroundings for a flat patch of ground. There was a space to their left where two trees could almost make goal lines. She didn't have a Knattleikr ball with her, but they could probably make one from rocks and some skins. She looked at Karn.

"What are you doing?" she asked.

He had dropped down to the ground and broken out some sort of wooden slab from his pack. It had a grid carved on the surface with a cross shape in the center made from inlaid pieces of darker wood. He was setting stone carvings on it. Karn looked up at her, puzzlement written on his face.

"I'm setting up the pieces."

"What pieces?" she said.

"The draug and the shield maidens."

"The what and the which?"

"The attackers and defenders. Don't they have Thrones and Bones in Ymiria?"

"We have plenty of bones. Not sure we have any thrones. Maybe in Trollheim. Look, what is that?"

"It's a board game," said Karn. "I thought we were going to play."

"A board game," repeated Thianna.

"Yes."

"Board game?"

"Yes."

"As in 'I'm bored by that kind of game'? Let's do something else."

"No. No, that's not it at all. It's a game. It's fun. Besides, what else is there to do?"

"We could play ball."

"Ball?"

"Yes, ball. Don't you have proper games in Norrøngard? Doesn't anybody play Knattleikr?"

"What?" said Karn. "Well, yes, we have that. I mean, I don't play myself. It's a bit . . ."

"Too rough for you, is it?"

"Rough? No. I was going to say 'simple.'"

"Rough."

"Hey, I once took down a mountain troll single-handedly."

"Sure you did."

"I did."

"The trolls are as tiny as the people where you're from?"

"It was bigger than you!" Karn shouted. Thianna's face darkened. This time he knew he'd said the wrong thing. Then Thianna's eyes lit up with a mischievous glint. She bent down and snatched the Jarl off the Thrones and Bones board.

"Bigger than me?" she said. "Then you'll have no trouble getting this back."

She turned and ran.

"Hey," said Karn, leaping to his feet. "Hey!" he called again. He started after her, paused, ran and scooped his remaining pieces into his satchel, and took off running after her.

"Careful with that! That's polished marble!" he yelled at her back.

Thianna laughed as she raced ahead of Karn. Again and again, she let him get close, and then just as he was about to catch her, she took off again with a burst of speed.

Thianna sprinted for the forest's edge on the eastern side of the camp. She glanced at him once before she plunged into the woods.

Karn couldn't believe it. Of course, he realized Thianna was having him on. He should probably just stop chasing her and let her tire of the game and bring the piece back. But what if she didn't? What if she just tossed it aside in the woods? The Jarl was the most prized piece of his entire set. He felt a surge of panic and plunged into the forest after her.

There was no path here, but there was plenty of underbrush, so Karn had to slow down and be careful of his footing. The trees were mostly pine, and the nettles scratched at him as he wove and dodged through the branches. At least Thianna would have to slow her pace as well. Wouldn't she?

He was suddenly aware that the only footfalls he heard were his own, the only heavy breathing his own panting. He dropped to a walk.

"Thianna?" he called. There was no answer. It was darker here in the shade of the trees than it had been in the open.

"Come on, this isn't funny."

No answer.

"That's the most expensive piece in the set, you know."

Maybe telling her that wasn't the best idea.

"I'm not even sure I could replace it if I had to. I might have to go all the way to Korjengard or Wendholm to even find another that nice."

Still no answer. This giant girl was infuriating.

"Scratch that. I won't have to go. You will. You want to hoof it all the way to Korjengard, big girl? That sound like fun to you? Well?"

Karn heard the crunch of a branch to his left. He turned to look.

And was knocked off his feet as Thianna barreled into him. They went down in a tangle of limbs.

He twisted onto his back to see the giantess's mocking face leering over him.

"Get off!" he yelled. Neth's sake, but she was heavy.

Thianna sprang right over Karn's head. He twisted around in time to see her rolling over and onto her feet. How did someone so large get to be so fast?

Standing, she dangled the marble playing piece over his head.

"Got to do better than that, Norrønboy." With a laugh, she was running again.

Karn sprang to his feet and took off. He wasn't going to let this girl get the better of him. His mind slid into that space he always went to during the best Thrones and

Bones games. Suddenly, the trees around him were playing pieces, the forest a game board. If he was to capture his opponent, he'd need to outflank her. Use her surroundings against her. Instead of chasing straight after her, he began to weave left and right. When he saw a tree up ahead in her path, he cut to the side, yelling as he did so. Thianna sensed him closing in on her right and moved in the opposite direction accordingly, straight into the path of the tree. The time it took her to readjust helped him close the distance.

He was really gaining now. Lunging at her left, he smiled as she dodged right but crashed into a wall of bushy branches.

"Ow!" she hollered as she extricated herself from the prickly nettles. But she was laughing now and so was Karn. He grabbed a fistful of Thianna's coat and yanked, hauling himself forward as much as pulling her back. They crashed into each other just as they tumbled together into a clearing.

"I got you," said Karn, gripping her broad shoulders as they both drew to a halt, but he saw that Thianna's attention had shifted. She passed the Jarl back over her shoulder absentmindedly. He took it eagerly, slipping it into his satchel. When he looked up, she was still staring ahead. The clearing wasn't empty at all. Karn's eyes widened.

"Where are we?" said the giant's daughter.

CHAPTER SIX

The Barrow

"This is a grave site."

Karn and Thianna stood at the edge of a clearing. It was maybe two acres in size, dominated by four small hills. The hills weren't naturally occurring, but were man-made mounds of earth. Three of the hills were smaller, with stone doors about a foot or two in height set at their bases.

"What?" asked Thianna. Her experience with the graves of frost giants was very different.

"Tunnel entrances," Karn said, pointing out the stone doors. "These are barrow mounds. Stone chambers covered with earth. The big one must be for someone important."

Thianna nodded, grudgingly impressed.

The fourth mound was indeed taller. It was surrounded by a ring of standing stones and had a larger stone door set into it.

Karn walked forward for a closer look. Thianna followed at his side.

"Listen," she said.

"I don't hear anything," he replied.

"That's just it. The air is so still here. Where are the animal noises? I don't even hear a breeze."

She was right. There was an uncanny stillness in this clearing. Not even a single insect buzzed. Karn felt a chill that had very little to do with the weather.

"Look at this," said Thianna. They had reached the ring of standing stones now, pausing to stare closely at one. It was taller than she was.

"It's a runestone," he said. The stone was covered in runic letters. He read them aloud. "'For if you stand you'll surely fall. And if you fall, stand you will for now and all.'"

"What does that mean?"

"I don't know."

The runes formed a half circle around an image, but grime and moss had filled in the inscribed lines and obscured it. Karn wiped away at it with his palm.

"It's of a man, I think," he said.

As the moss came away, more of the figure was

revealed. It was indeed a carved image of a man, a Norrønur by his dress. He was throwing his hands up and had a startled expression on his face. It wasn't a happy image.

Thianna walked to the next nearest stone. She brushed at the moss on its surface. "There's one here as well."

Karn joined her. The runestone had the same written inscription, but the picture carved on it was of a different person. This new figure didn't look any happier, and he had a wound on his neck. They moved on to the next stone, scraping the moss and grime away.

"They all seem to be on the losing end of a fight, don't they?" asked Thianna. Karn nodded. He glanced around at the other stones. The shape they marked out was more elliptical than round.

"It's shaped like a longship," said Karn. "Whoever was buried here must have been the captain of a drakkar, a dragonship. Only . . ."

"Only what?" Thianna asked.

"It's still missing a few stones to be complete."

"So some fell down," said Thianna.

"Then where are they?" Karn waved his hand. There weren't any fallen or broken stones anywhere in the glade. "I don't think even you could pick one of these up."

Thianna made a face.

"That wasn't a challenge," said Karn. "I guess someone could have carted one off if they really wanted, but no Norrønur would risk offending the dead like that when there are plenty of rocks to be had elsewhere. I don't think the ship shape was ever completed. Whoever put it up just stopped a few stones short."

"Why would they do that?" Thianna asked.

"I don't know. But that's not the only thing that bothers me."

Thianna shrugged.

"He's buried a bit far from the sea to be a ship's captain, isn't he?"

"Very good, nephew," said a voice. Karn and Thianna both jumped. "It seems I'm not the only clever one in the family." Casually, Uncle Ori stepped out from behind a runestone.

"Uncle Ori." Karn suddenly felt like he'd been caught doing something he shouldn't, though what exactly he had no idea. "What are you doing here?"

"I could ask you the same question." Ori sighed loudly. "But really, I just needed some time alone. All the revelry gets to be a bit much after a while."

Ori stopped in front of Karn, then made a show of turning his attention to Thianna.

"Um, this is my uncle," said Karn. "Uncle, this is Thianna."

"My, you're a big one," said Ori, who had to raise his eyes to look into Thianna's own. "What are *you*?"

"I'm a frost giant," said Thianna. Karn couldn't miss the defensive tone in her voice.

"Sure you are," Uncle Ori replied. "And all frost giants have that olive complexion, do they?" Thianna dropped her gaze but quickly raised it again. "No, you're a curiosity, is what you are."

Karn knew from his encounter with the wyvern riders in Bense that Ori harbored a dislike for the frost giants. He decided to change the conversation.

"What is this place?" he asked.

"Ah, well," said Ori, "you were right. It's the final resting place for a seawolf, a drakkar captain from over a hundred years ago."

"Isn't it a bit far from the sea for a captain?" said Thianna.

"Not if you know the story," said Ori, looking sidelong, if slightly up, at her.

"And you do?"

"I know it well. Better than anyone living, I suppose. I got it, if not from the horse's mouth, from the next best thing."

Ori waved for them to follow him, then led them to where a slight downward ramp was cut into the hill. Smaller slabs had been placed to either side of the ramp to keep the earth from collapsing inward. Ori sat on a left-side stone, leaning a shoulder back against the door. He patted the flat stone surface beside him, inviting them to join him.

Karn glanced at Thianna, hoping her irritation had subsided. She shrugged, so he walked down the ramp and sat near his uncle, but not too near. It wasn't Ori that bothered him so much as the stone door, which was covered with runes similar to those on the standing stones.

Ori looked past Karn to where Thianna still stood apart. The giantess shrugged again but came down the ramp, though she sat on the opposite slab and as far from Ori as possible. Ori nodded at them both and then began to speak.

"His name was Helltoppr," Uncle Ori began, "and he was a dragonship captain, the last of the true Norrønir raiders. In his day, he raided Araland and Ungland, though to mixed success." Ori glanced over his shoulder, as though looking into the hill. "I don't care how the legends tell it. I'm sorry, but it really was mixed success, nothing yet deserving of a song from the skalds." He shook himself as if dismissing a wrongheaded notion and turned again to Karn and Thianna. "At any rate, somewhere in there, he finds a sword, and not just any sword, but the legendary sword of Folkvarthr Fairbeard, the first true king of Norrøngard."

Karn's eyebrows lifted in surprise at this. "Really?" he asked. He looked to Thianna, but she pursed her lips and shook her head. The name Folkvarthr Fairbeard obviously meant nothing to her.

"Now, is this really a special sword? Perhaps." Again, Ori glanced behind him. "Or perhaps he only believes it is. Sometimes that's all you need to bring out true ambition. At any rate, Helltoppr's raiding takes a turn for the better. He proclaims himself Jarl and forces the other jarls to acknowledge him. Some he bribes, some he intimidates. They put up with him for a time, but that's not enough for him. He's a man of vision and broad appetite. He wants to be High King. Helltoppr slays three other jarls, and lays waste to a good bit of their holdings. He seems almost unstoppable."

The sun was setting now at Karn's back, and the runestones cast long shadows. In the strange stillness of the barrow mounds, it was easy to picture the fearsome dragonship raider as he marched across Norrøngard on a path of destruction.

"But no man shapes his own fortune," Ori continued. "Isn't that what they say? So just when Helltoppr is about to close his grasp on success, one of his own men betrays him. For love of a woman, no less. She tricks Helltoppr out of his legendary sword, gives it to his betrayer."

"Sure. Blame the woman, why don't you?" cut in Thianna. Ori scowled at Thianna's interruption, then went on talking as if she hadn't spoken.

"Without his sword, his confidence falters. The betrayer teams up with the remaining jarls. They face down Helltoppr and eventually they kill him." Ori's hands patted the stone beside him, but this time it was almost as if he were trying to reassure the rock. "Rather than doing him the honor of burying him at sea, his one-time followers carry him far inland and bury him in the woods. They bury three of his men with him—three who stayed loyal when the others surrendered or turned. And they put enough of his plunder in the grave that they hope he'll be content to do the decent thing and stay dead. But they remember his ambition, so they put a corpse door on the barrow just in case he isn't so inclined."

"A corpse door?" asked Thianna.

"Never heard of it?" asked Ori with a touch of derision in his voice.

"We don't bury our dead like you humans."

"What do they teach young giantesses these days?" Ori tsked. "A magically warded door, marked with grave-binding runes to keep the dead properly in their barrows. Like the one behind me now."

Ori reached across his shoulder to indicate the stone behind him. The woods were growing dark and the shadows were growing long, but Karn could still see Thianna's face clearly. Ori's face, though, was in shadow, limned in an eerie green light that seemed to be coming from the stone slab behind him. To Karn, the runes looked as if they were glowing, though they were hard to make out clearly. Surely, this was just an illusion of the twilight, his imagination playing tricks on him because of his uncle's ghost story.

"That's not really true, is it, uncle?" he said, hating the nervous tremor that had crept into his voice.

"Why don't we stay and see?" said Ori. "The restless dead are said to scratch on the doors of their barrows when the moons are high."

Suddenly, Karn wanted to be anywhere but sitting on a barrow in the moonslight.

"Actually, I think we should go back."

Ori stared at him a moment, and then broke out into a barking laugh.

"Oh, nephew," he said, "you really are wound up. Look at you, jumping at shadows. Does your uncle tell a good tale or what?"

Karn smiled weakly. "You tell a good one," he said.

"I'm told that my stories really are to die for," said Ori.

"We should get back," said Karn. "I don't want Korlundr to worry about where I am."

"But of course," said Ori. "It's burden enough being a hauld. I'd ease it for him if I could just think of how."

None of them spoke much on the way back. Karn kept pondering his uncle's tale. Perhaps there really was a dead raider buried in the hill, but surely Helltoppr couldn't return as an undead draug. Imaginative nonsense. Draug were fine as playing pieces on a Thrones and Bones board, but not something Karn ever wanted to meet in real life. Hadn't Ori said that it was all just fun and games? Glancing sidelong at his uncle, Karn remembered something else Uncle Ori had said. About games. Uncle Ori always played to win.

That night Karn dreamt that he was in the woods. A cat, a horse, and a bull were circling him. There was something wrong with the way they moved. The bull had a slick, black look to it, as if it were wet. Not with water but with something more disturbing, some liquid that only looked black in the dark of night.

Even though it was a dream, Karn could feel his heart racing and his sweat trickling. The moon and her little sister shone impossibly big in the sky, their rays creating isolated bars of light as the beams passed through the trees. The cat, the horse, and the bull moved slowly as the light and dark slid over them. But they kept their eyes fixed on Karn—malevolent, hungry, cold.

He didn't want to place his back to any of them. He kept turning around and around, trying to divide his attention between the cat, the horse, and the bull so that not one of them was out of his sight for very long. But each time Karn twisted around to glance behind him, he saw that one of the creatures had stepped in, tightening the circle. Their eyes never left his. The eyes said: Drop your guard for even a second, and we will get you.

Karn wondered how long he could keep his vigilance up. Sooner or later, one of them might pounce on his back. It seemed inevitable.

And then all at once, the cat, and the horse, and the bull began to sing.

Helltoppr his bold warriors heed:
Ship-ruler, man-slayer, he set to sea.

Ocean-proud longship that gleamed with his swords
was his storm-wrath's harbinger to lands manifold.

As Karn listened, the song seemed to recount the story
that his uncle had told him in the barrow. It was hard to
make out all the words, but he caught snatches of verse.
There was something that went "Helltoppr conquer'd
and great grew his power, till High King seat alone was it
left to devour." And something that sounded like a ref-
erence to his own father's sword: "The blade, storm of
white, treacherous dart, sharp-piercing its thrust through
Helltoppr's heart."

The verses rose and fell in volume like ghostly echoes
on the wind, the animals chanting it in singsong as they
circled around and around. But the final verse, when it
came, came loud and clear.

Stand you your ground, and stone you may be.
Sword-failing, battle-losing, none then hears your plea.
For if you stand, you'll surely fall;
and if you fall, stand you will for now . . . and all.

As the cat, and the horse, and the bull sang the last
verse, Karn woke up. He was still in his tent, twisted
in the furs that were his bedroll. Korlundr was snoring
beside him, a loud, heavy, familiar noise. The reassuring bulk of his father made him relax. As his heart rate
slowed, Karn laughed at himself. He was too old to be

frightened by nightmares. But then, faint enough that it might just be a trick of the wind or the babble of a distant brook, he heard a chorus of voices, just a dying refrain fading with the last shadows of night.

> *For if you stand, you'll surely fall;*
> *and if you fall, stand you will for now . . . and all.*

Karn shivered. It would be many hours before he would drift back to sleep.

CHAPTER SEVEN

Winternights

Karn's party spent a week trading and feasting with the frost giants. Karn thought that they could have conducted all of their trade in a single day, two at the most, if the parties involved had stuck to the actual business of trading. Instead, the days were generously punctuated with plenty of breaks—breaks for the singing of loud and boisterous songs, breaks for the telling of tall tales, and breaks for the staging of what few games were of the sort that a human and a giant could play together without one of them getting squashed.

The games mostly consisted of chucking axes and clubs at distant objects or bashing rocks with clubs and axes until they broke. The giants played a game of Knattleikr among themselves while the Norrønir placed bets on one side or the other; and the Norrønir invited the giants to the nearby stream to watch them in a swimming competition. Karn thought that Knattleikr as the giants played it was brutally pointless, while Thianna was disappointed to discover that Norrønir swimming competitions weren't races for speed. Rather, they involved one swimmer holding another underwater and timing how long it took him to drown. Midweek they did manage a good game of tug-of-war when Karn suggested that they could play if they agreed to a rule of three Norrønir for every one frost giant. Things got only a little rocky when someone suggested that Thianna either play for the Norrønir team or else count as only half a giant. She stormed off for a while, but the game itself was a big success with everyone else. When Thianna returned, she offered to show Karn her skis, which he thought might be her way of letting him know there were no hard feelings.

The last night was for the celebration of Winternights, the evening in which summer gave way to winter. It was the largest feast in a week of feasting.

Before the meal, two of Korlundr's freemen put on animal-hide masks and cavorted in a brief ceremonial dance. The giants looked awkwardly at this, and a few of them walked a little ways away.

"Where are they going?" Karn asked Pofnir.

"The dance is to bid Beysa, goddess of summer, farewell," Pofnir explained. "And to welcome Uldr, god of winter." Karn gave the freeman a blank stare. Pofnir winced. "The giants aren't comfortable with our invoking the gods in their presence."

Karn shook his head.

"The things you don't know, Karn. It was the first of the gods of the Norrønir who slew their father, the giant Ymir," Pofnir explained.

"Are they still mad about it?"

"Well, that was a long time ago. This is Winternight, and we should all stick close to our fires. When the world changes seasons, it is a time of transition for all things. Wild magic is in the air and anything can happen. Why, do you know there's a barrow mound not far from here? They used to say that if you sat on a barrow mound all night long on Winternights, you would gain magical powers."

Karn hadn't thought much about Helltoppr's Barrow since his first day at Dragon's Dance, and he had dismissed the memory of those eerie voices chanting in the night.

As the evening wore on, Karn thought he should find Thianna. He wasn't quite sure why. The giantess had only proved marginally good company. She was temperamental and reckless. But as they were close to the same age, they had found themselves lumped together off and on during the week, and Karn was smart enough to know that perhaps he was a little bit jealous. He longed to leave the responsibility of Korlundr's Farm behind. He imagined Thianna skiing down mountainsides with wild abandon, and he admired her boldness, even if she didn't see the value in playing Thrones and Bones.

Karn scouted amid the pockets of revelers, but he couldn't find Thianna anywhere. He made his way to Magnilmir's enormous tent. He peeked inside, but Thianna was nowhere in sight. He called her name anyway.

Someone coughed behind him. Karn spun and saw his uncle Ori.

"You always manage to creep up on me, uncle," he said. "Why aren't you off celebrating?"

Ori shrugged. "I've had enough of Ymirian company to last me until the spring. Probably longer. When I have my own farm, I'll dispense with this silly gathering."

Karn frowned, though he realized most of Norrøngard felt just as Ori did. Korlundr was the exception. Norrønir were generally suspicious of anyone who wasn't a Norrønur.

"I suppose you are looking for your little giantess?" said Ori.

"I thought I should say goodbye."

Ori pursed his lips. "I suppose I should tell you . . ."

"Tell me what?"

Ori sighed, as though he was going against his principles for Karn's sake.

"Thianna asked me to tell you to meet her at the barrow mound. She wanted some time alone with you on your last night."

"Why wouldn't she just wait for me to go with her?" he asked.

Ori gave Karn a long look down his nose in a way that made Karn feel like he was being naive.

"I suppose I can go with you, just to make sure you get through the woods safely at night. I won't stick around, of course, just see you there and off."

"Thanks," said Karn, who didn't like the idea of walking alone through the dark woods.

"Oh, don't thank me," said Uncle Ori. "I'm just doing what I have to do."

There was no sign of Thianna when Karn and Ori emerged into the moonlit glade. Both Manna's moon and her smaller sister were shining brightly. In the pale light, the standing stones were rendered in bright detail. Karn steeled himself and stepped from the trees.

"Where is she?"

Ori looked around.

"Maybe she's relieving herself in the woods," he said indelicately. "But she could be behind one of the runestones. Let's go check." With that, he walked boldly forward, heading toward the central mound.

They climbed the hill, passing through the ring of stones. Karn didn't see any sign of Thianna, though there were plenty of places where even someone of her size could be hiding. The thought wasn't a comforting one.

"Are you sure she's here?" he asked.

"Would I lie to you?"

Karn wasn't sure how to answer. Lately, he'd begun to suspect that his uncle might cheat at Thrones and Bones. Cheating seemed to be a form of lying, but he kept his opinion to himself.

Ori walked right down the ramp to the doorway to Helltoppr's Barrow. Then he turned to face Karn.

"Have you ever heard what they say about barrow magic?"

"I think they say a lot," said Karn, remembering the nonsense that Pofnir had spouted earlier.

"I'm sure they do," replied his uncle. "But here's one you won't have heard. Tap three times on a corpse door with a named blade and a wish will be granted."

"A named blade?" asked Karn, who hadn't followed his uncle down the ramp.

"You know. A sword from the songs."

Karn did know. The Norrønir were forever naming their favorite weapons. The songs were full of axes and swords and spears with supposedly magical properties.

"You could make a wish now while we wait," his uncle continued.

"Right," Karn said, chuckling uncomfortably. "Like I have a named sword."

"I don't suppose you do," his uncle said coolly. "Good thing I have one here. Come and have a look."

Karn hesitated. He really was as close as he wanted to be

to the barrow, and Ori was behaving strangely. As he dithered, he thought he felt eyes on his back and turned around. There was no one there. Just the stillness of the stones. His uncle watched him with a bemused expression. He was starting to feel exposed up on the hill alone, so he mustered his courage and walked down the ramp to join Ori.

"So show me," he said.

Ori grinned and drew back his cloak. There was a sword hanging at his side. Ori moved to draw it from its wooden scabbard. Karn recognized it by the hilt even before its blade was free.

"That's Whitestorm," he said in shock. Karn had never seen it out of his father's possession.

"Well, I wasn't going to walk through the woods at night without protection, was I?"

"You have your own weapon," said Karn accusingly. Theft was a serious crime in Norrøgard; theft from one's own folk, doubly so.

"An ax," said Ori. "And we both know I don't have the build to put much power behind it. No, what I really need is a sword. Big brother won't mind my borrowing it. Relax, nephew. It will be back before he knows it. And now we have a named blade so you can make your wish."

Karn wasn't convinced, but he didn't want to say so. Instead, he tried a different approach.

"I don't even know what I'd wish for."

"Really?" When Karn shook his head, Ori said, "Oh, I think we both know that's not true."

"Uncle?"

"In a funny way, I guess you're too much like me. We're both trapped by the accidents of our birth, aren't we, boy? If you had an older brother, like I do, you could come and go as you please. You wouldn't have to bear the burden that your father has laid on you. He never asked you if you wanted to be hauld of his farm. And I imagine he doesn't listen when you try to tell him how you feel."

Karn nodded, remembering his conversation with his father in the streets of Bense.

"It's hard to talk to him sometimes."

"Of course," Ori said. "It isn't fair. Such a responsibility. Such a chore for someone who can lift his head to the horizon and has the imagination to wonder what's beyond it. Wouldn't you like to see for yourself?"

"Like that's going to happen."

"Worth a shot, isn't it?" The boy made no move to take the sword. "Go on," said Ori. "It's already here. You're here. If we're going to get in trouble for swiping Korlundr's sword, we may as well do something with it. Take the sword, tap it three times, and let's see if any wishes get granted."

"This is foolish."

"Agreed," said Ori, "so what are you waiting for? There's a whole wide world beyond Norrøngard. Or do you want to be nothing but a farmer your entire life?"

His entire life. That was the crux of it. Karn nodded, giving in. He reached for the sword. Ori held it toward him point first, then realized what he was doing. He sheathed and reversed the blade so that Karn could take the hilt. As Karn's hands closed on the leather-wrapped grip, Ori held on to it for a moment.

"Remember, you must knock three times."

Karn nodded, and Ori let the blade go. His uncle stepped aside so that he could approach the corpse door.

"Three times?" said Karn. Ori didn't answer. Behind him, Karn heard his uncle walking back up the ramp.

"Uncle Ori?" he asked.

"Oh, didn't I tell you?" his uncle replied. "You have to be alone for the magic to work. No good if I'm there with you. But don't worry, I won't be far."

Ori disappeared around the hill. A chill ran up Karn's spine. It was dark, and it was cold. Karn wanted to run, to chase after Ori in the dark. But he did no such thing. To do so was to admit that he was afraid. Worse, it was to accept that a farmer was all he'd ever be. He steeled himself and turned to face the corpse door. The eerie green foxfire seemed to play across the stone. Better to get this over with quick, thought Karn.

"I wish I didn't have to be a hauld," said Karn. "I wish I could go far away."

Then he drew Whitestorm—the sword was surprisingly light in his hands for such a long blade—and knocked its point against the stone. Once—the sound of metal on stone rang in the air—twice, three times.

Nothing happened.

Doubtless his uncle was having a good laugh at his expense just down the hill from him now. Maybe Thianna was even with him, the two of them playing a joke on the farm boy.

Karn could hear his own breathing, heavier than he wished it was. Then he heard something else.

There was a scraping sound, like sand grinding on stone. Flakes of dust crumbled and fell from the corpse door. As he watched with mounting dread, the door split into widening cracks, the unearthly light shining through the gaps.

The corpse door broke into pieces and tumbled to the ground. Karn found himself standing before a gaping entrance, a tunnel leading into the barrow. It was lit up with foxfire, the walls of earth glowing green.

"Don't just stand there, boy." The voice was unnatural, dry, raspy. "Come in."

Ori paused at the edge of the forest. He arranged his clothing to look more disheveled. Then he slapped his own face to give it a nice, red flush. Lastly, he drew in a deep breath.

"Help!" he screamed, racing from the forest. "Korlundr, help!"

Ori raced up the hill toward his brother's tent, pumping his legs as hard as he could.

"Help!" he cried again, putting as much desperation

into it as he could stomach. Korlundr emerged from his tent, blinking at him in confusion.

"What's going on?" Korlundr asked.

"Karn is in trouble!" Ori yelled.

"Karn? What? Where?" the big man demanded.

"In the woods," Ori blurted. "Trouble. Come." He turned and ran down the hill as if someone's life depended on it. Someone's does, he thought.

"My sword—" Korlundr began.

"Karn has it," Ori said.

"Karn?"

"Come quickly!" Ori shouted.

Behind him Korlundr called out.

"What is happening with Karn? What trouble is he in? Tell me, brother."

"Don't worry, brother!" Ori called without turning or stopping, knowing his twin would follow regardless. This really was too easy. "Now that you're here, it will all be over soon."

Karn stood frozen, gazing down the tunnel into the barrow. The balefire flickered on the earth walls. But the slope of the tunnel kept him from seeing inside the chamber.

Karn took a step into the dark. He held the sword, Whitestorm, out before him and crept slowly along. The soil beneath his feet was damp and gave under his boots.

The tunnel smelled of dirt, mold, and the crawling things that live beneath the earth. But overwhelming all these smells was a rich, sweet, cloying scent. It was the stench of rot and decay. The smell grew stronger as the light grew brighter. Karn felt queasy, but he pressed on. He had to know what was inside. And then he did.

The chamber was round and low-ceilinged. The floor was of dirt, like the tunnel, but the walls were lined with stones, all carved elaborately with runes. There was treasure everywhere. The Norrønir always buried their dead with their prized possessions and those practical items—cooking utensils and favored weapons—that they might need to take down with them to the afterlife in Neth's caves, but Karn could tell that this grave was something special. This was a jarl's grave, a dragonship captain's grave, a grave of a very powerful and greedy man.

Swords and axes and shields and spears and armor. Ornately carved cups and fancy dishes. Jewelry. Drinking horns. Statuary, some of it foreign. Clothing. Furs. Knives. Cooking utensils. Even a gleaming, golden set of Thrones and Bones.

Karn's eyes only lingered on the treasures for a moment before something else caught his attention. There were real bones piled on a real throne.

On an imposing stone chair, a skeleton sat ramrod straight. It was still outfitted in what once must have been fine-quality armor, now shabby and dented. The leathers that it wore were rotting and ragged. The helm on its head tarnished. The great ax by its side rusting. Bits of gray beard still clung to its jaw like stringy cobwebs.

But that wasn't the worst thing. No. The worst thing was this: Ghostly green balefires lit the chamber—but those ghostly green balefires originated in the sockets of its eyes.

"Hu, hu, hu." The sound was like a gust of wind pushing through dead leaves. It echoed around the chamber. The grinning skull was laughing.

The skull lifted to face him.

"I swear, the challengers are getting younger and younger these days. How old are you, boy? Ten? Eleven?"

Bony fingers moved to grip the armrests of the throne. Karn stood, mouth agape, face to face with a creature out of legend. An After Walker. A draug.

"Well?" said the undead creature. Karn swallowed.

"Twelve," he said.

"A shame," said the draug. With an unnerving creak of bone, skeletal arms levered the corpse up to its feet. One hand casually reached down to grip the handle of the great ax that rested beside the throne. Knucklebones cracked as the fingers tightened on the shaft. "Not much of a talker, are you? Well then, let's get this over with."

"What are you doing?" said Karn.

"What am I doing? I'm Helltoppr." The draug leaned forward, as if the flames in its sockets were taking a better look. "Didn't you hear the legend? Don't you know the song? 'For if you stand, you'll surely fall; and if you fall, stand you will for now and all.' That not ring any bells?"

"That was real?" asked Karn, remembering his dream but dumbstruck by talking to a corpse.

"Of course it was real. I was betrayed and murdered one hundred and forty-five years ago. And men—boys now, I see—have been breaking into my barrow to chal·lenge me for my treasure ever since." Helltoppr hefted his ax and swung it lazily around to smack the shaft against his other palm, his fingers shifting into a strong, two-handed grip.

"I see you have brought your own weapon. Otherwise, the rules say you could choose one from among all of mine. It's just as well. I don't like other people touching my stuff."

"I—I don't want . . . ," Karn stammered. "I'm not here to challenge—"

"Nonsense," said the draug. He jerked his head to the side in what looked like an imitation of spitting. "You knocked three times. You entered my chamber, weapon drawn in challenge. Now we fight. If you win, you can choose from among my hoard. If I win, well, you know what the song says."

"What the song—?" said Karn, backing away rapidly from the corpse striding toward him. "No. No, I was told you'd grant a wish."

"A wish?" said Helltoppr, still barreling down on Karn. "Oh, a wish will be granted, boy, make no mistake. But what in Neth's name made you think it would be yours? Now, be a good boy. Stand still, and let's get on with this."

Helltoppr raised his ax, preparing for a swing. Karn didn't wait to see the blade fall. He turned and ran.

CHAPTER EIGHT

The Runestone

Karn burst up out of the barrow and into the open air. Still, he was a long way from safe. He could hear the After Walker trudging along behind him. He ran toward the ring of standing stones.

Then a shadow detached itself from the nearest runestone. Cold, fleshless hands reached out for him. Karn skidded to a stop. For a moment, he thought that Helltoppr had somehow managed to outflank him, but then he saw it. This draug was smaller. Also, its skin was a deep maroon color, darker than the blue-gray of the undead Jarl. This was another draug, not Helltoppr at all. Something from one of the three smaller barrows.

The desiccated lips pulled taut in a nasty smirk.

"The name's Snorgil, in case you're wondering," it said. "At your humble service."

"Th-thank you, n-no," Karn sputtered. He turned and bolted away from the creature, only to see a second figure leap from behind another stone.

"And that be my good friend Rifa," Snorgil said. The new After Walker held a bony hand to its chest and executed a mock bow.

"Your service," the one called Rifa said.

Karn heard a footfall behind him and realized that Helltoppr had emerged from his barrow and was walking down the hill. He was going to be surrounded if he didn't act fast. Still, Karn didn't look back.

He waited for Rifa to come closer, then he feinted to the left, and when the draug reached for him, he bolted to the right instead.

"Don't be like that," Rifa complained.

Behind him, he heard Snorgil laughing.

"Oh, he's a slippery one, he is," Snorgil roared. "Gave you the slip, did he, Rifa?"

"Shut your mouth," said Rifa. "Your teeth fall out when you flap your gums, you know."

"Shut your own," said Snorgil. "You've less teeth left than I do. Anyway, loosen up. You're the stiffest stiff I know, you are."

Karn took the opportunity created by their bickering to dart for a space between runestones, but a third undead After Walker reared up to block his path.

"Oooooooo," hooted Snorgil. "Seems you've met the last of our little band. Visgil, say hello to young Karn Korlundsson, will you?"

"The pleasure is all mine," croaked Visgil from his rotting mouth. Karn saw this one had very few teeth indeed. "Truly it is."

They had Karn surrounded and were closing in. He had four opponents. But the playing field had over a dozen obstructions. If there was one thing Karn knew, it was how to use the layout of a board against an opponent.

He took off running, heading straight for Rifa, then twisting at the last minute. Karn zigzagged in and out of the runestones. He was outnumbered. Every time he tried to get off the hill, one of them would appear to block his path. But while he stayed among the stones, he could twist in ways that kept them crashing into each other and the rocks. And he was learning. The draug weren't very coordinated, and there were limits on Helltoppr's movement. Anytime he approached the ship shape marked by the runestones, he winced and fell back. The ship of stones defined the boundaries of his domain. He scowled when he saw Karn had noticed.

Despite this disadvantage, Karn knew he wasn't going to elude the four draug for much longer. He was tiring and they didn't seem to be.

And then he slipped on some loose earth and went over, face planted in the ground. He scrambled immediately to his feet, spitting out dried grass, only to see that the draug had surrounded him on four sides.

"Enough running, boy," said Helltoppr. "Raise that blade and we'll get this over with."

"I don't want to fight you," said Karn. It sounded pathetic, but he couldn't think of anything else to say. He was desperate, and it was true.

"I bet you don't," laughed the After Walker. "But you haven't got a choice."

"Yes, he does," said a voice. Karn turned in time to see his father, Korlundr hauld Kolason, stepping from the darkness into the ring of stones. "Father!" exclaimed Karn, never so relieved in his life to see anyone.

"Give me my sword," said Korlundr, holding his hand out to his son while keeping his eyes trained on Helltoppr.

Karn started to hand the blade over when something stopped him. His arm was literally shaking with the effort to pass the blade, but it wouldn't obey.

"Karn, give me the sword," his father repeated.

"Don't blame the boy," the dragonship captain said. "He can't. It's the rules of the curse. The same rune magic that keeps me trapped inside the stones compels you all. You fight me with the weapon you bring, or you choose one of my own. The boy brought the sword—a very familiar sword, now that I see it clearly—so only Karn can fight me with it. If you want to challenge me, you'll have to use what you brought or pick one of mine."

Korlundr looked down at his belt. He had his sax knife,

but that dagger was pitifully small against Helltoppr's great ax. The After Walker smiled.

"Won't you come in," he said, gesturing toward the tunnel entrance. "I'm sure we can find something in your size."

"Father?" Karn's voice cracked with worry. Helltoppr looked up as if only just remembering him.

"Keep the boy here," he said to his three followers. "He'll be child's play after I've dealt with the big man."

"Don't worry, Karn," Korlundr called to his son. Then he squared his shoulders and walked bravely into the earth.

Karn flinched as a cold hand rested on his shoulder.

"Don't worry so," said Snorgil. "Some you win, some you lose. The important thing is to be a good sport about it."

Karn gulped and said nothing. All his thoughts were for his father under the earth.

Korlundr reemerged after only a few minutes. He had a short spear in his hand. Karn saw that the shaft was made of the same metal as the blade. Maybe it would give him a chance to block the draug's ax.

"How do we do it?" said Korlundr.

"Like this," said Helltoppr, rushing forward and swinging his ax in a great arc.

Korlundr leapt back, then jabbed at the draug with his spear. Helltoppr was quick, though, and darted away before the blade struck. Karn surged forward, but Snorgil's grip tightened on his shoulder, holding him fast.

Karn tensed up as he watched his father and the After Walker dance around the barrow. Helltoppr was supernaturally strong, swinging his heavy weapon without tiring or pausing. Korlundr blocked it or dodged it again and again. Karn felt a swell of pride for his father. His father was a hero, just like the great Norrønir in the songs of old. He'd never seen anyone fight so well. But Korlundr was tiring. Even in the cold night air, Karn could see the sweat standing out on his father's forehead. He'd have to do something soon.

Korlundr raised his shaft to catch the ax as it plunged down in an overhead swing. He kicked out with his booted foot. The blow caught Helltoppr right in his chest. The draug went reeling backward. Korlundr swung his spear around and drove it into the draug's side. Helltoppr gasped and dropped his ax, clutching the shaft buried in his chest.

Snorgil and the other undead shifted their feet nervously. Taking advantage of their uncertainty, Karn knocked Snorgil's hand off his shoulder.

"A very good blow that was," said Helltoppr, with something like genuine admiration in his voice. "And if ordinary weapons could harm me, you might have won." Then his left hand grabbed Korlundr by the neck. "Too bad the only named weapon here is in a boy's hands, not yours." Helltoppr tightened his grip on Korlundr's throat. "And so you lose."

"Karn!" called his father. "Run!"

Korlundr stiffened in the draug's grasp. And then the strangest thing happened. His skin hardened and grew gray. The air shimmered around him. As Karn watched in horror, a runestone appeared where his father had been standing. Carved on its surface, as if it had been chiseled there years ago, was a crude image of his father. But unlike the carvings of Helltoppr's other victims, who looked frightened as they were defeated, Korlundr's image still appeared proud and defiant.

"No! Father!" Karn cried. There was no answer.

Helltoppr walked around the new runestone, sizing it up.

"A nice addition to my collection, if I do say so myself," he said. "'For if you stand, you'll surely fall. And if you fall, stand you will for now and all.' Come on, boys. Place it in line with the others. Just need one more to see my curse lifted." Then the draug turned his eyes on Karn.

"One more."

Karn's scream was pure rage. Not only at the After Walkers, but also at himself. If he hadn't come here, if he hadn't knocked three times . . . He hefted Whitestorm in both his hands and swung it in a wide circle around him.

Snorgil, Rifa, and Visgil leapt away, hissing when Whitestorm brushed them. Karn saw, and he lunged out at the nearest. Rifa yelped and jumped back a pace. Karn followed. He'd cut them all down.

Suddenly Helltoppr was before him, the great ax lifting up.

"You may frighten my boys, boy," said the dragonship captain. "But you don't frighten me. After all, that sword used to be mine."

Karn's eyes widened. Then he couldn't help himself. He glanced down at the weapon in his hand. Whitestorm, Helltoppr's sword? The sword that was stolen from him when he was betrayed. But that would make Whitestorm the legendary sword of Folkvarthr Fairbeard. It was only called Folkvarthr's Fortune in the old legends. But swords could have many names.

"I'll be wanting it now," said Helltoppr. "That's right. Your great-great-great-great-grandfather took the sword off me, curse him and curse all his children. But it warms my undead heart to think it will be two of his descendants who complete my stone ship."

Helltoppr took a step closer, the ax still poised high above his head. Karn saw all the pieces. Saw their positions. He was facing uphill, which put Helltoppr at the advantage. Or did it?

Karn raised Whitestorm before him, as if prepared to fight. Helltoppr smiled.

Karn threw himself backward, drawing his knees in and somersaulting in reverse in a way that would have impressed even Thianna. His own momentum and the slope of the hill carried him over and over again. It wasn't graceful, and he had to struggle to hold Whitestorm straight out so the sword didn't trip him up or cut him, but he rolled down the barrow mound and through the stone. Above him, he heard Helltoppr hiss as the barrier of the longship kept him from pursuing.

"After him!" the draug screamed at his followers. Karn didn't wait to see if they obeyed. Scrambling to his feet, he cast one last look at the runestone where his father had fallen. Then he turned and ran.

At the edge of the forest, Karn skidded to a halt as someone stepped from the trees.

"Uncle Ori!" he cried out in relief. But his uncle was looking at him strangely.

"Oh, Karn," he said, "what have you done? For Neth's sake, boy, what have you done?"

"M-my father," stammered Karn. "Helltoppr, the draug . . ."

"I saw it all," said Ori.

"You saw?" exclaimed Karn. If his uncle had been there, why hadn't he helped?

"I hid behind the runestones," his uncle explained. "You had the only weapon I carried. We both know I'm not much of a fighter. But Karn—what you did."

"What I did?"

"You woke Helltoppr, challenged him to a fight. Your father—"

"It wasn't my fault," said Karn. "I didn't know—"

"Wasn't it?" said Ori, his eyes narrowing and his voice taking on an accusing tone. "You went to the barrow mound on Winternights, woke the draug, challenged him to a fight with his own blade."

"That isn't how it happened—it isn't . . ."

"Please, Karn," said Ori. "I'm your uncle and even I can see how bad it is. The Norrønir don't look kindly on those who betray their own kin. I really should turn you in . . . ."

Karn's heart pounded in alarm. He'd lost his father, and he was going to be blamed for it. Norrøngard justice was swift and harsh. His world was crashing down around him, and the earth felt shaky beneath his boots.

"I know I'll regret this," said Ori. He grasped Karn's shoulders in his own and looked deep into the boy's eyes. "But I'm going to help you. You need to run as far away as you can. Quickly . . . the draug are coming!"

Behind them, Karn heard footsteps. Snorgil, Rifa, and Visgil weren't far. Ori glanced at the sword in Karn's hands.

"Give me that," he said. "I'll hold them off while you flee."

Karn started to hand his uncle the sword, but something stopped him. His uncle couldn't fight any better than he could, and it was all he had left of his father. He shook his head defiantly. Ori reached for it anyway and Karn stepped back.

"Oh, very well," said his uncle irritably. "But go. Leave Norrøngard and never come back. It's what you wanted, after all."

The draug were close now. Clutching Whitestorm tight to his chest, Karn ran. He raced through the woods, pine needles tearing at his face and neck, tears streaking down his cheeks. He ran away from Dragon's Dance. Away from Korlundr's Farm. Away from everything he had ever known.

Ori watched his nephew disappear into the woods, listened as his footfalls faded into the night. Then he turned to the three figures that waited at the edge of the glade.

"He still has the sword on him," Ori said.

"Blast it, Ori," said Snorgil. "I knew that blade was going to be trouble."

"Trouble," said Ori. "No, I don't think so. He's never bothered to learn to use it. You'll get it back easy enough."

"Helltoppr won't like it if we don't," said Rifa, kicking at the ground with a rotting boot.

"Helltoppr should be quite happy with his latest runestone," Ori told the After Walkers. "Enough to keep him content for the time it will take you to hunt down the boy."

"Why didn't you catch him yourself?" asked Visgil.

"What?" sneered Snorgil. "Lazy ol' Ori get his hands dirty? Not on your unlife. Not when he can get someone else to do it for him."

"Yes, well," said Ori. "It's not like you three can get your hands any cleaner."

The draug all laughed at this.

"You do have a point," said Visgil, holding up a hand of rotting fingers.

"Always," Ori replied, blanching at the purple flesh. "Now, before my nephew gets any farther away . . ."

The three draug looked at him expectantly.

"You're called After Walkers, aren't you?" said Ori. "Shouldn't you be walking after him?"

"Oh, oh right," they said. Laughing again, they set off into the woods after Karn.

Ori sighed as he made his way back to Dragon's Dance. The draug were useful, but they weren't the brightest. Fortunately, he was. He had a bit more acting to do in the morning, something about how sad he was that Korlundr and his son had fallen. How he would only assume control of Korlundr's Farm with the deepest regret and the heaviest of hearts. He'd wait at least a month before he fired the freemen and replaced them with newly bought slaves. It would be only one of the many changes he hoped to implement. But his first act as the new hauld would be to do away with this ridiculous tradition of trading with Ymirians.

Speaking of the giants, that strange little giantess was looking at him when he reached the campsite.

"Have you seen Karn?" Thianna asked. Ori gave her an unfriendly glare. "We're leaving early tomorrow," she explained. "I thought I should say goodbye."

"My nephew and his father have already gone," said

Ori. "Korlundr decided to return to the farm early, and Karn went with him."

"Without saying goodbye?"

"I'm sure he didn't give you a second thought," said Ori. "We Norrønir only deal outside our own when we have to. Presumably, you were a pleasant enough diversion for a week, but I wouldn't flatter yourself he'll ever think of you again."

Thianna lunged at him and smirked when he started. Then she shrugged and walked away. Ori scowled as he watched her go. He didn't see how she could be trouble. But you could never be too careful. He didn't relish the idea of going up against a village of frost giants, or even one little one. But what was this creature with her strange half-giant height and olive complexion?

Glancing around to make sure no one was watching, Ori produced a horn from his satchel. It was smaller than the horn that Thianna's father had given her, but remarkably similar in design. Ori raised it to his lips and blew a single blast. No sound came out of it, but he had been told not to expect any. Unlike the single occasion that Thianna had blown her own horn, this blast wasn't heard by hundreds of creatures. It was only heard by one. And this creature wasn't thousands of miles away. No, this one was quite close by.

CHAPTER NINE

The Huntress

The final steps up to Gunnlod's Plateau made for the hardest part of the entire climb. Broad and high, built for giants and not humans, they were carved to look like part of the natural rock of the mountain. This made the steps hard to spot if you did not know what you were looking for, and they were even harder to use if you stood shorter than twelve feet. This was how the giants ensured that only their fellow giants ever visited the plateau.

Despite being too short to use the steps comfortably, Thianna still somehow managed to be at the head of the party of giants when they came in sight of home. Being among humans had been an interesting experience. Not as unpleasant as she had expected, but giants didn't belong down in green valleys; they belonged up in high, snow-covered peaks. She was glad to be back among her own and glad to return to life as usual. While she did not miss Thrudgelmir, she did miss beating him at Knattleikr.

As she took the last step, her father suddenly straightened up and came to an abrupt halt. Then his big hand gently but firmly pushed her behind him. She tried to move around, but Eggthoda stepped close as well. Not to be deterred, Thianna crouched and peeked through a gap between their limbs.

Creatures like nothing she had ever seen before, three of them, stamping their claws in the snow. They hissed and flicked their tongues out of their snakelike heads and twitched their batlike, leathery wings in discomfort in the cold.

"What are they?" Thianna asked, wide-eyed.

"Nothing that belongs here," her father replied. That was no answer, so she prodded Eggthoda in the back.

"Wyverns," the giantess said. "Nasty reptiles. Quiet, now."

Beyond the beasts, standing near the ornate door to Gunnlod's dwelling, Thianna saw three humans—humans on the plateau! It was unheard of. Her immediate thought was that some of the Norrønir had followed them from Dragon's Dance. But how would they have arrived here first? Plus, it only took an instant to see that these humans were nothing like the party from Korlundr's Farm. These newcomers were dressed in strange fashion. They were armed with swords and long lances and armored in bronze and black leather. They wore bronze helmets with black manes, and long, furred cloaks.

"Eggthoda," said her father, "get Thianna away from here."

"Dad?" said Thianna.

"See that she is not spotted," Magnilmir continued. "I will learn what I can."

"What's going on?" Thianna asked.

"Come, Thi," said Eggthoda.

"But . . ."

"You can help me unpack," Eggthoda said, swinging her packs from off her back and onto her side. The giantess kept them in front of Thianna as she ushered the girl swiftly toward her door, hiding her from the strangers' view. Inside the house, Eggthoda shut the door quickly.

"The women outside," said Thianna. "Who are they?"

Eggthoda ignored her. Instead, she tore open both of her packs and upended them over her workbench. The carefully wrapped foodstuffs and wooden items bartered from the Norrønir tumbled out in a pile. The giantess rooted through them, tossing the carved cups and containers aside, picking the dried meats and vegetables, her own cooking utensils, clothing, bedding. These she began to repack, adding in food and other supplies from her quarters.

"Where are you going? Are you going somewhere?" asked Thianna.

"Not me. Us."

"Us? We only just got back."

"I hope it won't come to it, but better to take warning early rather than late."

"Why? What's going on?"

At that point, Magnilmir strode into the room. His eyes found his daughter, and Thianna saw the hurt in them. He spoke to Eggthoda.

"It has been so long. I did not think to fear this day."

"Dad, who are these humans?"

"I do not know their kind, and they will not volunteer who they are. But their complexion, except for the hardness in their eyes, reminds me of your mother."

Thianna only had hazy memories of her mother. She knew her more as the still form under the ice in the Hall of the Fallen than as the warm woman who had held her as a child. Even so, she would never forget the dark look that crossed her mother's face whenever she was asked where she came from. Or the silence that followed. If the strangers were from her mother's past, they were to be feared, not welcomed.

"What are they doing here?"

"More to the point," said Eggthoda, "why now?"

"Good questions both," said Magnilmir. "And I can only answer one and only partially. They have heard rumors of a half-sized giant who is darker in appearance than a Norrønur or Ymirian. Gunnlod is warning them off, hoping that they will leave. But we must trust the whole village to keep silent."

"Thrudgey." Thianna spat out the name.

"Will not place humans over giants," her father said. But Thianna knew. Thrudgelmir did not consider her a giant. "We will trust that the village will keep silent and the strangers will fly away. But if it comes to it, I will lead them into my home first. While they are inside . . ." His voice trailed off, but he nodded to the two packs.

Magnilmir bent and hugged his daughter. Thianna could not relax for fear that her father was holding her for the last time. Too soon, Magnilmir let go, then he went back outside.

Eggthoda and Thianna crouched at the front door. They had the door open just a crack. Angry words came in from the plateau outside. Thianna was warmed that Gunnlod hadn't given her up. The old chieftess had never been particularly friendly, but her protection meant she must regard Thianna as a real member of the village. As to Thrudgelmir, she wasn't so sure. So far, Gunnlod's glares had kept his big mouth sealed. How long this would last, Thianna didn't know. Not much longer, would be her guess.

The voices outside ramped up into shouting. Several of the giants shifted their hands toward the shafts of their clubs. Thianna felt Eggthoda tense.

"Enough of this nonsense and prevarication!" the lead stranger yelled. Her two companions whipped their long lances around from their backs in smooth arcs so that they pointed dangerously forward.

"What are they doing?" asked Thianna.

"Being fools," whispered Eggthoda. "Those things are too long to be any good in close combat. And two against a village isn't good odds. Even if they weren't so short."

Thianna wasn't so sure. The strangers looked like soldiers, and soldiers wouldn't willingly walk into a situation they didn't think they could control.

Fire burst from the tips of the two lances. The two strangers lowered them to the ground and scorched a half circle of flame that continued to burn when it hit the snow. Steam hissed and rose into the air in white clouds. The giants stumbled back in alarm from the unwelcome heat.

"We know there is a half-breed among you," the woman said as the fire cracked around her. "Her mother is of our kind and our kin. Give her to us, and we can leave the rest of you in peace. Make me angry, and regret it."

One of the lances rose to point directly at Thrudgelmir's face.

Thianna's fear mixed with contempt when she saw the young giant cowering. Then his face hardened.

"Troll dung," he spat. "She doesn't belong here anyway. She never did."

The leader of the strange women smiled.

Magnilmir turned and bolted for his door.

"After him," the lead stranger called.

Thianna almost rushed into the open as well, but Eggthoda stopped her.

"He wants them to follow," the giantess explained. "Now." Eggthoda lifted the two packs and pressed one into Thianna's arms. Together, they burst through the door.

And came face to face with Thrudgelmir.

Thianna stared at him. Never a friend, often a tormentor. But rivals in Knattleikr didn't mean an enemy in life, did it?

"You never belonged here," the giant said. Then he yelled, "She's over here!"

Eggthoda knocked him over the head with her club. He dropped like a stone. It was too late, though. The strangers turned their way.

"There she is!" the lead stranger yelled.

A wyvern kicked up clouds of snow as it plunged down in front of her. Even Eggthoda flinched before the snarling serpent's head. The other two beasts dropped out of the sky on either side. They were trapped.

"Follow me!" shouted Thianna. She raced into Eggthoda's cave. Thianna skidded to a halt at Eggthoda's rear door, pausing only long enough to draw the heavy bolt and jerk the door open. She charged into the network of natural caverns under the mountain.

"You can't go there!" Eggthoda yelled when she saw

Thianna's destination. "You're running right toward them!"

"Can't be helped!" Thianna yelled. "Have to get something. Won't be a moment."

She yanked open her father's back door, and thank Dead Ymir, it wasn't bolted. She could hear her father's angry voice yelling at the intruders from the front caverns.

Thianna tiptoed, not daring to breathe.

Inside her bedroom, she went for her skis and poles, lifting them as carefully as she could, trying to keep them from knocking against each other.

She had almost made it to the back door when the woman turned.

"I see her," the woman called.

"Troll dung," Thianna spat. No need for caution now. She ran for all she was worth.

Eggthoda was ready at Magnilmir's back door. Just as the woman reached it, the giantess slammed the heavy stone door in her face.

Thianna stopped at a place on the ledge where the slope ran down to the stream on a less steep gradient than elsewhere.

"The stream," she called to Eggthoda, who was catching up with her on the ledge. "You say it comes out?"

Thianna dropped her skis to the ground and stepped into them, snapping them to her boots.

"On the other side of the mountain, yes," said Eggthoda. "But the passage is too low for a giant."

"Too low for a giant, yes," said Thianna with a wry smile. "Perhaps not too low for a little human."

"You don't know that."

"I don't know it's not, either."

"The water is too cold for you to swim in."

"I know. That's why you are going to freeze it."

Above them, they heard the sound of Magnilmir's back door crashing open.

Thianna kicked off and skied down the bank. Eggthoda slid awkwardly down behind her.

"Thi, this is mad."

"I know," said Thianna. "Be quick."

Eggthoda grabbed Thianna in a tight hug. Then the giantess knelt and placed her palms over the stream.

"Skapa kaldr, from the water shape ice, skapa kaldr. Skapa kaldr, from the water shape ice, skapa kaldr."

There was a loud, cracking noise as the underground stream froze over.

"It won't last long," said Eggthoda. "I'm not that strong a caster. You won't be able to stop."

"Can't stop anyway," said Thianna.

Eggthoda drew a chunk of phosphorus from her pack. It was fixed to a loop of cord.

"For light in the tunnel," she said, draping the cord around Thianna's neck.

Thianna nodded; then she kicked off.

"Stop!" cried a voice above.

Thianna didn't dare glance back. Skiing on solid ice was too tricky.

"I will hold them off!" Eggthoda shouted behind her.

Thianna swallowed, hating that she was the cause of this invasion. She gasped as the frozen stream cascaded over a slight fall. She was airborne for a second; then her skis struck the ice in a teeth-chattering impact.

She heard a roar and felt heat behind her. Flames curled around her on both sides. Her pack must be singed, maybe burning.

"I tell you, stop!" cried the woman again. "Stop!"

But Thianna was already around a bend in the stream. It was sloping steeply downward now, flowing into the tunnel mouth that carried it out of the caverns and into the heart of the mountain. She would draw the strangers away from Gunnlod's Plateau. She would pay any price to protect her home. Racing on slippery ice faster than she'd ever skied before, she sped into the unknown.

CHAPTER TEN

The Escape

Thianna raced down the hill. The snowfall, combined with the clouds that had settled onto the mountain, made for flat light and low visibility. She flew at breakneck speed into a field of white on white. Thianna was an intuitive skier, however. She could read the terrain through the feel of her feet. After skiing in the dark on a frozen stream, this was a cakewalk. Moreover, the thick powder meant that her occasional fall didn't hurt, and the cloud cover would shield her from her pursuers. But as the day wore on, the cloud would burn off, leaving her visible from their vantage in the sky. Hopefully, she would put some real distance between herself and Gunnlod's Plateau by then. In the meantime, the hard physical effort kept her mind off the magnitude of what she was doing. It kept her from thinking too long about the pain of leaving home, the concern for her father, and the thrill, she had to admit, of having made it through the mountain alive.

She had spent most of the night traveling under the rock until she had come out on the opposite mountainside. Eggthoda's magically induced ice ran out in the open air, and only the sound of rushing water had alerted her to the approaching plunge over a falls.

At least she didn't have to worry about her direction. Down. Down the hill. As far away and as fast as she could go. Anything to draw the strangers from Gunnlod's Plateau and those she loved. Thrudgelmir had been right that she didn't belong. Although she didn't understand exactly how, Thianna knew she was the cause of their trouble.

She would eventually need a source of food, as well as shelter from the cold. The latter concern wasn't a major problem for one of frost-giant blood. Food presented a bigger challenge. Not much grew at this altitude. She would have to hunt for game if she was going to eat. And all she had was a wooden sword.

Karn slammed headfirst into a wall of rock. He stumbled back, brushing dirt from his face.

He would have stopped before colliding if he weren't so tired. Karn had no idea how much time had passed.

He had run for what seemed like days, leading the draug through the thick woods. They weren't especially fast, but Snorgil, Rifa, and Visgil were tireless. They didn't stop to rest, or for any other reason, and so Karn could not stop either.

The After Walkers had come close a time or two, almost close enough to catch him. But he had always managed to break away. He studied the wall. It didn't ascend very high, maybe only twelve or fifteen feet. Karn looked for handholds in the rock face, then glanced at nearby trees, debating whether climbing or running made more sense.

A branch snapped in the woods behind him. Karn froze.

"Quiet, Rifa," hissed a voice Karn guessed was Snorgil's. "You're loud enough to wake the dead, you are."

"I've got news for you, Snorgil," Rifa whispered back. "We are dead."

"Then you are loud enough to wake me."

"But, Snorgil, you *are* awake."

Karn next heard a sound that a fist of dried bone might make if it were punching someone in a rotting nose.

"Ow," said Rifa. "What was that for?"

"You know what it was for," said Snorgil. "Now, be quiet or you'll get another one just like it."

Footsteps began crunching in the underbrush. The draug were getting closer. There was no longer time for Karn to try scaling the rock or a tree. Turning to the right, he ran as quietly as he could, moving perpendicular to the wall. Unfortunately for Karn, as quietly as he could wasn't nearly quiet enough. Twigs and leaves crunched, sounding to his ears like explosive bursts in the still air.

"What's that?" Snorgil called out. "Boy, is that you?"

Karn dropped any pretense of stealth and doubled his pace.

"Ha, ha," one of the draug roared. "The way is blocked. We have him." The draug had found the wall.

"It's just as well," said Snorgil. "My feet are killing me."

"But, Snorgil—"

"And don't say I'm already dead, unless you want another punch. I haven't forgotten."

The three After Walkers closed in on Karn. He ran as fast as he could now. He honestly didn't know where the energy came from.

"I think I see him!" yelled Snorgil. "Go ahead and run, boy. Run the fight out of you. Makes it easier for us to take you when we catch up."

Karn ducked his head and pressed on. The draug was probably speaking true. This really was the end. A stupid way to go, out here in the middle of nowhere.

Suddenly, the rock wall on his right dipped away. A natural overhang made a shallow cave in the stone. Karn's pulse quickened. There was a figure standing against the far wall. Karn yelled in surprise and stumbled to the ground. The After Walkers heard him cry and shouted excitedly.

They would be on him in seconds. There was no time to get away. Rolling over, Karn kicked his heels in the earth, propelling himself backward into the rock shelter and toward the figure. He had to hope whoever it was would be on his side. Either way, he couldn't turn his back to the draug. Karn brought his father's sword up before him, though he hardly knew what he would do with it.

His head crunched into hard stone. Looking up, he saw the figure looming over him. A statue.

The draug came pounding into view. They slid to a halt before the rock shelter, their rotten heads swinging back and forth.

Karn froze. At any second, he expected them to pounce. He held Whitestorm in front of him, tried to get his feet under himself so that he could stand, but his arms shook and his legs had no more strength.

Still, the draug didn't attack. Snorgil twisted his neck this way and that, a look of confusion on his rotten face. His gaze passed right over Karn where he lay at the foot of the statue, and didn't stop. Almost as if he didn't see it or the boy.

"Where did he go?" the draug asked. He stuck his nose in the air and sniffed. "I don't even smell anything."

"That's because you stink, Snorgil," Rifa said. "Your own rot drowns out everything else. Anyway, it's a good thing your nose hasn't worked properly in years or you'd know."

"How is *your* nose, then?" Snorgil asked.

"Just fine, thank you for asking."

Snorgil's fist crunched into Rifa's nose. Rifa screeched loudly.

"And now?" asked Snorgil. "How is it now?"

Visgil laughed at this until Snorgil shook a fist at him as well.

"Spread out and find the boy," he ordered.

"Relax, Snorgil," said Rifa. "He can't be far."

"Then where is he?" asked Snorgil.

"It's like he's just vanished," said Visgil.

"It's just our bad luck if he's gotten away," complained Rifa.

Frustration and confusion on their rotting faces, the three After Walkers walked on, and none of them so much as glanced Karn's way. They really hadn't seen him. Karn couldn't believe his luck.

As their footsteps died away, Karn sat up slowly and looked around. He saw that the statue stood on a small pedestal. It was crusted with the wax of long-ago-melted candles and littered with rusted coins and withered flowers. This was a shrine. The landscape of Norrøngard was dotted with them. Some were hundreds of years old. Karn rolled to his feet, anxious to avoid upsetting the offerings to a god.

Standing, he saw the enigmatic look carved on the figure's face: half smile, half frown. Then he took in the game board tucked under one stone arm, the acorns in the palm of the other. These were symbols of chance and fortune. The statue was of Kvir, the fickle god of luck. Kvir was said to frown or smile upon you, depending on his whim. Somehow this shrine had hidden him from the draug's view. Karn dropped to his knees in gratitude, glancing up at the stone face above him. He saw he had knelt on the frown side of the statue. That was when he heard the wolf howl.

The scream in the air set her teeth on edge. It must have been loud indeed for her to hear it over the wind whipping past her ears. The wyverns were high overhead, just dark silhouettes against the gray-white sky, but they were descending, heading her way. She'd been spotted.

The young giantess was speeding down an open slope. Of course she was easy to spot. There was no cover. Her dark hair and clothing must have stood out on the wide white mountainside. Her only hope lay in speed, and plenty of it. She tucked herself in tight, pointing the tips of her skis straight downhill. She remembered something her father said: Luck is one thing, brave deeds another. Well, Dad, she thought, I'm going to need a bit of both. Then she had no time to think at all.

Thianna raced down the mountain. She hit a mound— what they called a *mugl,* meaning "little heap." Her skis left the ground; then she made a hard landing on packed snow. Thianna tried to keep her legs bent and limber to absorb the blow, but still her teeth slammed together painfully. Each mound in her path sent shocks through her body, but she didn't dare weave around them. She had to stay straight. She had to stay fast. And no matter what, she couldn't—didn't dare—fall.

It was maddening—Thianna knew the wyverns were on her tail, but not how close behind. She couldn't help imagining leathery claws reaching down from the sky for her neck, or a scorching burst of a flame lance blasting her into charred bones on the white ground.

Then she saw something worse. A canyon ahead. A narrow fjord, carved by an ancient glacier. She was skiing toward a cliff that stretched as far as she could see from right to left. She would have to stop before the edge, and then she'd be reduced to poling without the momentum of a downhill run. The wyvern would overtake her easily, trapping her with a canyon to her back.

Thianna had made small jumps before, but she had never tried to cross a gulf as wide as the one ahead of her. She knew she didn't have enough speed.

She thought of Eggthoda's cantrips.

Thianna squatted down even lower and touched the wood of the skis.

"Skapa kaldr skapa kaldr skapa kaldr," she murmured. She just needed to summon enough cold to supercool the wood of her skis and form a thin layer of ice on their undersides. "Skapa kaldr skapa kaldr skapa kaldr," she chanted.

The skis shot forward. She was a one-girl avalanche

hurtling toward an abyss. Behind her, the frustrated cries of the wyverns told her how close they had been. Then the canyon's edge was upon her.

For a moment of frozen time, Thianna was airborne. Glancing down between her skis, she saw the rushing water of the fjord far below.

The skis slammed into the ground on the opposite side. Thianna let out a whoop of victory—a long, wild, triumphant yell.

Just ahead, a welcome sight. She had reached the tree line. Trees meant cover. She plunged into the woods as the angry wyverns roared. She heard screams from one rider as its mount fought to keep from crashing into the wall of the woods. She had to shift all of her attention to tight weaving between tree trunks. Skiing in deep woods was dangerous. You could slam into a tree and break a bone, or worse; and then there was undergrowth, rocks, and roots, which could snare a ski and tear it from your foot, sending you careening headlong into a trunk. But weaving between trees was nothing compared to dodging wyverns. At least for now, she had eluded her pursuers.

Karn was farther north than he would have planned. The golden colors of the changing season were giving way to the whites and grays of the snow-covered foothills of the Ymirian mountain range. The alpine trees and green grasses had been replaced by rocky outcrops and scrub.

Karn's feet slipped more than once on icy ground as he marched uphill.

He knew that traveling toward colder temperatures probably wasn't the smartest idea, but for now, Karn simply had to get away. Far away. What he would do and where he would go once he was free of wolves and After Walkers, well, he'd cross that fjord when he came to it.

Karn had vague notions that he might find a cave to hide in or maybe a promontory he could stand atop from which he might defend himself. He imagined himself tall, upon a large boulder, lobbing off draug heads and wolf snouts with his father's sword, Whitestorm. It was a heroic image. But not a very likely one. Not when he was shivering so badly he could barely stop his hands from shaking. If only his father were here.

His eyes began to tear up from more than just the cold wind. He fought them back.

"It's my fault!" he shouted to the mountains.

He had lost the draug at Kvir's shrine. At least that much luck was with him. But the wolves—the wolves were harder to shake. The pack had kept up with him. The beasts were staying mostly out of sight, and always out of range of a good stone's throw, but they weren't giving up or going away.

Karn's feet slipped again as loose rocks shifted under his boots. He bit it, landing facedown on the snowy slope. He spit snow and rubble from his mouth. He was so tired, he almost didn't get back up. But lying still for a moment, he could hear soft, padding noises that weren't of his making.

Karn spun around. There was a wolf just downhill. Karn wished he had a good bow or even a spear. He didn't pretend his sword would do him much good against this many. His hand scrambled for another loose rock. He pried one up and flung it hard behind him. It missed the wolf, which nonetheless leapt away with a yelp. But two more wolves appeared downslope. This was bad.

Karn tossed more rocks as he rose and ran. He scrambled up the hill, but it was slow going on the difficult terrain and the wolves weren't dropping back this time.

Ahead, Karn saw a lone fir tree clinging to the mountainside. It was his only choice. Behind him, the wolves must have realized the same thing. They charged.

Karn pounded his feet on the slippery slope. If he fell, it was over. He didn't fall.

Reaching the fir, Karn jumped to grab the lowest branch, his cold fingers managing to grip the ice-encrusted bark. Using the very last reserves of his strength, Karn hauled himself up as the lead wolf slammed into the trunk below him hard enough to shake the branches and rain ice down on its furry head. Karn reached for the higher branches as the wolf below him leapt. Teeth snapped a handspan below his feet as he climbed higher into the tree.

Karn knew that his problems were far from over. Below

him, the pack began circling. They knew that sooner or later he would have to come down. Karn was trapped.

Karn studied the wolves. They twined among themselves as they paced around the tree. Their movements were graceful, fluid. Majestic. Great, Karn thought, it's not like being eaten by majestic animals is any better than being eaten by trolls.

He'd outwitted the troll. Maybe he could outwit the wolves. Karn studied the pack. Two were clearly bigger, a male and a female. He saw how the other wolves seemed to take their cues from these two. These would be the alpha male and the alpha female. The other wolves would be their children. They would follow the alphas' lead.

He couldn't drive the whole pack away, but maybe he could drive away the alphas. If only he had something to throw. He scanned the fir tree, looking for cones he could lob at the wolves, but it was too late in the year, too cold on the mountainside. Unfortunately, the firs here were deciduous, shedding the scales of their cones. If only he'd climbed a pine or a spruce, then he'd have something hard and sharp-edged he could toss at the wolves. Here, in the fir, he had nothing.

With a sinking sensation, Karn realized he did have something he could throw. If only he could bear it.

Reluctantly, he unlatched his satchel and dipped his hand inside. He ran his fingers over the cool pieces, feeling the texture of the marble and the whalebone. He hated the thought of parting with any of them.

He wondered which would be easier to replace, the whalebone or the marble. There were fewer marbles, just nine defenders to the sixteen attackers. But marble was heavier.

Karn sighed and lifted a marble shield maiden up to his eyes. Then he looked down at the hungry eyes of the alpha male wolf.

"I hope you appreciate my sacrifice."

Karn put all his resentment at having to ruin his prized Thrones and Bones set into his swing. He chucked the shield maiden hard. It struck the wolf a solid blow right on the snout. It yelped and jumped back.

"I hope you know this hurts me more than it does you!" Karn yelled. He pulled out another shield maiden and drove it hard at the wolf.

This time the animal saw it coming and dodged quickly to the side. The playing piece sank straight down into a bank of snow, gone.

"Oh, for Neth's sake!" roared Karn, who usually wasn't given to such language. "If I'm going to toss away my prized possessions, the least you can do is have the decency to stay still."

The next one he was more careful with. He took it out slowly, keeping it cupped and hidden in his palm. Then he pretended to ignore the wolf. He crawled out a little on the limb, trying to change his angle. Then he threw.

The hard marble made a good, solid *thunk* as it struck the wolf in the haunch. The animal howled now, losing its cool. Several of the younger wolves looked at it in puzzlement.

"Yeah," said Karn. "Big, bad wolf doesn't seem so tough now, does he?"

There was a growl below. The alpha female had stepped up to the trunk of the tree. She looked meaner than the male.

"Normally, I don't like to fight ladies," said Karn, "but under the circumstances, I'll make an exception."

His next throw caught her square on the snout.

"Yes!" He laughed, bouncing on the limb. It was too much weight this far from the trunk. It broke.

For a moment Karn was in free fall; then he caught hold of another branch. Wolves leapt at his feet, now dangling within their reach. He felt one brush his boot.

Karn scrambled up.

"Okay, won't try that again."

He put his back to the trunk and made sure his feet were steady across two branches. Holding on with one hand, he swung two more shield maidens in quick but precise succession.

This time both male and female ran away. Karn's victory was short-lived. They returned immediately. But he could see he was wearing them down.

One more shield maiden each. *Thunk, thunk.* The wolves were whining now. And he was out of shield maidens.

Reluctantly, Karn pulled out the Jarl. It was an oversized marble piece, the prize of his collection. But there was something fitting about using the alpha male of his Thrones and Bones set to take out the alpha male of the wolves. Karn lined up the shot. No, not the alpha male. The female wolf was the tougher, meaner of the two. Wolves weren't like people. Karn thought of Thianna, remembering the tough half-giant girl. Maybe wolves were like people. He remembered Gindri's lesson about how his own assumptions could blind him. He aimed at the alpha female.

He put his best throw behind the Jarl. The playing piece had served him well in hundreds of games. It served him well here.

Howling, the alpha female turned and fled. Taking just a stunned second to watch her run, the alpha male bolted after her. The rest of the pack was right behind.

He'd done it. The wolves were leaving.

Karn waited a long time before he climbed back down. It was getting dark as he hung from the lowest branch and dropped, his feet crunching in the snow. He dug in the thick drifts, hoping to find his playing pieces, but he could only find two of the eight he had thrown, and neither was the Jarl. The Jarl was lost forever. Then he took another look at all the paw prints in the snow. His loss could have been far worse.

CHAPTER ELEVEN

The Wilderness

Thianna sat leaning against the rough bark of a tree. Twilight was coming on swiftly, and she wanted to take stock of her backpack before nightfall. She pulled out a small pouch of hazelnuts and set it carefully on one leg. Next came a knife. Good—knives were essential gear. Some cooking utensils. Root vegetables. She found a whole leg of roast goat wrapped up in skins, which set her mouth watering. She'd need to ration herself; she didn't know how long her supplies would have to last. As long as possible, obviously. There was some greasy mutton—not as welcome as the goat, but beggars couldn't afford to be choosy. Two small pebbles that were warm to the touch and had the stamp of the Dvergrian Mountains on them. A bit of rope. A small wheel of cheese, undoubtedly from

Korlundr's Farm. Thianna had to smile at this. Eggthoda had actually managed to bring some cheese all the way home. None of Magnilmir's cheese wheels had survived the trip back uneaten. The bottom of the pack held a tightly wrapped bedroll and an empty waterskin. And that was the sum total of her wealth.

Thianna carefully repacked all of her meager supplies, placing the bedroll on the top—she would need that soonest—and then climbed reluctantly to her feet. She hefted the pack onto her back, then plucked her skis from the snow where she had planted them. She tied them together and slung them over a shoulder.

Climbing a hill in thick powder—even her long legs sank nearly past her shins—was rough going. Halfway up the hill, she gave in to her growing hunger. One hour and a pouch of hazelnuts later, she had just about reached the summit. There, she found a small crevice below the lip of the hill where she could rest for the night.

Using a little of her precious cheese and some branches, Thianna spent a good while setting traps for small animals. Returning to the crevice, she dug into the surrounding snow and built up a hard-packed wall in front, both to trap warmth and to provide concealment. Unfolding her bedroll, she settled down for the night. After a week camped at Dragon's Dance, it didn't seem as rough going as it could have, though she was lonely and worried about her father and Eggthoda. Her flight had drawn the strangers after her, so hopefully they wouldn't return to the village. She worried about what they wanted from her until she slipped from exhaustion into slumber.

Once, during the night, she awoke. Gazing up through the small opening at the night's sky, she could see Manna's moon and her little sister. Suddenly, a dark shape flew across Manna's glowing expanse. A wyvern. But only one. Her pursuers must have split up to chase her. They must think that increased their chances of capturing her. They were wrong. It evened the odds.

Karn was starving, thirsty, tired, and cold. He'd been stumbling through the snow for hours, most of it in a daze. He'd seen neither wolves nor draug, but he hadn't seen much of anything else, either. He had no food and no supplies.

His thirst, at least, he thought he could do something about. He grabbed a handful of white powder and stuck it into his mouth. It was bitter cold, so cold it was painful, but the warmth of his mouth soon melted the snow. It gave precious little water. He scooped more handfuls of snow onto his tongue, hoping to get enough meltwater to slake his thirst.

What he got was chattering teeth and a frozen tongue. Karn pulled his strike-a-light and pouch of torchwood fungus from his satchel, then used hands, numb with cold, to break enough twigs and branches for a fire. It was a struggle to light the cold wood, but he knew he would pass out soon one way or another. If he collapsed before the fire was lit, he might not wake up again.

Thianna saw the smoke from atop a hill. Nothing out here would catch fire and burn by itself. Smoke meant something man- or giant-made. She realized that it might be her pursuers, but then again, it might not be. And if they were grounded, the frost giant's daughter was pretty sure she'd spot them first. Kicking off, she aimed her skis in the direction of the fire.

It wasn't long before she saw the source of the smoke. A lone figure was huddled over the remains of a small fire. It looked to have gone out recently, the puff of dark smoke the last gasp as the flames gave in to the cold.

Thianna didn't see any wyverns nearby. The figure wasn't dressed in the strange garb of her enemies either, but wore the skins and furs of a Norrønur. Surprising that someone would be alone in the wilderness, but not as surprising as what happened next. As she watched, the figure kneeling before the fire fell over. It lay in the snow, unmoving.

Growling, Thianna skied the rest of the way down the slope. She'd come looking for help herself, not to save some crazy fool without sense enough to stay out of the Ymirian cold.

Something about this one was familiar, though. Thianna turned sharply, skidding to a halt.

She stepped out of her skis, planting them upright in the snow to keep them from sliding downhill. She approached the still form.

"Hello?" There was no answer. "Hey, are you okay?" Thianna felt a chill that had nothing to do with the weather. Whoever it was might be beyond help.

Cautiously, she reached with her hand and poked the prone form in the back.

"Uhhhhhh," it replied. She started, then poked again. This time the figure twitched but didn't cry out.

"Okay," said Thianna, "Don't bite me or anything." Gripping a shoulder, she rolled over whoever it was. The face that flopped into view was familiar.

"Karn?" It was the boy from Dragon's Dance. The Thrones and Bones player who was such a stick-in-the-snow when it came to anything fun.

Karn's eyes opened.

"What are you doing here?" Thianna asked.

"Ffff—"

"What?"

"Ffff—"

"Fishing? Furriering? Falling, obviously."

"Ffff—"

"Farting?"

"Freezing, you silly girl," Karn suddenly spat.

"Oh," said Thianna. "Why didn't you say so?" She noticed his ice-blue lips and equally cold fingertips.

"Oh, Karn, you weren't eating snow, were you?"

"I was thirsty," he said weakly.

"Oh, you idiot. Don't you know that drops your body temperature?"

"Freezing. Thirsty," he managed.

"Okay, hang on."

As Karn lay there, Thianna dug in her pack. She pulled her bedroll out and tossed it over him. Then, after a moment's reflection, she rolled him over twice so he was wrapped up in it like a sausage in bread dough. She grabbed one of the warm pebbles next. She shook the stone to activate it, feeling a rush of heat in her hands. She dropped the stone in her waterskin, then scooped several handfuls of snow in after it. The stone was dwarf-heated. Ideally, it would be used to melt snow for drinking, but she'd given it a good shake, overcharging it. The melted snow in the skin would soon be a hot-water bottle. She tucked it into the blanket against Karn's chest. Then she set about her next task.

The hot waterskin began to revive Karn a little. He cracked an eye and stared at his rescuer. Thianna was busy piling snow and then packing it into large square bricks.

"Hey," he said, "I'm freezing here. Don't you think you could build your snowman later?"

She gave him a stern look.

"Does the boring southern boy want saving or not?"

"I'm not southern."

"Does the boring southern boy who argues with his rescuer want saving or not?"

"Okay, okay," said Karn. "I'm just asking."

Thianna had a good number of her snow bricks now. She hauled them over one by one and began to set them in a wall around Karn, using the slope of the hill as the back wall.

"Not more snow!" Karn cried out. "I'm freezing as it is without you burying me in it."

"I'm not burying you. I'm building us a shelter," she said.

"I'm not a frost giant. I can't live on ice like you can."

Thianna smiled. She liked the way Karn thought of her as a giant.

"You can," she said. "It's something my father learned from the Bear Folk. The walls will block the wind and once the roof is on, our body heat will warm it up nicely. Well, maybe not nicely, but near enough."

Karn was too tired to argue. He lay still and watched in amazement as she built the structure over him. He did recall something of the Bear Folk. They lived in the wilderness across the Cold Sea. This structure was called an igloo or something similar. He rested while Thianna finished building.

Before long, they were both inside the igloo. There was barely room for them both, and not enough for the giantess to sit up. But Thianna explained that the cramped space would heat up quickly. Thianna considered Karn a moment, then she dug in her pack and pulled out something that had his dry mouth fighting to salivate.

"Is that—?"

"Goat leg. Yup. I was trying to make it last, but, well, you need to get some strength fast if you are going to make it. Let's eat it now and worry about tomorrow's meal when we get there."

Karn nodded, too grateful to think beyond the immediate need of food. They split the leg. Thianna insisted on dividing it evenly even though she was clearly so much bigger than he. They both ate greedily, and when the waterskin began to cool off, they drank it down between them, careful not to swallow the precious dwarven pebble. As he filled up with food and drink and warmth, Karn found his strength returning. Thianna noticed, and she had questions.

"What are you doing here?"

"I don't want to talk about it."

"You don't want— You can't say that. You're alone in the middle of nowhere with no equipment and no supplies, freezing to death. *You.*" The way she said "you" spoke volumes about her low regard for his wilderness-survival skills.

"What about you?" Karn snapped back. "You often walk around in the middle of snowy nowhere alone?"

"I live here."

"Here?" Karn gaped. "You mean this is Ymiria? I've gone that far?"

"You don't even know where you are?"

"I was running, okay?"

"To where?"

"For my life."

That hung in the air.

"Is your village nearby?" Karn asked after a moment. A frost giant village might not be his ideal destination, but it would have food and shelter and a lot of very big giants he could place between him and any draug.

Thianna glanced through the small doorway in their ice shelter to the range of icy peaks that framed the horizon.

"Not near enough," she said wistfully. "Anyway, I can't go back there."

Karn gave her a questioning look.

"I don't want to talk about it either."

"Well, that doesn't leave us much to talk about."

Thianna shrugged. The Norrønboy wasn't of much use. He didn't have any supplies of his own, so he'd be a drain on hers. But . . . he couldn't survive out here without her. And it was good to have someone—anyone—to talk to.

"How about what we do now?" she offered.

"Find food and safety. But first, find food, obviously."

"Well, isn't that something," said a large voice from outside. "We go looking for food. And here we find food looking for food itself."

A large gray-green hand reached into their shelter to grip the ice block that formed the lintel of their small doorway. They saw broken and dirty fingernails, then the hand—and then the arm it was attached to heaved. The ceiling of their shelter was tossed effortlessly aside, landing with a *whump* in a bank of snow. Five ugly, hairy, warty faces glared down at them from above. Five faces, but only three bodies.

"Oh great," said Karn. "More trolls."

Thianna leapt straight up and out of their ruined shelter. She cleared the low ice wall and landed on her feet. The trolls hollered in surprise.

"Grab her!" one yelled.

"She's got more meat than the other," his second head added helpfully. They all sprang after her.

Karn hauled himself to his feet. He didn't feel fully recovered, but while the troll's attention was on Thianna, he thought maybe he could sneak away. It wasn't like he could fight them, and he'd seen how the giant girl moved. She had a better chance than he did, so he had to take the chance he'd been offered. He clambered over the wall.

"Hey, now, where are *you* going?"

One of the trolls, a two-headed one, had spied him

when one of its heads looked back. Now both heads swung to his attention.

"Food doesn't get to get away," one head said.

"I've got cheese!" Karn yelled. But he could see the teeth in both sets of mouths and none of them seemed to be broken.

"Good," said the troll. "We can toss it in to flavor the meat in the stew."

The troll reached down, and before Karn could move, he found himself gripped by the ankles and hauled up into the air. The creature shook him once, then brusquely patted him down, looking for weapons. It snatched Karn's father's sword and shoved the blade in its own pack. When the troll was satisfied the boy wasn't carrying anything else sharp enough to give it trouble, it swung him over its back.

Karn kicked and struggled, but the troll was moving swiftly, hurrying to join its fellows in the hunt for Thianna. Bouncing around, with his face colliding frequently with the troll's smelly bum, Karn couldn't tell what was going on, but he could hear the sounds of their exertions. Shouts of "Grab her" and "Get her" and "Squash her" were mixed with cries of "Curse her" and "Blast her" and "Ouch" and "What did you go and do that for?" It sounded like Thianna was giving as good as she got. Karn began to feel hopeful, but three against one was poor odds. Soon the noises quieted down and the trolls' shouts turned to wicked laughter.

The troll carrying Karn came alongside another one. Thianna suddenly appeared on its back, hung upside down by her ankles just like Karn.

"You ran," he said, somewhat stung she'd deserted him.

"You didn't," she shot back angrily.

Karn started to protest but the trolls were talking.

"We could eat the little one and take the big one captive," one of them said.

"The big one would make for better eating," another offered. "And I doubt she'd make a very good slave."

"You got that right, ugly!" Thianna shouted. "I'm nobody's slave."

"See?" the troll said. "Eat her now."

"Shut up," hissed Karn. "Are you crazy?" Then he called out loudly to the trolls, "She'd make a very good slave. She's strong."

"But she won't break easily," the troll objected.

"She will. She'll be grateful not to be eaten. Tell them you break, Thianna."

From her upside-down predicament, Thianna scowled at him.

"Tell them," Karn stressed.

"I break, I break."

"See?" said Karn hopefully.

"Anyway, we've still got a good bit of that moose we caught yesterday," said the troll. "We can haul these two back to Trollheim and let the king decide if they're for eatin' or slavin'."

This was generally agreed by all five heads to be a good plan, as the Troll King was sure to reward them for the capture, and his favor was thought to be worth considerably more than the scant meat they could get off their two prisoners.

"Plus," said one of the trolls, "you two will like Trollheim. Finest city there is. Everybody should see it once before they die."

"Which in your case," offered another helpfully, "might be pretty soon after seeing it."

"But count yourself lucky you'll get to see it first," the third offered.

So it was that Thianna and Karn were bundled along, dangling upside down behind two smelly trolls. Even worse, Karn's troll was flatulent, forcing him to jerk his head to avoid great blasts of smelly air from spraying him in the face. As desperate as their situation was, Thianna couldn't help giggling at him.

"You're impossible," he shot at her. "As bad as things are—"

"They aren't as bad as all that," said the troll carrying Karn. "You get to see—"

"Trollheim, yes, I know," said Karn. "Before I get eaten."

"Oh, cheer up. You're a little one. The king probably won't eat you for a few years yet. When you've gone and grown bigger."

"There is that," said Karn.

"See," said the troll, missing the sarcasm, "you've just got to look on the bright side." Then he let loose with a burst of flatulence.

"Ugh." Karn winced. "Any side would be better than the one I'm facing."

Thianna giggled again.

Karn glared at her.

"I know things are bad, Karn," she said. "Believe me."

"However bad they are for you," said Karn, "they're worse for me."

"Really? I suppose you just fled your village to draw the fire of mysterious, flying foreigners away from your home, did you?"

Karn couldn't think of a response to that. Not one he wanted to share anyway.

"Foreigners can fly, can they?" asked Karn's troll.

"Nobody can fly," said Thianna's troll.

"These can," said Thianna. "They are riding wyverns."

"Wyverns?" asked Karn's troll. "What's that?"

"Like little two-legged dragons."

"No such thing," her troll replied.

"Anyway, you'll be safe from them where you're going."

"Trollheim?" said Thianna.

"Into a cooking pot, most like," said her troll.

"Anyway," said Karn, "you have to look on the bright side...."

Things went on like that for most of the day. Occasionally, the trolls would haul them around right-side up and shake them "so the blood going to your head don't kill you 'fore you see the glories of Trollheim," they explained, and then they would be swung unceremoniously over the great, warty shoulders and carried some more.

Karn and Thianna tried to whisper to each other, but it was hard to be heard over the troll's conversation, bouncing around upside down, and they weren't always side by side. But during one of their shakings, when they were proceeding up a precarious ridge between two hills, Thianna thought she noticed something—a swirl of snow like the vortices that Eggthoda had shown her.

Thianna puckered her lips. She let out a strange, high-pitched warbling whistle.

"Ow," said her troll, giving her a quick shake. "That hurt my ears."

"What did?" asked Thianna, all innocence.

"That noise."

"This one?" she asked. Then she let loose another loud whistle.

"Yes, that one," said the troll. "Stop it!"

"Stop this?" she asked. She whistled again.

"Yes, stop it!"

"So, to be clear," said Thianna, "you are asking me to stop doing this." She whistled again.

"Yes. Will you stop doing that?" said the troll, clearly getting angry.

Karn wondered what she was doing. Then he noticed the strange way the snow flurries were swirling around them.

"Skapa kaldr skapa kaldr skapa kaldr skapa kaldr," Thianna called out.

The snow in the flurries thickened. Karn could see shapes. They looked like eels made of snow, spinning in the air.

"What?" he asked.

"Frost sprites," Thianna answered. "Friends of mine."

"Friends of yours?" said a troll.

"Yes," said Thianna. Karn could see her grin. Karn was beginning to realize how dangerous her grin was. He kept quiet. She let loose another burst of "skapa kaldr" chanting.

The trolls gawked at the cavorting sprites. As Thianna cooled the air, the frost sprites grew more agitated. This worried the trolls, who ducked and batted at the sprites as they swooped around them. Inevitably, one of the trolls took a swing at one of the creatures. His great hand tore the sprite in half, but the snow that formed it quickly regathered into its previous shape.

Thianna beamed in self-satisfaction.

All at once, the sprites turned on the trolls. In an instant, the playful creatures transformed into savage monsters. They struck at the trolls again and again, taking vicious bites out of the trolls' hides with teeth sharp as icicles. Karn even saw one sprite shoot up a troll's nostril,

only to reemerge from its other nostril as the unfortunate troll howled and clutched its nose in pain. Amid all
this chaos, Thianna and Karn were forgotten, dropped
to tumble in the snow along with most of the trolls' gear.

Screaming and yelling, the three trolls ran and tumbled down an escarpment as the sprites pursued them,
icicle teeth snapping and biting.

Karn couldn't help himself. He cupped his hands and
yelled.

"Remember, you have to look on the bright side!"

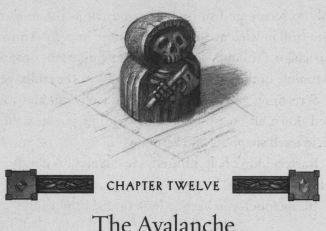

CHAPTER TWELVE

The Avalanche

"We've got plenty of meat," said Karn, digging in the trolls' discarded packs. "I wish it weren't moose meat, but we're better off than we were this morning."

"The bright side?" said Thianna with a smile.

"Exactly." He thought a minute. "You knew the trolls would upset the frost sprites, didn't you? You were banking on them not being respectful."

Thianna nodded, remembering the lesson that Eggthoda had taught her, which seemed so long ago.

"All creatures behave according to their nature," she said.

"Yeah," said Karn. "Well, I'm glad your nature is on my side."

When they had gone through the packs, they found

they had a week's worth of meat, a stone ax, several bundles of kindling, some threadbare blankets that smelled of troll, and a couple of poorly skinned hares. They found Whitestorm, to Karn's relief, as well as Thianna's pack, though her skis had been left behind. This put Thianna in a glum mood.

While Thianna sulked, Karn used some of the kindling to start a small fire. He set about roasting the hare—they weren't desperate enough to eat moose yet—and considering their next steps.

"We should head back south," Thianna said. "More chance of food and shelter."

"I can't go south."

"I could even pick up my skis."

"I can't go south."

"Can't or won't?"

Karn glared at her.

"Well, I won't go north," she said.

"You really fled your village?"

"Yeah."

"From wyverns?"

"Yeah."

"What—?"

"I don't know why they were after me. Something to do with my mother."

"Your mother?"

"Yeah. She was like you."

"Like me?"

"Human, I mean. But she wasn't a Norrønur."

"What was she?"

"She never said. Wouldn't say."

Karn noticed her use of the past tense.

"I'm sorry, is she—?"

"It was a long time ago. Anyway, if you wondered why a frost giant was so short and dark . . ." Thianna let her voice trail off. Karn looked for a way to divert her thoughts.

"But these foreigners are after you?"

"I think they come from wherever she came from. I think she was fleeing them when she first came here. I don't know why they've come back now, though."

"Rabbit's ready," said Karn. The meat was too hot to hold in their hands, so they passed the spit back and forth and tore into it with their teeth. As they ate, their moods improved.

"This is the best rabbit-on-a-stick I've ever had," Thianna said, only half joking.

"You think?"

"Sure. When we get wherever we're going, you could open a tavern. Stick Rabbit à la Norrønboy."

"That's a mouthful."

"So is this," said Thianna, ripping into the hare and tearing off a big chunk. "But I bet you'd totally put whoever the local rabbit-on-a-stick guy is out of business."

"So I open the Norrønboy Tavern. What will you be?"

"Not your serving wench, that's for sure."

"Wouldn't dream of it. You could be my doorman. Uh, door woman? Door giant?"

"Keep the customers in line? Break the kneecaps of anybody who tries to leave without paying? I could do that." She fake-glared at Karn from under her dark bangs. "What's this job worth? What kind of coin do you pay in?"

"Well, I don't have any money," laughed Karn, "but I can guarantee you a steady supply of Stick Rabbit."

They fell into easy laughter then. Karn pulled the other hare from the fire and took a great bite of it.

"Truth, though? This rabbit needs something." He wished they had some salt.

"Hold on," said Thianna. She dug in her pack and pulled out the wheel of cheese. "A little piece of home."

Karn's face fell when he saw Korlundr's famed cheese. He pictured his father as he had last seen him, a rune-stone on a barrow mound.

"Karn," said Thianna, seeing the look in his eyes. "What is it? Did something happen to your father?"

"The story Ori told us. It's true. I woke Helltoppr. I called him out. I did, my fault. Those stones in the long-ship shape are all people. When you lose a fight with Helltoppr, you turn into one."

"Oh, sweet Ymir," Thianna said.

"And . . . and there's a new standing stone now."

"Korlundr?"

Karn nodded.

"It was supposed to be my fight. My father took—" Karn's voice broke. It was all he could do to stammer out his next words. "H-he took my place. That stone. It should have been me. It should be me."

"Oh, Karn, I'm so sorry."

"I can never go back, you understand?" He met her eyes and she saw how haunted his were. "How could I tell them what I've done? My mother, my sisters—I've ruined all our lives."

They sat by the fire a long time, nibbling slowly at the second hare and, yes, eventually some of the cheese. Karn told Thianna more about Helltoppr and the events in the barrow. Thianna told him about life on Gunnlod's Plateau, about Thrudgelmir, and then finally about the huntress in bronze and gold. Karn sat up straight at the mention of wyverns.

"Her name is Sydia," he said.

"She didn't give her name," Thianna replied. "I don't know it."

"I do. It's Sydia."

Thianna gripped his arm.

"You've met her?"

"She was in Bense—that's a town we trade in. Weeks ago. She was asking about—"

"About me?"

Karn thought back to his altercation with Sydia at Stolki's Hall.

"No. At least I don't think so. She said she was looking for something, not someone."

"Something? You're sure?"

"Yes," said Karn. "Something that was lost long ago."

"She must have meant my mother. She didn't know she was dead. I don't know why she's after me, though. Unless she thinks I'll lead them to her."

"Can't they find your mother in the Hall of the Fallen?"

"The ice is foggy without a cantrip. And no giant, not even Thrudgelmir, would desecrate that hall by clearing it for an outsider. So, if I stay on the run, Sydia stays away from the village. But if I go back, Sydia will invade my home again. So I can't go north."

"I can't head south," Karn said.

Thianna nodded.

"We should head east," she said. "For a bit at least. We can cut south when we're clear of Norrøngard. Then we can head down into Saisland, or Araland."

"Sydia, her two lackeys, three draug, Thrudgelmir." Karn ticked them off on his fingers. "That's a lot of enemies between us."

"We could even try for Escoraine."

"I hear they have good cheese there." Karn snorted. "And probably no Stick Rabbit. Anyway, the farther, the better."

"Agreed."

Thianna constructed another shelter, teaching Karn how it was done as they worked. She had no trouble plunging her bare hands into the snow, so he made use of the trolls' ax and one of their blankets to help shape the bricks. That evening they were almost warm as they lay inside their makeshift shelter. The smell of the trolls was strong, but not as strong as it had been when they were dangling against their backsides. Thianna produced a small phosphorous stone that gave off a wan light when it was shaken. Now that they had a large stock of fresh meat, they ate heartily of Thianna's mutton, and she again used her dwarf stone to melt water for Karn. He noticed she only used it for him. When she was thirsty, she could melt the snow in her mouth, untroubled by the cold.

"Can you even go south?" he asked.

"What do you mean?"

"You're eating straight snow. You're a giant. The cold doesn't bother you. Does the heat?"

She shook her head.

"It doesn't seem to. Cooking fires, hot springs, sunny days—all the things the other giants steer clear of."

"Best of both worlds, huh?"

Thianna stared at him.

"Never thought of it that way. Being able to take the heat just marks me as different, you know. Not fitting in."

"Nonsense," said Karn. "You can take the cold as well as any of them. Taking heat too just marks you as special."

"Thanks." She leaned back on her elbows. "So, what about you? What's special about you, Norrønboy?"

"Not much, really. I never really had to be."

"There must be something."

"No. Well, I'm good at Thrones and Bones."

"Oh yeah, your boring game."

"*Board* game."

"What did I say?"

"Well, I'm good at that."

Thianna sat up, careful not to bump her head on the low ceiling.

"So how do you play?"

"Like you care."

"Like we have anything else to do."

Karn shrugged. He rummaged in his pack and withdrew the board. Then he lifted out the pieces.

"Oh," he said. "I used the defenders' team to chase off some wolves. I only have the attackers now."

"Wow. You lost your precious playing pieces." Karn nodded sadly. "What did the defenders look like?"

"Eight shield maidens. One Jarl."

Thianna reached under their blankets and scooped up a handful of snow. She molded it into a crude figure, then pressed the snow together in her hands, muttering a cantrip as she did so. When she uncupped her hands, Karn saw the snow had hardened to near-transparent ice.

"Will that do?"

"Yes, if you make seven more, and a larger one. But you'll have to play the defenders. I'm not freezing my fingers off moving those around."

Karn and Thianna played until late into the night. She wasn't particularly good at Thrones and Bones, but he found that teaching her was a different kind of fun and he enjoyed showing off his talent to the frost giantess. They slept late afterward, then rose to a glorious, sunlit morning. The air was clear, the sky a brilliant blue. They set out east, working their way carefully down a broad bowl of loose powder that shifted and slid under their boots, and felt considerably brighter.

"There's not much of a bright side to things today, if you ask me." The speaker was the optimistic troll head who had tried to console Thianna and Karn when they were his captives. His other head just grumbled and swore as their shared body stumbled along through the snow. They and their two companions were bleeding from multiple savage bites. The frost sprites had chased them for miles, mercilessly nipping at them again and again. The trolls were a hardy lot, but they were still stinging from their frost-sprite wounds.

"No one did ask you," said another troll.

"The next time we find humans camped out here," said the third troll, "we squash first and ask questions later."

"But if we squash first," said the optimistic one, "how

can they answer questions later?" No one answered but his own second head, butting him savagely in the temple for that bit of stupidity.

"Ow!" he hollered. "That really hurt! Then again, looking at the bright side, how could this day get any worse?"

As if in answer, a huge black-winged reptile plunged down from the sky, landing in the trolls' midst and kicking up a whirlwind of snow. A woman in bronze and black armor sat astride the beast. She looked cruel and hard, respectable troll traits to be sure, and the creature was unfamiliar, and thus threatening. But they were three in number (with five heads between them) and they'd already hit on "squash first" as their preferred policy for dealing with humans.

The trolls fanned out, trying to outflank the creature. It snarled and swung its long neck back and forth, glaring at first one of them, then another.

"I'm looking for someone," the woman said.

"What do you think it is?" said one troll to another, as if she hadn't spoken at all.

"Is it good to eat?" asked the optimistic one. "Because if we are going to squash something, we should eat it."

"Excuse me, boys," said the woman. "I said I'm looking for someone."

"If two of us grab a wing each, the third can smash its head with a rock while it's pinned down."

The creature hissed and jerked its head back on its neck as if it understood.

"Would it taste like chicken, or snake?"

"That's practically the same taste."

"I don't have time for this," grumbled the woman. "Boys, your attention please."

"I don't see any rocks. Will a large tree branch do?"

"Anything big and heavy, really. Just crush its skull."

"Perhaps you didn't hear me. I said, your attention now."

The woman sighed. Almost casually, she unslung a large lance from her back. The trolls were still giggling when it shot out a burst of flame that struck the single-headed troll squarely in the chest. In a blink, he was utterly engulfed in fire. He ran off, screaming and howling, a blazing ball of flames tumbling down the white hill, leaving melting snow and nasty ash in his wake.

"Do I have your attention?" the woman said.

The four heads of the other two trolls looked at each other, then at her.

"I'd say you got it now, miss," said the optimistic one.

"Good," said the woman. "My name is Sydia. As you might have guessed, I'm not from here. But I'm looking for someone. A young girl. Unusually tall, though not I suppose from your perspective. Dark complexion. Athletic."

The trolls thought about that.

"Maybe we seen her," one said at last. "If that's the case, what's in it for us?"

Sydia smiled.

"That's a good question. I'd say, what's in it for you is that you don't have to burn up."

It wasn't as big an upside as they'd hoped for. But no troll likes fire. They decided to cooperate.

"We captured someone like that earlier today. Come to think of it, she might have mentioned someone like you was chasing her. Only she got away from us."

"She got away? From three of you?"

"She was tougher than she looked. And she had help."

"Summoned some frost sprites, she did," said the other. "They bit into us something fierce."

"You didn't kill and eat her, then?" asked the woman, her eyes narrowing and her grip tightening on her lance.

"Not as such, no."

"It's lucky for you you haven't harmed her yet."

"You don't want her harmed?" asked a troll.

"I didn't say that. I don't want her harmed before I find her. But that's my business. Yours is to tell me where you last saw her and what direction you think she was heading."

"Hard to say."

"Harder to say with your head on fire, you mean." Sydia leveled her lance and thumbed a trigger. The end gave a little burp of flame that set the trolls cringing.

"It was west of here, on that ridge." A troll pointed.

"We ran north, northwest from there," the other troll said helpfully, stating the obvious.

"She wouldn't have followed you, so we can rule this direction out."

"No, I don't suppose so, and the going's hard on the southwest side of the ridge. They would have headed east."

"They?"

"Yeah, don't you know? There was a boy too. Scrawny little human feller."

"I didn't know she was traveling with any boys," said the woman.

"Just the one, ma'am," said the optimistic troll. He'd added *ma'am* to be polite, since she had just set his friend on fire.

"She was alone when she fled her village," Sydia said. She leaned forward in her saddle. "Tell me everything you can about this boy."

"He was scrawny."

"So you said."

"He was most inconsiderate about my body odors."

"Ghastly manners, but hardly germane."

"He did say he had some cheese."

"Okay, but still not really relevant," said the woman. "I'm afraid that you aren't helping me, boys." She thumbed her lance menacingly. Her mount snorted in a way that was as unsettling as the lance itself.

"I think the girl called the boy 'Cairn' or 'Corn' or something. Maybe it was 'Karn.'"

"Karn," said Sydia. "Now that is something. Very well, thank you for your help. You can go now."

"Nothing for our troubles?" said the other troll. He rubbed his fingers together.

"No further troubles for your troubles," replied Sydia. "But if you like, I could light you up."

"No, no, ma'am," the trolls said hastily. "We'll just be heading away."

"See that you do."

Sydia closed her eyes as if in prayer. When she opened them a moment later, her mount suddenly reared up, screeching and beating its wings. The trolls ducked as the creature took to the skies. They watched her climb higher and higher, until she was a dot in the white sky.

"That was something."

"Well, maybe now it's safe to say the day can't get any worse," said the optimist.

"Oh, I wouldn't say that," said a new voice. "I'd say there's always lower you can go."

Three creatures strolled into their midst. They were human in appearance, but rotting and decayed like walking corpses. The draug. And they were slinging rusted but wicked-looking weapons casually back and forth in their bloodless hands.

"Now," said the undead speaker, "how about you boys tell your good friend Snorgil here who that was you were just speaking to and everything you just told her."

"Hold on now," said a troll head. "What's in it—?" He was about to say "for us" when his companion punched him in the gut, shutting him up. The optimist, it seemed, had finally learned his lesson.

The snow continued to shift and slide under Karn's feet. The bowl was full of loose powder, and a misplaced footstep could send them tumbling down the hill. It wouldn't be long before the sun dipped beneath the high crags and draped the bowl in long shadows. It would be even harder going in the dark, but rushing was just as dangerous. The trolls had carried them a surprising distance—farther north and higher in altitude than they wanted to be. Now they had to make up for lost distance and time.

Sometimes Karn hated snow. Then it struck him that where they were heading might not even have snow. Even though he had always wanted to leave the farm, this was not the way he'd imagined it, running for his life in shame and grief. He looked at the giantess. Despite her bulk, she moved with a lighter, more assured step than he did. She was so much more a creature of this frozen land than he could ever be. And yet she was leaving it just as he was.

"What was it like?" he asked, glancing northward at the Ymirian mountain range. "Growing up in the mountains, I mean."

"Best place ever."

"That doesn't really tell me anything. What's it like *living* there?"

Thianna pursed her lips as she studied the ground, choosing her footing.

"You spend a lot of time looking up," she said at last.

Karn laughed, uncertain if he was supposed to or not. He couldn't tell if she was making a joke. Seeing her smile back was a relief.

"I'm serious, though," she said. "The mountains—they are incredible and they go on forever. Right to the top of the world. The sky is so big when you are up there. You really feel like a giant. And also really small. Of course, everyone's taller than me. But everything is just bigger, you know. Big games. Big celebrations. Big arguments. My dad, though—he's the biggest thing around."

"I know what you mean," said Karn. Strange to think of this enormous person as a small girl having to survive by her wits and dexterity among much larger, rougher folk.

"So this rabbit-on-a-stick tavern," said Thianna, snapping him out of it. "Is that all it's going to serve?"

"What do you care?" laughed Karn. "You're just the door giant."

"Door giantess. Get it right. But we door giantesses have to eat."

"My mother makes a mean skyr," Karn said, thinking of the creamy, soft Norrønir yogurt. "Maybe I could try to re-create her recipe."

"Yeah? I might like that better than cheese. Go on."

"Only . . . I don't have any skyr with me, and it takes skyr to make skyr. You have to mix in a little of the old batch to get the new batch to taste right."

"That's too bad. Maybe we could score some on the way across the border."

A sudden screech in the air overhead made Karn miss his footing. He waved his arms to keep his balance, then cast his eyes skyward.

Three wyverns and their riders.

They looked around wildly. Apart from a few rock outcroppings, the terrain was smooth and featureless. There was no cover anywhere.

They ran along as best they could, hurrying down the slope. The wyverns dipped closer and closer, then dropped to the ground, aiming to surround them on three sides, but their hasty landing sent the snow sliding and slipping under them. They flapped their wings in an ungainly manner as their riders struggled to stay mounted. *You're not used to this—no snow at all where you come from,* thought Karn. He filed that information away.

When the wyverns had found their balance, the lead woman turned her attention on Thianna.

"So," said Sydia in her peculiar accent, "you are the one that's giving us so much trouble."

The woman and the girl studied each other. Thianna stared into the face of her enemy for the first time.

"Only trouble is what you brought," Thianna replied.

"If only that were so," said Sydia. She gave a regretful shake of her head.

"And you . . ." She looked at Karn. "Aren't you the boy whose father fraternizes with giants? Even so, it's odd to find you alone here together."

"Nothing odd about it. We're just taking a stroll, enjoying this lovely weather. But what are *you* doing here?"

"Hunting for this one," she said, indicating Thianna. Her wyvern stretched its neck toward the giantess in a threatening gesture, but this unbalanced the creature. The reptile hissed as the snow shifted under it.

Karn noticed. And he noticed the drifts of snow around them. Taking stock of the game board, he thought. Very slowly, he began to step backward up the hill. He met Thianna's gaze, willing her to understand, but she was focused on Sydia. Typical, unsubtle Thianna, looking for a fight.

"Hunting for my mother, you mean!" barked Thianna.

"I don't think so," said Karn, who was putting things together in his mind even as he was trying to get Thianna's attention. When she met his eyes, she wrinkled her brows in confusion. Not understanding. Hadn't she learned anything from their Thrones and Bones session? The playing field was everything.

"What do you mean?" said Sydia, her eyes narrowing.

"You said you were looking for truth," Karn said. "But I don't think you were speaking it. In Stolki's Hall. You said then you were looking for something that was lost years ago. *Something,* not someone." He spoke to the giantess. "Thianna, what are you carrying? What did your mother give you that this woman wants?"

"Nothing," said Thianna, frowning. Then, withdrawing a small metal horn from her satchel, she said, "This?"

All three wyverns grew agitated. More snow slippage. More claws scrambling for balance. Hissing.

Sydia hissed too.

"Give it here," she said. "Hand it over and we can all go home."

Thianna examined the horn curiously. She had thought it was a trivial, inconsequential thing.

"My mother died a long time ago," she said, almost to herself.

"Talaria was always trouble. Years before she went and started this ruckus. But we were never after her. We were after what she stole. The Horn of Osius."

"What is that?"

"Nothing that matters to you. But long ago it was in my charge. My honor was stained by its loss. Now give me the horn, and we will leave and forget all about you and Talaria and the trouble she caused."

Thianna was still pondering the horn in her hand. The Horn of Osius, not that the name meant anything to her. It really didn't matter to her very much. Or did it? Then there was Sydia. The woman who had chased her mother. Her mother who had fallen from the sky.

She took a step back up the hill toward Karn.

The wyverns advanced on them, stomping clumsily forward on shaky legs.

Karn grabbed Thianna's arm and pulled her up beside him.

"Blow the horn," he whispered.

"What?"

"Aim downslope and blow the horn."

"What?"

"Just do it," Karn insisted.

"You're right," she said, addressing Sydia. "This horn really doesn't matter very much to me."

Sydia smiled and reached a hand forward.

"But you matter even less."

Thianna placed the horn to her lips and blew.

Karn was surprised when no sound came. He and Thianna were both surprised when all three wyverns grimaced and howled and plunged their heads to the ground at their own feet. The three women could barely control their mounts.

"I thought it didn't work," said Thianna.

"Too high-pitched a sound for us. Not for them."

Thianna nodded.

"Not too high-pitched for the mountain either, I'm hoping."

"The mountain?" asked Thianna.

The snow directly below them creaked; then a chunk of the mountainside came loose.

Karn's grip on Thianna's arm tightened and he hauled her backward.

"Upslope!" he yelled. "Move! Fast!"

They scrambled to get as far uphill as possible, while mere footsteps below them, the mountainside was erupting in churning powder.

Karn had a glimpse of the beasts and their riders as they were swept away in a surging current of white—and then he had his own problems. The ground under his feet was beginning to give way as well, sucked down by the shifting snow downslope.

While Sydia and her minions had no experience in snowy climes, every true son or daughter of the north knew what to do in an avalanche. Hanging on to each other tightly, Karn and Thianna struggled to make their way upslope and away from the center of the flow of snow. But fissures were running through the ice, huge sections tearing loose and shifting away. They had only gone a few paces when the ground under them gave out.

Karn's grip on Thianna's arm was torn loose as his legs flew out from under him. He landed on his back, but immediately flipped himself over onto his stomach. He drove his fists into the snow, trying to anchor himself, but everything under him was moving.

Karn fought hard, swimming as if he were in the sea, trying to stay atop the crest of the wave of snow. To stay atop was to stay alive.

He couldn't see a thing—there was almost as much

powder in the air as there was beneath him—and then the light diffused further as he went under.

Frantically, he thrust his arms out, punching his way to the surface and air, sliding like a human sled down the slope. The bulk of the avalanche had been below, but he was still in danger. He swam again, fighting to stay afloat.

He felt the snow start to slow down. Finally, he came to a rest. He lay still, trying not to disturb the snow around him while he caught his breath, and was totally unprepared when a huge wave crashed over him.

Karn struggled to curl up into a ball around his own arms, an effort to make as big an air pocket as he could. He was encased in a soft, white glow. Buried alive.

CHAPTER THIRTEEN

The Cliff

"Get up, Karn."

Karn gasped with relief as the snow above him was shoveled away. He looked up into Thianna's big face as the giantess scooped up handfuls of powder in her bare hands.

"This is the second time I've rescued you. I'm going to have to start charging."

"You rescued *me*?" said Karn indignantly. He sat up. "I seem to recall you being menaced by three angry lizards and their riders."

"Yeah, well, get on up. We can argue about who rescued who later."

Karn grabbed Thianna's arm and allowed her to haul him out of the snow.

"You weren't buried?" he asked the girl as he clambered to his feet.

"I'm a frost giant," she replied in a way that said she thought he was being an idiot. "We bodysurf in this stuff. For fun."

Karn grunted and looked around.

"Where's Sydia and her lackeys?"

"Somewhere in that." Thianna pointed downslope at the newly settled mounds of snow. There was no sign of anyone.

"Think they made it?"

"I'm not waiting around to find out."

"Agreed."

They made their way carefully out of the bowl, heading sideways, not down. If angry wyverns were going to be bursting up from the powder shortly, they'd rather be elsewhere. The sun had set enough now that night was rapidly coming on. Soon Karn and Thianna wouldn't be able to see anything downslope, but they *would* be hidden in its shadows. For the moment, they were safe.

After a short night and a long day of hiking south and east, Karn and Thianna were once again below the tree line. Where exactly they were below the tree line, though, was another matter.

"We're lost," said Karn.

"We're not lost," grumbled Thianna.

"So where are we?"

"Downhill from where we were."

"That's all you got?"

"What else do you need to know?" She turned around and pointed. "Sun's over your left shoulder. Keep it there; you'll be good."

They kept on like that for a while, until they came to a cliff's edge. Far below them, they could see sluggish, ice-choked waters flowing through a steep-sided valley.

"I think if we follow this, it will connect to the Argandfjord," said Thianna. She was speaking of the glacier-carved inlet that marked the easternmost border of Norrøngard. The Argandfjord was the greatest of the fjords and separated both of their homelands from the vast and inhospitable Plains of the Mastodons to the east.

"You've been to the fjord?"

She shook her head.

"Magnilmir told me stories about mastodon hunts when he was young."

Karn whistled. He couldn't imagine anyone actually attacking one of the enormous creatures. But then, Thianna's father was three times his size. He looked to the south.

"Hard to believe that we've come so far."

"That's usually what happens when you start walking in a direction and you don't stop for days. You get somewhere."

At Karn's glare, she gave him an apologetic smile.

"Anyway," he said, "this is way past the farthest I've ever been from home."

"Yeah, I'm right with you there, Norrønboy," Thianna said. "This is new territory for me too."

They stood awhile atop the cliff, looking down at the breathtaking view. "You think the southlands have anything this grand?" he asked.

"How could they?" she replied.

Several days' journey southward would lead them out of Norrøngard and into Araland, a land Karn only knew from tales of druids and warrior women. Rather than think about the adventures ahead, he found himself absorbing every detail of the walk, memorizing the features of his homeland for what was probably the last time.

At one point, they spotted a herd of reindeer drinking from the cold water. They would have welcomed the meat, but there was no easy way down to the valley below. Besides, they had no spears or bows, and swords would be useless for hunting the animals.

The temperature warmed as they progressed. Now the ice in the river thinned and the water swelled and picked up speed. The air was cold but clear and the sun shone bright above. Karn soon felt hot inside his clothes even as the exposed skin of his face froze. He saw that the frost giantess was sweating. She caught him staring and tossed her head.

"I'm fine," she said. "Just takes getting used to, is all."

It was as if there were two sides to Thianna, her giant

side and her human side. Karn wondered if that was like playing a Thrones and Bones game against yourself. Being both winner and loser.

"It would be better if we could find a way down," he said. The valley could offer them shelter and concealment, but so far the cliffs had been too sheer for them to risk the descent.

Picking up on his concern, Thianna said, "Still, we haven't seen any sign of pursuit in a while."

"You think maybe the avalanche . . . ?"

"Maybe," Thianna said. "Or maybe we just lost them."

Karn was just opening his mouth to tell her not to jinx them when they heard the screech.

The blast of flame from the fire lance came right on their heels.

Karn threw himself aside, striking the ground and rolling over. This was no warning shot. The rider had meant to kill.

The wyvern descended but didn't land. It hovered over their heads, out of their reach. Rider and beast had survived the avalanche and learned to be wary of their quarry. Karn had a sword, for all the good it did him, but no bow, spear, or throwing ax. He remembered the artifact Thianna carried, and the seemingly painful effect it had on the creatures.

"Your horn!" he cried to Thianna. "Use your horn."

The giantess fumbled at her pouch, but a second blast from the flame lance sent her leaping out of the way.

Even as Karn's heart beat, his head cleared. Only one rider and mount. Had the others perished in the avalanche? He didn't think so. The shot aimed at Karn had meant to blast him from the earth, but the ones fired at Thianna were meant to keep her from using her horn. So this rider was still under orders to capture Thianna alive. Perhaps scouting ahead while her boss was going back for reinforcements, or had they all split up to cover more territory? It didn't matter. Karn suddenly felt far less hopeless than he had before. He understood his opponent. So he could predict her moves.

"Thianna!" he shouted. "Stand your ground!"

"What?" The snow around her had been burned away, the rock underneath scorched. The ground around the girl was a muddy mess. Her usual catlike grace was useless in the slippery melt. But it just confirmed Karn's suspicions.

"Stand still. She won't shoot you."

"Are you crazy, Norrønboy? Shooting me is exactly what she's doing!"

"You stubborn girl. Trust me. Stand still and use your—"

The rider yanked her reins and twisted her mount around to face Karn. She leveled the lance, a snarl forming on her face as she thumbed the trigger.

He flung himself at the only safe place on the

mountain—Thianna. The rider jerked the lance up, the flame going over their heads.

Karn gripped Thianna's arms above the elbows, steadying himself and keeping them close.

"She'll shoot me. I'm not who they're after. But she won't shoot you. Or it." He indicated the contents of her satchel. "Use it now." Thianna pulled the horn out.

"Don't be stupid, girl," said the woman. "Just give me that and you can go home."

"What about Karn?" Thianna said, draping an arm over the boy's shoulder.

The woman's eyes narrowed. Karn saw how badly she wanted to burn someone. But she shrugged.

"Who cares about him? Just give me the horn. Then you can both go."

Thianna nodded, like she was mulling it over. The wyvern, beating its wings to stay aloft, glared hatred at both of them. Or was the hatred really for them? Its eyes were full of anger, but just who was the target?

Thianna glanced over the cliff's edge to the river below. The ice was mostly gone here and the water ran deep and swift.

"Only thing is," said Thianna, "we've been through this before. I don't like you very much, and I still don't trust you. So you want the horn, here it is."

She lifted the horn up to her lips and blew. Again, it made no sound. And again, the wyvern snarled and flung its head down as if it was in pain. Its rider was nearly flung out of the saddle and over its neck, but she hung on.

"Forget you," the woman spat. "If the horn melts, I don't care."

Flame shot again from her lance, but she was having trouble aiming with the wyvern wincing and bucking under her. Heat flared above their heads. At the same time, Thianna's left arm clamped Karn about the waist.

"Hang on," the frost giant said. Then Karn was off his feet, snatched like a rag doll, a yell building as Thianna leapt off the cliff's edge and into the sky.

Cold winds whipped past them, and then they were tumbling and spiraling in the air. Karn saw the face of the mountain flying past, saw the rushing water rising up to meet him. He opened his mouth to yell.

And then they hit. The breath was knocked out of him by the impact. The shock of the cold was almost as bad. Karn tumbled in the strong current of the river, dazed and numb. Then he was fighting for the surface. His woolen clothes, weighed down by water, seemed like they were full of stones. His father's sword dragged at his waist. His boots were heavy, making his feet almost useless.

Karn reached the surface and gasped for air, only to be plunged under again and tumbled head over heels. He couldn't see Thianna—or anything else but the white foam of the waters. The cold was horrendous. It was a struggle for each breath. He kicked and paddled and tried to make the bank, but the current swept him onward, over rapids and small falls. His feet struck rocks on the riverbed. If his ankles became stuck in a rock and the current dragged him on and over, he could be trapped under water by the force of the river. He would drown in an instant.

He pulled his feet in, but that resulted in more tumbling. Flipping onto his back, he tried to point his feet downstream, not to fight the current, but to let it carry him. This seemed to work better. He shot like a little longboat down the rapids. But he was still freezing.

No longer struggling, he took in more of his surroundings. He heard someone hollering. Craning his neck, he saw Thianna a little ways upstream, spitting and gagging and invoking all manner of troll dung as she cursed the water. He almost laughed.

"Don't fight it," he said. "Aim your feet and ride it out."

"What?"

"Aim your feet downstream!"

She must have heard him because the yelling subsided. Glancing overhead, Karn was relieved to see no sign of the wyvern. The river was carrying them so fast they would be far from the spot where they had jumped. But they would need to get out soon or he would freeze. He would have to wait for a break in the current and then make for the bank. The Norrønir had a saying: "If a man's time has not come, something will save him." But rushing down the freezing rapids, he thought of a more ironic saying: Out of the cooking pot, and into the fire. Fire, he thought as his limbs went numb. If only.

CHAPTER FOURTEEN

The Blasted City

Karn and Thianna lay on the bank, recovering their breath. The river had broadened as the mountains gave way to a wide valley, the water slowing enough for them to swim to shore.

Thianna pushed herself up onto her elbows and knees on the rocky bank and looked around. They were a long way south from where they had leapt from the cliff, but where they were, she couldn't say.

She stood, shaking water from her hair. Her clothing was heavy with water as well. It was uncomfortable, true, but she could handle it. Karn would be worse. She'd need to get him somewhere warm so he could dry off, or he would freeze again. She hadn't realized how fragile it was being human.

"Karn?" she said.

"A minute," he gasped, huddled on the ground and hugging himself. So she took the minute to examine their surroundings further. The river had carried them to a strange location. The valley before them was barren. It was not what she expected this far south, where the trees should be plentiful. Blackened trunks dotted the landscape, burnt to cinders as if they had been charred in a great fire. Beyond their dead trunks, she could see what looked like a vast wasteland of crumbling stone.

Thianna had never seen any settlement but Gunnlod's Plateau and the camp of Dragon's Dance. Thus it took her a while to realize that she was gazing at the remains of a dead city, long since toppled into decay. She knew that the people of Norrøngard built their towns and homesteads primarily out of wood. Whoever built this city had quarried stone. That meant it wasn't Norrønir. She had a sinking feeling that she knew where they were. They should leave immediately. If Karn didn't need shelter, if their pursuers hadn't found them . . .

She looked upstream, back toward the mountains, and she thought she saw a dark speck whirling in the sky. A speck that was growing larger as she watched. Then it didn't matter where they were. They had more pressing concerns.

"We need to hide," she said. When Karn didn't answer immediately, she grabbed him by the arm and hauled him to his feet. "We need to hide now." Then she pointed. "She's still following us. We need to get out of the open."

Karn nodded. His teeth were chattering. "Wh-wh-where?" he stammered.

Thianna gestured toward the ruins in the blackened valley ahead. Karn's eyes bulged.

"I-is that what I th-think it is?" asked Karn.

"Yes," said Thianna. "It is."

"S-S-Sardeth," he stuttered.

"The one and only, Norrønboy. Welcome to the Blasted City."

Nothing moved in the dead forest but a chill wind. Thianna helped a shivering Karn between rows of blackened trunks without seeing so much as a bird or squirrel. The ground underfoot was ashy, soft, like fresh powdered snow, but there was nothing natural or wholesome about it. She felt she trod in the dust of a dead past.

The trees gave way to mounds of weathered, gray stone. Here and there a tall, fluted column still stood, or a partial wall. Thianna wanted somewhere they could hide, a house that hadn't collapsed. She needed a roof to shield them from the sky.

The eerie quiet reminded her of the barrow mounds. Only this dead city was far larger. If ever a place were haunted . . .

As they drew nearer the center of the city, the buildings

appeared more intact. Here two walls and a partial roof, there an entire portico—though the dwelling behind it had collapsed. They passed statues standing solitary in what must once have been public squares. Many of the walls and arches were covered in elaborate carvings.

She saw statues of a woman with a lion-drawn chariot. A man with crescentlike horns protruding from his shoulders. A figure riding a horse bareback and wielding a staff. A creature with the upper body of a woman but the lower body of a fish. Bulls, lions, images of the sun and moons. The images made no sense to her. They weren't of any god, giant, or hero that she knew.

If anything like this city existed in the wider world, and still stood, the world was a much bigger and stranger place than it had ever looked from her mountaintop. It made her feel small. Thianna hated to feel small.

"The Gordion Empire," said Karn.

"Hey, aren't you freezing to death?"

"S-sure," Karn answered, his teeth chattering right on cue. "But this is the f-first time I've ever seen anything that isn't from Norrøngard or Ymiria. I m-mean, anything besides a traveling m-merchant. Or his wares."

"I think we're still inside the Norrøngard border, technically."

"Yeah, but we didn't build this. Soldiers of the empire did. Over a th-thousand years ago."

Thianna whistled.

"Don't you kn-know this stuff?" Karn asked.

"I've heard of Sardeth, sure," she said. "Just not the history expert you are." She looked around at the ruins. "You think anybody's been here since?"

"Of course. Every so many years some adventurer comes here looking for treasure."

"They ever find any?"

"Don't know. N-n-nobody's ever come back."

"Well, that's encouraging."

Thianna looked at the sky. She could see the black speck again, grown larger as it drew closer. It was more of a dot now. It ranged back and forth. The wyvern and its rider were obviously searching for them. It wouldn't be hard to work out where they had come ashore. She took a good look at Karn.

"Karn," she gasped. "You are turning blue."

"Is it a g-good color on me?" he asked, grinning bravely.

"That settles it. Shelter. And fast."

Thianna broke into a slow jog, dragging Karn with her. They were approaching the center of the ruins now, several of them smoldering as if they had been burned recently.

"Is there a fire?" Karn asked.

"We'll worry about that later."

Thianna pulled Karn to the looming, black doorway of what appeared to be a temple. It was rectangular in shape, with one narrow end facing what must have once been a main street. The stone above the doorway was carved with an image of a man with horns on his shoulders. A god, then. Ymirians didn't go in much for gods. She hoped this one didn't mind them intruding on his ruins.

Inside, a cold stone floor was littered with debris. There was the altar for the same god toward the back of the room, where the horn-shouldered guy stood over a large metal brazier.

Thianna left Karn to explore. The brazier was empty. She was hoping one of Karn's fabled adventurers might have left something in their explorations that she could burn. There was nothing on the temple walls but fungus.

She went back to Karn. His pack had survived the plunge into the river. She pulled out the strike-a-light and the remains of the torchwood fungus. The strike-a-light was still good. The fungus was sodden and disintegrated in her hands.

"We have to get a fire going," Karn said unhelpfully.

"Yeah, that's what I'm trying to do, Norrønboy."

"Why don't you?"

"Nothing left to burn that isn't burned already."

"Anything in the brazier?"

Thianna winced. He must be pretty far gone not to have realized she just checked it.

"Nothing?" he asked.

"No. Nothing."

"N-nothing you can burn at all?" he asked again. He was desperate.

"Nothing," she snapped. "There's nothing here at all but fungus."

She glanced down at the soggy, melted fungus smeared on her fingertips.

"Hey . . . wait!"

Shortly, Karn and Thianna were huddled around the brazier while a pile of torchwood fungus blazed merrily. Torchwood burned hot and fast, with little smoke and a lot of heat. Thianna hoped the scant smoke wouldn't give their position away amid the other fires smoldering around the dead city. They had shed their outerwear and stretched their clothes across the edges of the brazier. Karn was taking turns with each of their boots, roasting them one at a time on the end of Whitestorm like a sausage on a spit. The fire wasn't hot enough to hurt the famous blade, but he hoped the sword wouldn't mind the indignity.

Thianna suddenly burst out laughing.

"What?"

"You. You've gone from rabbit-on-a-stick to boot-on-a-stick. I'm having serious second thoughts about being the door giantess at your tavern."

Karn flicked Whitestorm and sent a hot boot flying into Thianna's lap. She just rolled over with it, laughing.

"It's done then, is it?" she laughed. "I'd say the sole is a bit undercooked!"

After a bit, Thianna's laughter subsided.

"We need to figure out our next move."

For an answer, Karn pulled his boots back on. He got up and began to walk the perimeter of the room.

"If we go outside now," the giantess continued, "we risk being spotted."

Karn was running his hand down the temple walls as he walked, studying the stone, but he kept silent.

"If we stay here, we risk getting pinned down if we're caught."

Karn had made a full circuit of the room. Now he was studying the statue of the horn-shouldered guy, looking up at the face of the statue and then letting his gaze fall all the way to the base.

"We're down to our last bits of soggy meat. So we'll need food soon."

Karn walked around the statue now, disappearing from sight.

"Plus, we want to make sure we don't end up as food for whatever lit those fires we saw coming in."

No answer from Karn.

"If only there was another way out of here."

Still no answer.

"Karn? Karn, are you listening? I said, If only there was another way out of here."

Karn reappeared from behind the statue.

"You mean like a secret passage under the altar?" he said.

"Yes, that's exactly what I mean. Why do you ask? Oh—"

Thianna leapt to her feet. She ran to the back of the statue. Karn was kneeling beside a low opening at its base. He had slid aside a thin panel of stone, revealing a passageway. The ground sloped sharply downward into the dark, with rough steps hewn into the rock.

"Shall we?" Karn asked.

Thianna looked at her bare feet.

"Let me get my boots."

She slipped back into her footwear, and they donned their newly dried coats. Karn looked at the rapidly dwindling pile of fungus.

"Wish there was something we could use as a torch."

"Like this?" Thianna held up her wooden practice sword. "It's not like I'm going to impale any wyverns with it." She stuck the end of the wooden sword into the fire, spearing some of the leafy fungus. "One torch coming up."

Their makeshift light didn't illuminate much in the passageway under the statue.

"Probably just a storage room," said Karn.

"One way to find out," said Thianna. Passing Karn the torch, she ducked through the opening.

"Hurry up with that light, Norrønboy," she called back. "We've fallen off enough rocks for today."

Karn grinned and followed her under the earth.

The passage led not to a basement chamber but to a tunnel. It was narrow enough that Karn and Thianna couldn't walk comfortably side by side. As she was already in the lead, he passed her the torch.

"So you think we should follow it?" she asked.

Karn shrugged. "Might as well." He didn't see any evidence of animal dwellings, and draug would be in Norrønir barrows, not in Gordion ruins. Of course that didn't mean *something* didn't live down here. Just nothing he had learned how to recognize.

It was awkward not being able to see much past Thianna's broad shoulders, and Karn kept looking over his own shoulder at the wall of darkness trailing them outside the circle of torchlight. The passage ran roughly straight for a ways, then it veered sharply to the right, opening abruptly into a bigger chamber. Thianna stepped out into the dark space with uncharacteristic caution.

They were in a large chamber with multiple columns that were laid out in a grid, supporting the stone ceiling overhead. Between every other pair of columns, metal bars had been fitted. It divided the room up into a number of cages, with open spaces that allowed walking between them.

"A dungeon?" Thianna asked.

Karn narrowed his eyes.

"I don't think so," he said. He pointed at the low stone

troughs that were still in evidence in several of the nearby enclosures. "Those would have held water or feed. More like a stable. These are animal pens."

Thianna nodded, but then her eyes fell on something hanging in another cage. She pointed to a pair of shackles chained to a set of bars.

"Not all of them were."

Karn nodded, stepping closer to examine the shackles. They had definitely been made to fit around a person's wrists to chain that person upright to the bars. Walking around, he found several more cages clearly meant to hold people.

"So," he said at last. "Cages for men. Pens for animals. All underground."

"What *is* this place?"

Karn shook his head. Somehow it was more disquieting being here than in the narrow corridor. Beckoning Thianna to follow, he led them across the room to the wall opposite the one they had entered. There, they found a wide hallway leading away into more darkness.

After twenty paces or so, the floor of this hallway suddenly sloped upward. There were no steps, but the stone was cut with shallow horizontal grooves to help a foot, or perhaps a hoof, gain traction.

The light of Thianna's torch fell on an open doorway set into the wall on their left. She poked the torch, and her head, into the opening. They saw an antechamber off the hallway.

"Look at this."

The room was small, maybe ten feet square. The ground was littered with detritus and rubble. But all four walls were ringed by rows of stone pegs, some of which still held an assortment of items. Picking their way through the rubble, they saw that the wall pegs held weapons, including clubs, barbed chains, what looked like metal darts, and most exciting to Thianna, actual swords.

She ran her hand quickly over several rusted weapons, then, smiling, she lifted up a finer blade.

"Hold this," she said, passing her torch to Karn. Then she gave a few quick experimental thrusts.

"Hey, watch it," he said, stepping back.

Thianna grinned and whipped the sword around in a wide arc. Then she held the sword out to examine it in the torchlight. The metal gleamed and cast back the firelight.

"It's called a spatha," said Karn.

"Spatha?"

"Yeah. It's what the Gordion army used."

"No surprise there. We're in a Gordion town. But it looks like your sword."

"Yeah, well, most Norrønir swords are patterned after Gordion spathae." When she gave him an odd look, he continued, "Hey, we know a good thing when we see it."

Thianna nodded.

"Can I see Whitestorm?" she asked.

"Why?"

"I just want to compare them."

Karn drew his father's weapon and handed it to her.

Thianna held the two weapons out side by side.

Both were straight double-edged swords. Both had plain, column-style grips, round pommels, and oval guards. Whitestorm had a groove down its length, called a fuller, but the spatha had no such groove. Whitestorm also had a red-gold glint that the other blade lacked. And while both swords were on the longish side, this one was also somewhat shorter than Whitestorm.

"It's lighter too," said Thianna.

"Of course the shorter sword is lighter," said Karn.

"No, I mean Whitestorm is lighter. A lot lighter."

Karn blinked and looked again at the two weapons.

"How can that be?"

"I don't know," said Thianna, flexing both wrists to test the balance of each blade. Karn ungraciously wondered if Thianna would want to keep both weapons, but she suddenly handed him back his father's sword.

"I think you've got yourself a very special weapon," she said. "At least there's something special about its metal."

"You think?" said Karn, looking at his father's sword anew. "I mean, I knew it was special, but—"

"I doubt it was forged around here. Maybe it's elven or dwarven made. It's lighter than it should be otherwise. Anyway, lucky you."

Karn nodded, glad to have Whitestorm back in his grip, even if he didn't really know how to use it. For her part, the giantess didn't seem unhappy with her quite ordinary weapon. The long blade and the weight were clearly not a problem for someone her size. She danced around the room, experimentally thrusting and cutting with the spatha.

"About time I had a real sword," she said.

"Yes, you weren't reckless enough without it. No, really, it suits you."

"Yeah, well, my wooden one's on fire." She grinned. Then she ducked out of the antechamber into the broader hallway. When Karn followed through, she rushed at him. "Defend yourself," she called. Then she was on him, swinging her spatha in a lazy arc. Karn leapt away and raised Whitestorm on instinct. The blades clashed, the sound of metal on metal ringing in the dark. Thianna laughed and swung at him again.

"You're crazy, you are!" he said, but he was grinning.

Laughing, they danced around, the two blades clashing and clanging over and over again as they chased each other around the hallway.

Thianna sprinted ahead. Karn ran after her, remembering how he had pursued her through the woods after his pilfered Thrones and Bones playing piece. Then he remembered where that chase had led. Helltoppr's Barrow. And here they were running again, and being very loud about it. That was when he heard another noise. Sliding or scraping or maybe shuffling. Maybe slithering.

He came up sharp.

"What's wrong?" Thianna asked.

"Shh," he said.

She tilted her head.

"For a minute there," he said, "I thought I heard something."

She listened.

"I don't hear anything."

"My imagination, then," said Karn, but he wasn't quite convinced.

Moving more cautiously ahead they came to a pair of large iron doors. Thianna put her shoulder to one of them and shoved. The door slid open a crack. The two slipped through to emerge blinking into the light.

Karn found himself on the rim of a vast labyrinth. The stone flooring where he now stood had crumbled away before him, so that he looked down into an elaborate maze of chambers and hallways, once underground and now exposed. But glancing around, he saw that they were actually at the bottom of an enormous, bowl-like structure. What looked like the remains of tiered seating rose above them in an elliptical ring.

"What is this place?" asked Thianna.

"It's an amphitheater," said Karn, who was just working it out. "This is a Gordion coliseum. The empire built these everywhere they went. At one time there were hundreds of them."

"What's it for?" she asked.

"It was a kind of entertainment. Those are the stands,

where the audience sat. They played games down here on the floor."

"Floor?"

"Well, the floor's fallen in, but here is where they had a sand-covered field for the games."

"What games? Like Knattleikr?"

"Yeah, but more brutal." Karn remembered the roughness of the giants' favorite pastime. "A little more brutal, anyway. They had people called gladiators who fought to the death. And they matched slaves against wild animals."

"Barbaric," Thianna said. Karn knew that her culture had used to keep human slaves. Many Norrønir still did, although his father usually freed his, but neither Norrønir nor giants would force anyone to fight to the death just for fun. He looked down at the subterranean level beneath them. The sun was deep into the west now and a section of the lower level lay in shadow.

"That's the hypogeum," said Karn, pointing into the maze below. "They would keep slaves and animals down there and bring them up through trapdoors when it was their time to fight. The room we came though with all the cages was probably where they kept the extras. Also, the tunnel to the temple makes sense."

"How so?"

"Well, some of the same animals would be used for sacrifice. And the priests might want to visit the games without having to go out into the street."

Thianna nodded.

"You know a lot about it."

Karn shrugged.

"Yeah, well, I always wanted to see a bit more of the world. Anytime anybody came by with a story . . ."

"Guess we're seeing a bit more of it than either of us planned on now." Thianna glanced at the sky. "So where do we go from here? It will be dark soon. Should we head back to the temple for the night?"

Karn wasn't sure he wanted to go underground again. He pointed to a place where the arena wall had fallen in. "We can make it up to the first floor there. Then we can find an exit out."

"Sounds good."

Karn and Thianna had to walk across the exposed tops of the chamber walls of the hypogeum. It was exactly like walking on the walls of a maze. Though the going wasn't hard, Karn found himself being extra cautious. He didn't want to fall in. It wouldn't be an easy fall. He thought he heard the sliding-shuffling-slithering sound again, but he couldn't pinpoint it, and it didn't linger.

They reached the gap in the wall and clambered up to the first level of seating, picking their way up the tiers toward an entrance.

Thianna paused. Despite having grown up in a frost giants' village, she was having a hard time just getting a handle on the size of the coliseum. It was hard to imagine how many people could have filled the stands of this amphitheater. Hundreds? Thousands even? Were there really so many people in the world?

"I've already seen the top," she whispered defiantly to the stones of the coliseum. "This is just downhill."

"Hey, you coming or what?" Karn hollered, snapping her back to the present. She skipped quickly after him.

A broad archway led them into an elaborate chamber with a roof and walls on three sides while the fourth was open to the arena below. Karn explained that it was a private box for the use of a wealthy patron or government official. The box had a great view of the field, but couldn't be seen by people in the stands. Thianna wasn't sure why anyone would want to hide away from others at a sporting event, but she shrugged it off as a "human thing." Karn studied the walls in the light of his torch.

"Look at this," he said.

He held the torch up high, casting its light on the elaborate carvings.

"What is it?"

"It's a map," he explained. "Of the empire." Karn pointed out details as he spoke. "This is the continent of Katernia."

"I know that," snapped Thianna, when, in fact, she hadn't. She knew nothing of the wider world. She certainly didn't know how wide it was. She had never wanted to be anywhere but atop her mountain.

"They've put horse heads as markers for everywhere

they've been," said Karn. He replied as if Thianna hadn't snapped at him. She felt a little guilty about that.

"Here in the upper corner, wolf heads are clashing with horse heads amid a mountainous landscape. Norrøngard," he said. Thianna was silently grateful that he had pointed it out before she had had to ask where it was. "The empire never got very far into our borders."

Thianna could see a great many more horse heads spread out in the lands below Norrøngard. In fact, horse heads stretched over most of Katernia.

"So, all this is Araland and Saisland?" she asked.

"What?" said Karn, stifling a snort. "No. Saisland is here," indicating a very small portion of the upper left corner, "and here is Araland."

Not much bigger. Thianna felt a real sense of vertigo now. How could a land of such little people feel so big? How could it make a giantess feel so small? She hated to be small.

"Now," Karn was saying, "if you'll come over here—"

Karn stopped on the far-right side of the wall, where the continent of Katernia met the sea. He pointed to a line of icons carved in the waters.

They looked like serpents. Winged serpents. Wyverns. And was there something else among them? Thianna saw that there were thin lines raised in the wall, leading from each wyvern to converge on a single crescent shape. It was almost like . . .

"Your people," said Karn proudly.

"What?"

"I think this is a clue to where you are from."

Thianna felt her spine go rigid.

"I'm from Ymiria," she said frostily.

"Yeah, I know, but I mean where you are *really* from."

Karn realized his mistake almost as quickly as the words were out of his mouth.

It was too much. This world she didn't want to be a part of, this world that had come crashing into her mountain and robbed her of her life, this horrid reminder that no matter how hard she tried, how many games of Knattleikr she won, she would always be different. Always be an outsider in her own home.

"I am a Ymirian!" Thianna yelled. "I'm not Norrønur. And I'm not human. Not from wherever these lizards are from. I'm a giant!"

"Okay," said Karn. "I get it. You're a giant. Like anyone could forget that."

"What do you mean?"

"Nothing. It's just that, I swear, you go around trying to outgiant the giants!"

"I *am* a giant!"

"Then stop trying to prove it!"

For a moment, Karn thought Thianna was going to hit him. Instead, she turned and stormed out of the room.

CHAPTER FIFTEEN

The Dragon

Karn hadn't been sure if he should go after his friend or
not. In the end, he decided to let her work it out for herself, and he occupied himself with studying the wall map.
He thought the object carved with the cluster of wyverns
was a horn, and that the lines between it and the reptiles
were like reins of a sort. What if Thianna's horn drove
the beasts rather than just irritating them? Perhaps they
weren't using it right.

"I found this." Thianna's voice sounded uncharacteristically tentative. The giantess held something out to
him, carved stones on a stone board. "I thought maybe it
could replace your missing pieces."

Karn's eyes lit up. He came over to see what she held.
It was a board game, all right, though not his favorite.

"It's Gordion chess," he told her.

"It's not Thrones and Bones?"

"No," he said. Seeing her sudden downcast look, he added, "It's very cool, though."

"We could play?"

"I don't know the rules."

"Oh."

"Hey, but maybe we could play Thrones and Bones."

"With this?"

"With some of it. I still have my board and half my pieces. We could use their footmen to replace my shield maidens. The pieces are a little larger, but, well . . ." He looked up at her and grinned. "I'm starting to get the strategic value of having tall women on your team."

Thianna smiled. "You're on, Norrønboy. But don't expect me to go easy on you this time."

Karn chuckled and set the board down. The footmen indeed made for good shield maidens, and its king piece was a good substitute for his missing Jarl. This time, he played the defensive side, while Thianna took the attackers.

Karn tried to explain a little bit about the importance of the game in Norrøngard. He wanted her to realize that he wasn't alone in his passion, that it was something of a national pastime.

"Plenty of Norrønir are even buried with their game."

"Yeah?"

Karn nodded. He thought he recalled seeing a set

in Helltoppr's Barrow, but that brought up unpleasant memories, so he concentrated on beating the giantess.

Thrones and Bones was an asymmetrical game: one side (the attackers) had more playing pieces than the other. Thianna commanded fifteen draug minions and one draug leader, called the Black Draug. She had played ably for several moves, impressing Karn with her learning ability, when she asked about the Black Draug.

"What's this one do again?"

"He can reenter the Barrow Mounds after he exits it. The others can't go back in once they step out. He can also occupy the Jarl's Throne. No one else can do that."

"Right. I remember that. But there's a cost for bringing him out, right? I lose if he's captured, right?"

"Yes, game's over if I capture him."

"That's dumb."

"What do you mean?" Nothing about his beloved board game was dumb.

"Why can't the others keep fighting? I mean, if somebody took out Gunnlod, I wouldn't just roll over."

"Well, of course you wouldn't."

"So why do these minions give up? Do they melt or something?"

Karn thought about it.

"There's actually a term for it. You say they've been 'released.'"

"Released?"

"Yeah. But the point is, your side loses if that happens."

"That sounds like they were under his spell or something."

"Yeah. But you lose."

"So the Black Draug has his forces under a spell, and when you defeat him the spell is broken?"

"Yes," said Karn, who wasn't sure why she was so interested in the spell. "They are under a spell. And they are released when he's defeated."

"Like your dad?" Thianna asked.

Karn looked up at that. "You mean . . . he might not . . . he might be . . . He might not be . . . dead?"

Thianna nodded.

Karn was speechless, which was just as well because that's when the dragon interrupted them.

"I do so love visitors," rumbled a deep voice that seemed to originate nowhere but echoed off the stones all around them. Karn and Thianna froze. There was no mistaking who the voice belonged to. Even though he hadn't been seen in centuries. A figure more out of legend.

"Don't think that I don't," the voice went on. "I love visitors. But they come so seldom these days. It's been simply ages since I ate the last one."

Neither Karn nor Thianna dared to breathe as they stared into each other's eyes. "I would have introduced myself sooner," said the voice, "but you were having the most agreeable conversation and I hated to interrupt."

Karn broke out of the paralysis first. He scooped his Thrones and Bones set, complete with the new pieces, into his satchel. Thianna shook her head. Even under the threat of imminent death, he wouldn't leave his precious set behind.

Getting away from the open wall of the private box seemed like a good idea to both of them. Quietly, slowly, they stood up and began to move backward to the door leading to the corridor.

"The bickering was entertaining enough," the deep voice continued. "But I was especially interested when the talk turned to tabletop games. You might even say I'm a bit of a gamer myself. Would you like to guess my favorite?"

They had just about reached the exit. They were almost away. Then a great shape rose up from outside the box, nearly blocking out their view of the sky. It was a head. An enormous head. Covered in white, gray, silver, and blue-white scales. Some scales glittered and some were dull and dark. The head sported long, vicious horns. It was framed by ears scalloped like bat wings. It had a mouth that could swallow a horse. Worse, it had teeth the size of spears. With fires smoldering in its great nostrils and balefires burning in its eyes, the face was lit with its own harsh and angry light.

"Come now. My favorite is . . ." His huge lips frowned in annoyance. "No guesses? Well, I suppose I'll tell you, then." Eyes the size of Thianna's large fists held them transfixed. Eyes that seemed to burn holes right through them.

"My favorite is Cat and Mouse."

"Orm," said Karn, finding his voice at last.

The head dipped in a slight bow, graciously receiving the acknowledgment. Then Orm Hinn Langi, Orm the Largest of All Linnorms, Orm the Great Dragon, Orm the Doom of Sardeth, smiled at Karn and Thianna.

"You do know how Cat and Mouse works, don't you?" rumbled the dragon. "No? My, oh my. What are they teaching the younger generation these days? The rules are quite simple. The cat chases. That would be me in case there is any doubt. And the mice—that would be you two dears—the mice . . . run."

Karn and Thianna bolted from the room. Karn hesitated in the corridor outside, unsure which way to turn. Thianna grabbed his hand and jerked him to the left. She had explored more of the coliseum when she went off to sulk. He hoped this meant she had an idea where they were going.

"Oh, you do understand the rules," the dragon sang out enthusiastically. "How delightful! It's always a pleasure when you don't have to waste time breaking in a novice."

Karn and Thianna hurried down the corridor, their feet ringing too loudly on the stone floor. They had left the smoldering remains of their torch behind. Now the only illumination came from what little daylight spilled through doorways or fell in shafts through holes in the crumbling stone walls. They ran as fast as they could and hoped they didn't trip or turn an ankle.

There was a large archway up ahead, another exit to the seats. Suddenly an enormous, scaled snout pushed through it.

Orm twisted his neck so that he could face down the hallway in their direction.

The dragon opened his mouth, but he didn't speak. Just opened his jaws wide.

Thianna yanked Karn aside. He lost his footing for a second, recovered his balance, and saw that she had pulled him onto the bottom step of a stairway, one leading to a higher level.

"Up?" questioned Karn.

"Anywhere but here would be good, don't you think?"

The wisdom of her idea was made clear when a cone of white burst from the dragon's mouth. Karn would have thought it was a blast of snow and ice if he hadn't felt the searing heat. Orm's fire was so hot it burned not red or orange or yellow, but white. The stones of the corridor where they had stood until seconds ago glowed in the heat. Up the stairs they ran.

"Step it up, step it up. You're doing fine," called the dragon in mock encouragement. "You know what they say, no lamb for the lazy wolf."

"What?" panted Karn. "Why in all the wide, wide world is everyone so obsessed with lambs and wolves?"

"Don't know. Don't care," said Thianna.

They were atop the stairs now, one level up. They ran down this new corridor, their hearts leaping every time they passed an open archway. Another blast of dragon fire exploded.

There was a hole busted in the wall about head height. Karn paused. He felt compelled to look through it.

He could see more of the dragon, not just its massive head. Orm had risen up out of the shadows of the hypogeum and had his face pressed into an archway. His long, white serpentine body coiled around the amphitheater like a great, pale snake—if snakes had massive plate scales running down their spines and two savagely clawed forelimbs.

"He's . . . so b-big," Karn stammered.

"Let me see," said Thianna. He didn't budge.

"You really don't want to," he said, unable to take his eyes off a creature so large.

Orm pulled his head out of the arch. Then he brought his neck around and one cold eye bored into Karn's own.

The dragon grinned. As fast as a serpent strikes, it dove for them. Karn leapt back. Then he shoved Thianna forward, tripping over himself to get out of the way.

Stone burst from the wall as Orm smashed his head straight through it. Dust filled the corridor and loose stones fell from its ceiling. Orm rocked his snout back and forth to free it of debris.

"I seeeeee you!" the dragon sang.

More steps up. They took them as fast as they'd ever run. Karn heard a great intake of breath.

"Here it comes," he said.

The steps in their wake disappeared in a haze of white fire.

They ran on.

The rings of the upper levels of the coliseum were naturally wider than the lower levels, and the arches to the seats were spaced farther apart. Unfortunately, up was the wrong direction.

"We have to get back down," Karn said. "He can play Cat and Mouse with us forever. And the light will be fading soon. We'll be at even more of a disadvantage then."

"Why? You think he can see in the dark?"

"Well, it would be worse for us if he could. So yeah, I figure he does. Plus, you saw how his eyes reflect the light. Like a cat's. But if we can get down, we can get out. He'll have a harder time finding us if we have the whole city to hide in."

"If we can get down."

"I'm working on it."

"You do that."

They kept running.

"No private boxes up here," Thianna observed.

"Yup," Karn acknowledged. "We're in the cheap seats."

"Then why do I feel like we're the show?"

"Again, working on it."

Through another gap in the wall, Karn caught a glimpse of the dragon thrusting his head into another archway. It wasn't near them, thank goodness. Karn had an idea. He murmured to himself.

"Einn, tveir, þrír . . ."

"What are you doing?" Thianna asked.

"Shh. Counting. Fjórir, fimm." He listened to the dragon draw breath, followed by the roar of the flames.

Karn stopped counting and stopped watching Orm. Instead, he looked across the amphitheater to the tiers opposite. He couldn't see the archways on the tiers below their own position, but he could guess where they should be by the archways he could see on the opposite side of the field.

"Orm takes five seconds for the whole process. Stuff his head in a hole, draw breath, blow a blast of fire, pull it out. And we know when he is about to blow because he has to stop talking and draw a deep breath."

"Okay. Where are you going with this?"

"I'm going out."

"Out?"

"We both are. Next time he does it, we're going to race out to the seats."

"Out there? With him?"

"He'll have his head stuffed in a hole. We'll have five seconds to drop a level and get back inside."

"That sounds risky." This was true, but Karn didn't

have time to argue about it. So he put on his best gamer smirk.

"Not if you're fast, big girl," he said with an edge of challenge in his voice.

Thianna met his eye, her lips curling up.

"Okay then."

They found an archway with a small hole positioned near it, just large enough to be a peephole, near enough to be of use. Karn watched from the shadows as Orm considered where to thrust his snout next. When the dragon chose and drew breath, he took Thianna's hand.

"Here we go," he whispered.

They ran out of the archway into the seating area. Orm's huge body was coiled beneath them, his neck forcing his head into a corridor.

"Einn," Karn muttered to himself as they hurried down the steps. Running down the tiers was harder than running down a mountain slope would be. One misstep and they'd be done for, sprawled in the seats with no chance to make it to shelter in time.

"Tveir, þrír," he counted. It was hard to fight the feeling of being utterly exposed, to keep from quavering at the sight of the dragon's enormous bulk. No creature had a right to be this size.

"Fjórir." They were above the archway of the next-lowest tier now. Karn took three steps and then jumped down the rest of the way.

"Fimm." His feet hit the stones. Thianna landed beside

him. The dragon began to withdraw its neck. Karn didn't wait. They raced back into the shelter of the corridors.

"Oh," the dragon said. "Someone's being clever!"

Karn glanced over his shoulder. Outside in the amphitheater, Orm had risen up high into the air, his neck arched almost as if he were sitting back and reclining. He looked like he was enjoying himself entirely too much. Karn realized that some part of him would really like to fix that.

Here, on the lower levels, stairs, exits, and side chambers were more numerous. They made it down another level using inside staircases.

Next was a stretch of dark hallway covered with rubble. The dragon was suspiciously quiet. When they came to another archway leading to the seats, Karn risked another peek.

Orm was gone.

"What do you mean he's gone?" Thianna asked when Karn whispered the news to her. "Gone where?" She pushed past him to gaze into the arena. There was no sign of the dragon. "Where did he go?"

"How should I know? I was with you, not him." Karn looked up, but there was no sign of Orm in the sky. "Maybe he hopped the wall and he's waiting for us to exit so he can pounce on us."

"He could be just above us," said Thianna. "In the seats, I mean."

There was no way they could see the tiers above them

unless they walked out of the shelter of the archway and turned around, and then, if Orm really was above them, it would be too late. Orm could gobble them up before they even had time to yell, let alone race back inside.

"We can't risk going out," he said. "Not when we don't know where he is. We'll have to find a way down inside."

They picked their way on through the corridor, passing more boxes and side chambers. The dragon's continued silence was unnerving. Karn wondered if Orm had grown tired of them and wandered off. He knew that that was too much to hope for, but then how to explain the creature's disappearance?

Finally, they came to a staircase leading down. If Karn had mapped their location correctly in his mind, then the level below them should be ground level. There would be exits to the street outside as well as a few passages to the hypogeum below. Either avenue would get them out of the coliseum and lead them to places where they could hide from the colossal linnorm.

They were halfway down the stairs before they saw it. The sunlight was fading, and the lower levels naturally got more shadow than the upper tiers. But the ground beyond the steps wasn't ground. It was scales. Karn's heart sank.

Orm had squeezed his long, snakelike bulk into the corridor. Filling it with his body.

They ran back up, not bothering with silence. The dragon was so large; it seemed impossible that he could fit inside the coliseum. Unfortunately, he was long, not broad.

A quarter of the way around the amphitheater they came to another stairway. And the linnorm's body lay at the foot of it too.

"He's coiled around the entire level," said Karn. "He's circled the whole stupid arena. We can't go down anywhere. He has us trapped."

A chuckling sound came up from the level below. From everywhere below. As of course it would. The dragon was laughing down its entire long, coiled length.

"I did give you two lambs ample opportunity to get away," Orm said. "I waited and waited before I sprang my trap. It was more than a reasonable chance, I'm sure you will agree."

"Is that how you deal with all the heroes who come here looking for you, Orm?" Karn called out. He was frustrated at the unfairness of it all. "With dirty tricks?"

"Come now," said the dragon. "Outflanking can hardly be called a dirty trick."

"But you do what it takes, don't you?"

"Naturally."

"Just like those Gordion legions you ate?"

"A history buff, are you, boy?"

"Something like that."

Something was working in the back of Karn's mind. "Outflanking" had made him think of military tactics and the Gordion legions Orm had attacked when he first came to Sardeth. The Gordion legions brought to mind the wall map, which showed the empire and the place where Thianna's people hailed from. And Thianna's people made him think of the horn. Yoked to the wyverns. Reptiles. They weren't linnorms, but they were at least distant cousins. Could the magic of the horn be used to annoy linnorms as well as wyverns? Or to control them?

"Keep him talking," he said to Thianna. "I need time to think."

"Keep him talking?" said Thianna. "Everything I've ever heard about dragons says you do not want them talking to you."

"You think them eating you is better? Keep him talking."

"What if he charms me or mesmerizes me or something?"

"Please. I really doubt he could." If Karn knew anything about Thianna, it was that nothing so impressed her as herself.

"Um, hello, Mr. Dragon," Thianna called out uncertainly.

"The mouse wants to talk?" laughed Orm. "You realize you've lost and want to give yourself up?"

"What do you want with us anyway?" she called.

"What do I want with you?" He sounded incredulous. "You treasure seekers come here, invading my home and my slumber, looking to steal from my hoard. That you end up as my sport instead is fair play."

"We didn't come here on purpose," Thianna said. Naturally, the dragon replied that he didn't believe her.

Meanwhile, Karn thought about the horn. A blast from it had driven the wyverns crazy. Even though it made no sound that humans—or giants—could hear, it was obviously earsplittingly painful to the reptiles. But was that its only use? The wall map had shown the wyverns yoked to the horn, as if they were being driven and controlled by it. So why hadn't it worked like that when Thianna blew it?

"You stupid, fat worm!" the frost giantess was shouting. "If you weren't so big, I'd roast you on a spit and feed you to my . . ."

Of course. Thianna blew the horn like she did everything else. Loud, brash, with all the force of her personality. Whatever sound was coming out the other end was sure to be painful. What if she tried a lighter, softer touch?

"Thianna," he called. She was still yelling at the dragon. "Thianna!" he shouted louder until she shut up. "Use your horn, but this time don't blow so hard on it. Try and . . . try and play music."

"Try and what?"

"Play music."

"I don't know how to play any music."

"Well, at least blow softer."

"Softer?"

"Trust me on this. I think I know how it works."

Thianna looked at him askance. But she pulled the horn from her satchel. "Whatever you say, Norrønboy."

Thianna placed the horn to her lips. She drew in a huge breath. Karn raised a warning finger. She took the horn away from her mouth and exhaled half the breath, giving him an annoyed look as she did so. Then she placed the horn to her lips again.

"Softly," Karn admonished her.

She scowled but nodded. And blew a gentler breath.

As before, the horn made no sound that Karn or Thianna could hear. But the linnorm was strangely silent.

"Again," said Karn.

Thianna blew another quiet note, then another.

And then she heard it. A voice so faint that it sounded like one of her own thoughts, except that it was no thought that she would ever have.

What is this? the voice said. *What presence is this in my mind?*

"Who are you?" Thianna whispered back.

"Who is who?" Karn said, thinking that she spoke to him.

"Shhh," she replied.

Mouse? asked the voice. *Is that you? How did you get in here?* Thianna was suddenly aware of a wave of irritation, so powerful it made her sway on her feet. *You have no right to be here!*

"Here?" asked Thianna. "You mean, in your mind?"

"Who are you talking to?" asked Karn. "Are you talking to it?"

Get out! Orm roared in her head. *How dare such a tiny, ephemeral little thing as you invade the greatness of my mind? You live and you die in the batting of my eyes. You cast a wavering shadow on the snow for a day. I cast my shadow over empires across eons.*

The force of Orm's scorn hit Thianna like the trunk of an oak swung by a giant. She was knocked off her feet, crashed into the wall of the corridor. Karn ran to her. She waved him away even as he helped her to her feet.

Thianna gritted her teeth. She was tired of big things pushing her around. What was so special about dragons and trolls and even giants? Bullies. Braggarts. She'd taken Thrudgey down with her brains. She'd taken the trolls down the same way. And in here, in her mind, size didn't matter. She drew in a deep breath.

"Not so big," Karn warned, but she shook her head to silence him. She wanted the dragon's attention.

She blew as hard as she ever had.

Orm roared. The coliseum shook. The ground quaked, tossing Thianna and Karn off their feet. Dust and loose stones fell from the ceiling.

"Stop that!" bellowed the dragon, no longer talking in her mind but shrieking his words loud and clear. His voice echoed throughout the coliseum.

Thianna blew again, as hard and strong as the first.

More stones crashed to the ground as Orm thrashed his body violently in the tight corridors.

"He'll bring this whole thing down on our heads!" Karn shouted.

"No, he won't!" Thianna shouted, loud enough for the dragon to hear. "He's lived here over a thousand years, haven't you, big guy? It's the only place in these ruins large enough for him. The only place within a thousand miles, I bet. He's not going to ruin his home over a little earache caused by a mouse."

"I wouldn't bet on it," growled the dragon.

"Well, I would," said Thianna. "Especially since there's a much better alternative."

She blew the horn again, but softly.

What is it? What gives you access to the innermost chambers of my mind?

"Something that my mother stole, long ago, from far away. Her people have come here, looking for it now. I don't understand much of it, but I don't think she liked what they used it for. I think she was trying to keep it away from them. I think that's why she left home. They chased her. Now they are chasing me. I told you we didn't come to Sardeth on purpose. We are trying to keep the horn away from them. Believe me, whatever they want it for, it can't be good for your kind."

Thianna felt the dragon's immense mind sifting through hers, running over her thoughts. But softly.

I believe you, Mouse. But I can't let a treasure seeker leave here unmolested. After all, I have my reputation to think of.

"I told you, we aren't treasure seekers."

No? And what of that sword at your side? Don't tell me you had that when you came.

Thianna glanced down at the Gordion spatha. She had taken it, but she hadn't known it belonged to the dragon. And hadn't he stolen it first? She didn't think either argument would get her very far with him. But she had another idea.

"Call it a loaner," she said. Next to her, Karn listened intently, trying to piece together what was happening from just one side of a conversation.

A what?

"A loaner. I'm not stealing it. You are loaning it to me. I'll bring it back one day."

You'll return it? And when will you do this?

"You count the days in eons. I'm half-giant. We measure it in centuries. Plenty of time to keep my promise."

And the horn, will you destroy it?

Thianna hesitated. That was harder to promise. The horn was her only connection to her mother.

"I can't."

It is a hateful thing.

"When I'm done with it. When I know what it has to teach me about my mother."

Again she felt the dragon's thoughts slide across her own.

I could swallow it now, and you with it. I could bring the stones of this place down on you.

"I could blow it again."

She felt the dragon's anger wash over her like a wave.

But it was a wave that broke and dissipated. Then she felt something else. Amusement.

"You offer me something new," Orm spoke aloud. "In fifteen hundred years, I have never loaned anyone anything. I have taken, and I have eaten. Once or twice, I have even given advice to jarls and wizards who came seeking it. But to loan something—I admit, I am curious to see if you will keep your promise. The novelty is worth a single sword." Orm paused, and Thianna felt a twitch of irritation from the linnorm. "I believe the proper response is 'Thank you.'"

"Thank you," she said, and meant it.

They found a gap in the walls and saw the dragon sliding from the corridor and into the arena, but he didn't stay in the open. He slithered into the shadows of the hypogeum and disappeared from sight.

"Go now," he said aloud. "Go now before I change my mind. And never blow that hateful thing in my presence again, or I swear by my sacred fire that I will swallow it and its bearer whole."

They didn't have to be told twice. As night fell, Karn and Thianna raced from the coliseum, into the streets of the Blasted City, and away from the might of Orm.

 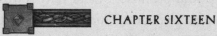
The Return

Miles away at Dragon's Dance, Karn's uncle slid grate-fully out of the wyvern's saddle. Ori was glad to have solid ground under his feet again after a harrowing ride spent clinging to the back of one of Sydia's soldiers. Though he would not show it to the foreigners, he had been afraid to be so high in the air. And these scaly creatures made him nervous. He had never been very fond of animals—a drawback, admittedly, for one born to work a farm—and the wyvern seemed strangely intelligent for a dumb beast. It didn't bother to hide its dislike of him.

"My leader waits at the top of the hill," the soldier said. But she didn't move to accompany him. Ori walked up the slope to the crest alone. At night, when the camp was empty of all the boisterous Norrønir, it was an eerie place. The crossed poles with their stone dragon heads cast odd shadows. Like he was in a graveyard. Not that he had anything to fear from barrows.

A light burned in one of the wattle-and-daub cabins at the summit. "Leave it to these foreigners not to know how to pitch a proper tent," he scoffed.

He raised his fist to knock.

A wyvern thrust its head from around the corner of the cabin. It hissed at him. Ori jumped. But he recovered in time to sneer back at the thing.

The cabin door opened before he could knock again.

Sydia stepped out. Neth's sweet sake, did the woman sleep in her armor?

"You wanted to talk," he said, hating how his words gave her the upper hand. "It's not easy sneaking away from a longhouse unnoticed in the middle of the night."

"You were well paid for your information," Sydia replied scornfully "What's a little inconvenience now that you are hauld of your brother's farm?"

"Yes, well, thanks for that," said Ori, wondering how he could turn this summons to his advantage. "But money only goes so far. Not all the freemen were happy about the change in leadership. I had to let a few of them go and replace them with slaves. More compliant, you understand. They don't have to be paid, true, but they still have to be fed."

Sydia narrowed her eyes.

"Don't think you can worm more gold out of me,

northerner. It is because of your kind's interference that I am still in this gods-forsaken ice hole you call a land."

"Interference?" said Ori, his hackles rising at the foreigner's tone.

"Your nephew, the one called Karn."

"What of him?" snapped Ori. But inwardly he felt a sinking feeling. Karn should be long gone. Disposed of by Helltoppr's minions or the harsh elements. He might play a mean game of Thrones and Bones, but his nephew was hardly the rugged survivalist type.

"He and Thianna are traveling together. Aiding each other."

"They are what?" shouted Ori.

"Somehow the two young fools are managing to elude my soldiers."

"How do you know they haven't just left Norrøngard altogether?" Or been killed by draug, he thought.

Sydia glowered.

"They've been spotted. Almost captured a time or two."

Now it was Ori's turn to scowl. So those incompetent After Walkers hadn't done their job. Maybe there was something of his brother's fire in Karn after all. Either way, this wouldn't do.

"And so you've come to me to . . ." He let the question hang open in the air.

"I'm trying a new tactic," Sydia replied. She gestured to the three large standing stones at the hill's summit.

The stones were in shadow but . . . were there forms huddled at their bases? Large forms? Ori raised an eyebrow.

"Insurance," Sydia went on. "Something to pluck the girl's heartstrings. Karn also must have someone on the farm he would hate to see hurt."

Ori didn't like where this was going. His sister-in-law was still grieving over the news of Korlundr's and Karn's deaths. It had been easy to blame the attack on trolls. And she was a strong Norrønur woman, brought up in the harsh realities of a cold and unforgiving land. She would come around to accepting the new order. As for Karn's sister Nyra, parting with her wouldn't be so bad.

"It would be hard to sell another story about a third disappearance so soon after the last two. Trolls can only eat so much. Whereas slaves, slaves eat every day. . . ."

Sydia spat into the ground.

"Is gold the only thing you care about?"

"Gold and what it buys me." Ori smiled his most charming smile.

"Help me with your bothersome nephew," Sydia replied, "and we'll talk about more gold."

Now the upper hand was his, and Ori knew how he could strengthen his grip. He glanced at the hissing wyvern beside the cabin. Maybe it was his turn to startle the foreigners.

"Deal," he said. "But before we plot any further, take a walk with me."

Without waiting for a response, he started down the hill, heading in the direction of the barrows.

"Where are you going?" the woman called after him.

"It isn't far," Ori replied. "There's someone I think you should meet."

The lands south of Sardeth were hilly, but nothing like the Ymirian range. The going had been easy the last few days. Physically easy, at least. Now that the excitement of the dragon was behind them, Karn kept thinking of the Thrones and Bones game with Thianna. When the Black Draug piece was captured, all his minions were "released." Could that really mean that if Helltoppr were somehow defeated, his father could be restored? But how could Karn defeat Helltoppr? Even with a sword like Whitestorm, he was useless at blade work.

Every step south took him farther and farther from his father. Karn stopped short.

"I have to go back," he said.

"What? Are you crazy? We just got away from Orm!"

Thianna was looking at him aghast.

"Not to Sardeth," he explained. "To Norrøngard. To the barrow. I have to rescue my father."

"Karn, you can't stand against Helltoppr."

"How can I not?" argued Karn. "If there's even a chance that my father's not dead?"

"But . . ."

"You'd do it. If Magnilmir was in trouble, you'd go back."

Thianna locked eyes with him.

"Yes, I would."

"So then . . ."

"But, Karn," the giantess went on, "I can't go with you. I've got to keep this horn far from Ymiria. Far from Sydia. I don't know why she wants it so badly, but whatever she wants from it can't be good."

Karn nodded. "Then this is goodbye." He felt oddly formal. He held out his hand. She stared at it, the wind blowing her hair across her dark eyes. "I appreciate all you've done for me," he went on.

Thianna threw herself at him, gripping him in a fierce hug.

"Spine! Cracking!" he hollered. But he was laughing. To think that someone so strange and irritating had become so close to him . . .

Thianna set him down. She brushed at her cheeks. "Wind in my eye," she mumbled.

"Mine too."

"Good luck, Short Stuff," she said, giving him a friendly punch on the shoulder. He put a foot forward to keep from stumbling. It was going to be hard to travel alone without her, but now that he'd made up his mind, there was no choice.

He pointed his feet toward home. He could feel Thianna's eyes watching him, but he didn't turn around.

After a few moments, he could hear her footsteps carrying her away.

The frost giant made it a good ten paces southward before she stopped.

She knew Karn wasn't going to make it without her. She'd had to rescue him from the snow, from the trolls, from the avalanche, from the cliff, from the water. But he'd saved her too. From Sydia. And from the dragon. True, she'd rescued him more than he'd saved her, but she had to admit, the dragon counted for a lot.

What was facing down a few draug when you'd already bested Orm? She had to keep the horn away from Sydia, but the woman already knew she was heading south. Maybe doubling back could throw Sydia off her trail. She would just toss the horn into the sea if it wasn't her only link to her mother's past. She'd never cared about that past as she was growing up, but now . . .

Thianna barreled into Karn before she even realized she'd made up her mind. He gave a startled yelp as the two tumbled to the ground.

"Surprise, Norrønboy! I'm coming with you!"

Thianna helped him to his feet, dusting him off almost protectively.

"We'll face our threats together," she said. "Whatever they are."

"Okay then." He smiled. "Let's go home."

"Wonderful," said a voice. "That's just where we plan on taking you."

The bronze-and-black-armored woman had her lance ready, pointed right at them. Even so, Thianna held her horn, poised to use it to torment the mount.

"We've been in this standoff before," said Thianna.

"No cliff for you to dive off this time," said the soldier woman.

"Never a cliff when you need one," groused Karn.

Thianna blew a quick blast from the horn.

The wyvern bucked, almost throwing its rider from the saddle. She shot a burst of flame into the air over their heads. They recoiled from the heat.

They ran, drawing swords as they did so.

"Keep piping on that thing," said Karn. "Keep her from controlling her mount."

"Way ahead of you," said Thianna between blasts. "Hard to run and blow." But she only had to keep the wyvern disoriented enough that it couldn't follow them.

They crested a small hill. There was a small herd of wild cattle at its base. The cattle moved uneasily as Karn and Thianna thundered into their midst.

Something darted across the ground at their feet. A cat, its fur strangely wet-looking. As Karn passed it, a hand gripped his sword arm. A clammy hand. It dragged him to a halt.

"Boo!" said Snorgil, leering through his rotten teeth.

Karn tried to wrench his sword arm free, but the

draug's grip was unbreakable. He punched Snorgil in the face with his free hand. The feel of the soft, decaying flesh was sickening, but the blow didn't seem to hurt the After Walker at all. The herd shifted around them, nervous. Where was Thianna?

Karn spared a glance and saw the frost giant struggling with two of the cows. Why, at a time like this? No, not cows. A bull. And a horse. Their hides were filthy and also wet. Like the cat . . . A cat, a horse, and a bull—they were the animals from his dream. The ones who had sung "The Song of Helltoppr" to him. He could identify the wetness of their hides now. Their flanks ran with thick black blood.

"Draug," he said. He looked back at Snorgil. "You were the cat."

Snorgil grinned. "A convenient form for dream-walking." The draug cast an unfriendly glance at the sky. "And daytime travel."

Thianna was swinging her sword at the bull. It had reared up and was kicking at her with powerful hooves. At least one struck a glancing blow on her shoulder, but the big girl just shrugged it off. There was strong, and then there was Thianna strong.

Inspired by his friend, he kicked Snorgil savagely in the leg. The draug almost lost his footing, but he clung to Karn and stayed upright.

"None of that, boy," he snarled. "You've had your fun,

but it's over now. You've given us enough trouble to last me for the next century or two." The After Walker head-butted him then, sending him crashing to the ground.

Then a lance poked Karn in the throat.

"Enough," spat the soldier, who had dismounted and stood on the ground, her finger on the trigger. She pushed the point of her flame lance sharply into Karn's flesh. "I'm pretty sure I won't miss at this range."

It was over. They'd caught him. Karn nodded. He saw that the bull was still a bull, but the horse had turned into Rifa. That meant the bull was Visgil.

"Enough!" the soldier said again, shouting now at Thianna. "I will boil this boy if you do not lay down your arms!"

When Thianna saw Karn's predicament, her shoulders sagged. She growled at the soldier but lowered her sword.

"Drop it," the woman insisted. "On the ground." Reluctantly, Thianna did so. "Now the horn. Drop the horn as well."

Thianna hesitated.

"Drop it now," the woman commanded. Her thumb moved on the trigger of the lance.

Thianna tossed the horn to the ground.

Rifa smiled and picked it up.

"Give that here," said the woman.

"When we reach Helltoppr's Barrow," Snorgil said,

"then we can all get what we want." He looked at Karn and smiled unpleasantly. "Well, not what *you* want, obviously. But what's coming to you."

Karn spat at the draug.

"Oh, cheer up, boy," the undead Norrønur said. "You want to be reunited with your old man, don't you? This way, you and he get to be together for all time."

Karn was thrown over the back of the bull, his wrists and his ankles bound by a cord stretched under the creature's rotting belly. It was sickening. But worse was the feeling of hopelessness and failure.

His position of being strung over a bull's back also afforded him with a good view of the ground. It was flying by with alarming speed. No real animal could travel this fast.

He felt the cat's claws dig into his flesh to steady itself. Snorgil had changed into a smaller form for the trip.

"Watch it," Karn complained.

"Sorry, boy," the cat replied, not sounding sorry in the least. "Wouldn't want to cause you any unnecessary pain. Then again, you led us on quite a chase. So necessary pain is probably okay."

The claws dug into Karn's back again. Maybe he should keep his mouth shut. Anger made for bad decisions. He needed to keep his wits about him. He'd meant to return anyway, and now he was heading home, and fast. He just had to work out his next move. The draug had left Whitestorm in its sheath. They seemed afraid to touch the blade, but with his hands tied it didn't do him any good. Unfortunately, his pack had been abandoned, along with all of his supplies and his prized playing set. He always thought he'd be buried with it. Even Helltoppr had a Thrones and Bones game among the hoard in his barrow. Karn shook off the thought—getting a new game would be the least of his worries if he made it through the day alive. But then he had an idea. It was ill-defined, just the beginnings of a plan, but it was a ray of hope in the dark.

Thianna rode in front of the soldier with her hands bound behind her. It was disconcerting. The woman had far too relaxed a grip. Thianna wondered how much trouble the woman would be in if she fell. Maybe the soldier was considering the same thing. Probably better to keep her big mouth shut and not antagonize the woman.

"Hunch!" the soldier said, shouting in her ear against the wind.

"What?" she called over her shoulder.

"Don't sit up straight. I can't see where we're going over your bulk."

"Not my fault you foreigners are so tiny," Thianna replied. So much for keeping her big mouth shut and not being antagonistic. The woman shoved her hard, jostling her in the saddle.

"Okay, okay." Thianna bent her torso over the wyvern's neck. It wasn't comfortable, but it was better than falling to her death.

Long way down, said a voice in her mind.

"What?" Thianna replied.

Not out loud. She'll hear you. Just think to me.

Think to who?

To me, idiot.

You're the mount, um, the wyvern?

Do you see anyone else up here?

No need to be snarky.

There's every need. You allow the instrument of our slavery to return to our masters.

You mean the horn?

Of course, the horn. Are all giants as thick-skulled as you?

Thianna thought about that: Probably. But the horn, she asked the Wyvern, what is it?

I told you. The tool of our masters.

Yeah, but how does it work?

You already know. It compels us. Without it, we could cast off these yokes.

But it's been missing for years.

One song, played by a master with the proper skill, lasts a long time.

It's been missing my whole life!

I said, a long time, didn't I?

So what happens without it?

Its effect begins to wear off. We begin to think for ourselves. We were hoping it would stay lost. Then you had to go and blow it.

So why are you helping Sydia recover it?

There you go again, showing off your thick skull. I said it compels us.

Then what's the point? Why are you even telling me this?

You have blown the horn many times now. You have carried it for days.

Yeah, well, I'm sorry about that.

Bah, spare your pity. You don't understand my point. You compel us too.

So.

So, you are a master. And never have our masters been at cross-purposes.

"Oh," said Thianna out loud.

Quiet.

Sorry. But you are saying that while you still have to obey your masters . . .

Having two masters at odds with each other gives me a bit of latitude in interpreting my orders.

What would you have me do?

I can't have you do anything. Aren't you paying attention? But you can have me do something. If you demand it of me now, while my rider isn't giving me other orders.

Ah. Okay. Well then, let me go.

Can't. I'm under a compulsion to return you to Sydia.

Then what good are you?

You can order me, as long as it doesn't conflict with my other orders.

I see.

You do not.

I'm beginning to. Give me a moment.

Thianna grinned.

I bet you are one impressive flyer.

Of course. But hardly relevant.

Oh, I think it is. I'd like to see a demonstration.

She dug her heels in tight to the wyvern's side.

Show me a loop.

Inside her mind, Thianna thought she could almost feel the beast smile. Then it gave a beat of its wings and reared up, so steeply that she was thrown against the woman. This wouldn't work if the soldier gripped her. She tossed her head backward as hard as she could, teeth gritted against pain as her skull smashed into the woman's face. Thick-skulled, indeed.

Then they were upside down. Thianna gasped as she saw the world overhead. She dug in with her knees, but it was harder to stay on than she had imagined. She felt the reptile's flanks slip away under her. Then Thianna, like her mother before her, was falling from the sky.

CHAPTER SEVENTEEN

The Game

Cold air whipped around her. Thianna was frozen in a moment of sheer terror. Below her, the white earth was rushing upward far too fast.

Was this it? With both "masters" gone, was the wyvern free to fly off wherever it wanted? Or was it still bound to fly northward to Sydia, carrying the horn in its saddlebag to its enslavers? Either way, she wouldn't be around to find out.

Through her panic, she wondered if this was what it had been like for her mother thirteen years ago, when Talaria fell from the sky. Did plunging to your death run in their family?

The ground loomed large before her. This was it.

Then large claws snatched Thianna from the air. Large, scaled claws.

She hung by her shoulders in its grip, her feet dangling above the earth.

"I wasn't sure you'd catch me," she said both aloud and in her mind.

I can't let my master fall.

"What about your other master?" she asked. There was no sign of the soldier woman. Thianna glanced down at the ground and shuddered.

I can't catch but one at a time, the wyvern replied with a mental shrug.

It slowly glided to the ground, dropping Thianna when she was perhaps five or six feet from the earth, then flapped its wings to settle in front of her.

Thianna picked herself up, glad to be alive and in one piece.

"Now what?" she asked.

I am still under a compulsion to return to Sydia.

"That's okay. We're heading that way anyway. Karn's going to need somebody to rescue him."

She turned around, raising her wrists to show the beast.

"But before we get going, think you could run a claw through these ropes?"

❈

Night was falling when Karn reached Dragon's Dance. There were lights at the summit of the hill. Not ghostly balefires, but the lights of a camp. The yellow glow of natural fires made his heart swell with longing for his father and the time when his only complaint was slopping pigs. But this was no Norrønir camp.

The bull leapt the small stone wall encircling the hill without pausing. As they approached the summit, Karn caught a glimpse of figures huddled at the base of the three standing stones, as the pretend animal stopped short. Karn felt the ropes fastening him to the creature go slack; then he was tossed unceremoniously off its back.

Visgil transformed into his rotting-corpse form, grabbed Karn by the arm, and hauled him to his feet. His wrists were still bound together, though it felt good to have his legs free. He wondered how far he'd get if he tried to run.

The door of one of the wattle-and-daub cabins opened. Sydia.

"Finally, the thorn in my side has been plucked," she said in her strange accent. "You should listen to your uncle, boy, and stay away from giants."

Karn shook off Visgil's hand and straightened to his full height.

"My uncle! You just be glad that my uncle isn't here, or he'd have a thing to say about you abducting his family members."

"I doubt that," Sydia said, smiling cruelly. "But you can ask him yourself."

She stepped aside from the cabin's doorway. Behind her, a Norrønur walked forward into the moonlight.

"Uncle Ori!" Karn shouted in excitement. True, Ori had warned him to flee and never return. But once he explained that Korlundr wasn't really dead, then they could find a way to set things right together. But what was Ori doing with Sydia?

"Karn, Karn, Karn." Ori was shaking his head sadly. "What have you gotten yourself into? You were warned away, nephew. You could have slunk off to Araland or anywhere. The farther the better. But you had to go and involve yourself in things that are none of your affair."

"What are you t-t-talking about?" Karn stammered. "This crazy woman has been after us—look, Korlundr isn't dead. If we can beat Helltoppr, we can get him back." But Ori wasn't listening.

"You've never cared for anything but your precious Thrones and Bones before, boy," his uncle went on. "Why bother yourself with matters of the farm now? Oh, what to do with you? What to do with you?"

"Uncle?" said Karn.

"We are not kind to kin slayers here," Ori said, speaking to Sydia as if he were apologizing for the rustic ways of his quaint people. "Blood for blood and all, you understand."

Sydia nodded.

"But . . . but Korlundr isn't dead. We can release him."

"Got his father turned into a runestone, he did," continued Ori. "It's only fitting he stand beside him."

"Aren't you listening?" Karn yelled. "I tell you, my father isn't dead!"

"Delightful," Ori replied. "Then you've nothing to fear from sharing his same fate."

Ori nodded to Visgil, who gripped Karn from behind. The boy struggled to throw off the draug, but Snorgil and Rifa appeared beside them, again in their corpse forms.

"Ha, lazy ol' Ori," laughed Snorgil. "Still getting us to do your dirty work. No matter. All's well that ends well, they say."

Karn looked from the draug to his uncle.

"You *know* them?"

"I always found it useful to have friends in low places," Ori said with a shrug.

"They're undead!"

"Nobody's perfect," Snorgil mumbled, sounding genuinely hurt.

Karn's mouth moved, but he was speechless.

"Oh, don't take it so hard, nephew," Ori said. "It's not that I don't like you. Just think of this as a game. I warned you before, I don't like to lose."

Fire burned in Karn's eyes.

Then a very real fire burst out of the sky, setting the wattle-and-daub cabin aflame. It went up immediately, burning so fast that the fire could only have one source.

As Ori and Sydia leapt back from the bonfire, Karn turned his attention to the sky.

Thianna held the lance expertly in one hand. She gripped the reins of the wyvern with less assurance in the other. But she still managed to look heroic hovering over their heads.

"Let him go," she ordered, pointing her lance at Sydia.

To Karn's surprise, Sydia didn't seem upset.

"Thianna, good of you to show up. We've been expecting you," the woman said. "In fact, we've arranged a little homecoming for you. For you both." She nodded toward the crest of the hill where the three standing stones marked the summit of Dragon's Dance.

A second lance spat flame into the night. Sydia's remaining soldier lit a bonfire amid the stones. As the fire rose, the stones were illuminated, revealing the three figures bound to their bases. Karn and Thianna gasped in unison.

Magnilmir, Eggthoda, and Karn's sister Nyra were gagged and tied to the stones. Nyra glared defiantly, but the two frost giants writhed before the unwelcome heat.

Someone thrust a burning pole into the faces of the giants.

The newcomer was large, a giant himself.

"Thrudgey," Thianna said.

Thrudgelmir favored her with a wicked smile.

"You're a traitor to your kind," she hissed at him.

"You aren't my kind," he spat back. "And they are traitors to their kind for not seeing it. With you gone, we'll be free to live our lives without any of these little people interfering ever again."

"You're a fool, Thrudgey," Thianna said. Why she had ever craved the respect of giants like him was beyond her.

"Land," ordered Sydia.

"I can roast you from here," Thianna replied.

"You can't roast us all, not before your families go up in flames. Now land."

Thianna seethed with anger at the woman. Then she faced Karn.

"You tell me what to do," she said.

"Go ahead and land," he said. He saw Thianna's confusion. "Trust me on this, it will be okay."

"Ha," snorted Snorgil beside him. "You have a funny definition of 'okay,' don't you, boy?"

"Don't worry," Karn said. "This game has a few moves left."

Thianna looked into the eyes of the Norrønur boy. Giving up in a fight was never her style. But Karn didn't seem to be giving up. She remembered how he sometimes made sacrifices in a game of Thrones and Bones. I hope you know what you are doing, she thought.

She lowered the lance and guided the wyvern to the ground.

Karn and Ori stood before the broken corpse door on the earthen ramp leading down to the barrow's entrance. A little ways off, Thianna was held between Thrudgelmir and two other frost giants. Behind them, and guarding against escape, stood Sydia's remaining soldier, the three draug, and four hard-looking men who answered to Ori, or at least to his coin.

"Now, no trouble, nephew," Ori said. "The rules say you have to be the one that knocks, so I've got to free your hands."

Karn nodded. Everything rode on his being able to pull off the next few moments successfully.

"No trouble," he said. He held his wrists out. Ori stepped forward to untie the knots. Karn looked upward at the moon and its own smaller moon, both full overhead. In his mind, he whispered a short prayer to Kvir. He hoped it was true that the god of luck favored daring strategies.

"You knock three times, remember?" Ori said. "Then you enter. Cheer up, Karn. You might best Helltoppr in a sword fight."

Karn put on his most confident game face.

"I just might," he said. "Thanks for leaving me my sword, uncle. None of the draug seem to like White-storm. And I've had lots of practice with it."

Ori glanced down at the blade at Karn's side. Carefully, Karn gripped the hilt and drew the blade partially out of its sheath. The metal gleamed with a reddish-golden radiance in the moonslight. It was easy to believe it was a charmed weapon.

"Thianna says it's a special sword," Karn went on, forcing himself to sound grateful and naive. "Dwarven or elven make. It's lighter than weapons a foot shorter. And perfectly balanced."

He could see the lust in his uncle's eyes. The man had tried to pry Whitestorm from his hands before.

"Sorry, nephew," said his uncle. "The rules say you can pick up another weapon inside." He knocked Karn's hand from Whitestorm's hilt, then drew the blade.

Karn pretended to look reluctant as he allowed his uncle to take Whitestorm from him. Ori swung the blade experimentally in the air.

"Only fitting that a weapon like this be in the hands of the hauld of the farm, don't you think?" He lowered the blade and gestured at Karn with the point. "Now knock. Three times. I'd hate to impale you with your own father's sword, but I will if you try any tricks."

"No tricks," said Karn, raising his fist to knock. No *more* tricks anyway.

He knocked. Once, twice, three times.

Down the dim corridor, ghostly green balefires were lit. The sound of old bones rustling drifted up from the ground.

"Well, well, well," a dry, raspy voice called. "Welcome back."

Karn wrinkled his nose at the cloying stench of rot inside the barrow. The unnatural presence of the undead dragonship captain was acting on his nerves. But despite his fear, his mind was working fast.

He emerged from the tunnel into the round, low-ceilinged chamber. Helltoppr sat on his thronelike stone chair, still wearing his rusting armor and rotting leathers. Karn spared him only a glance, then ran his eyes around the room. He took in the swords, axes, shields, the spears and armor, the cups and dishes. All the treasures the draug had accumulated in his lifetime of warring and plundering.

"Impressive, isn't it?" Helltoppr said. "You can't take it with you, they say. Maybe that's why I refused to go. Hu, hu, hu." The After Walker laughed, dust swirling from between his rotting teeth.

With a creaking of old bones, Helltoppr levered himself to his feet. More dust fell from the draug as he strode forward. Knuckles popped as he gripped his great ax in dead hands and swung it up into the air.

Karn beamed. He saw what he'd been looking for.

"Why the smile, boy? You that eager to die?"

"Eager to win," Karn replied, meeting Helltoppr's fire-lit eyes for the first time. The green balefires burning there weren't that different from the eyes of other overconfident people Karn had faced.

"Then draw your sword," said Helltoppr, choking out another laugh. He gestured with the shaft of his ax at Karn's sheath.

Karn pulled his coat aside, showing the draug that his sheath was empty.

"I seem to have mislaid my weapon," he said. "I guess that means the fight is off."

"Off? For Neth's sake, you still can't remember the rules! If you don't come with a weapon, you are free to choose from among my hoard."

Karn looked around at the piles of treasures, deliberately casting his eyes over the more impressive swords and spears.

"Anything?" he said.

"Anything," replied the draug. "You have my oath. But be quick about it. I'm eager to bury my ax in your skull."

"No worries," said Karn. "I've already made my choice."

He strode forward to where a small table stood against the wall. Atop the table, the gleaming, golden set of Thrones and Bones that he had remembered.

"I hope you can play a decent game," said Karn. "I don't want to be too bored."

"What?" roared the draug. "That's no weapon."

"I beg to differ," said Karn. "Our stories say that a game of Thrones and Bones can be as vicious as any other battle. And you know you're not a true Norrønur unless you can swing a sword, hurl an insult, and play a game of Thrones and Bones. Are you a true Norrønur, Helltoppr?"

"None truer," growled the After Walker. "I was its greatest jarl. Why, the high kingship was almost within my grasp. I am a proper son of Norrøngard, not like these peace-loving thin-bloods that blight her snows today."

"Then what are you afraid of?" Karn gestured to the board. "Prove your heritage. Prove your worth and beat me at the game board. As many battles as you commanded, it ought to be easy for you. And I have your oath that I could choose any weapon in the barrow."

The green fires of Helltoppr's eyes flared in hatred. But then the draug's dead lips curled.

"Very well, Karn Korlundsson. I will beat you at this game, and then you will take your place as the last runestone in my longship. My collection will be complete, and so will be my revenge on the children of my enemy." He strode to the table.

"I will play the bones," he said.

"I kind of expected that."

Magnilmir was furious with himself mostly. If he'd never given Thianna the horn, none of this would have happened. He hadn't realized that it was anything important to anyone other than himself. He hadn't even realized it was more than just a drinking horn. He'd only wanted his daughter to appreciate her human heritage, and now that heritage was going to get them all killed.

He should have kept her hidden away, up at the frozen top of the world where no one could ever find her. But Thianna deserved a bigger life than his small world afforded. He flexed his great muscles and again tried the ropes binding his wrists.

"Will you hold still?" fussed a voice behind him. "How do you expect me to untie you if you don't quit moving about? I'll knock your great, shaggy head with my hammer if you pinch my fingers, I will."

"Is someone there?" Magnilmir asked, or tried to. His voice was terribly muffled by the gag on his mouth. There was a rustling at his neck and suddenly the gag came free.

"Thank you," he said. "I said, Is someone there?"

"Well, of course there's someone here, you big lug," said the voice. "Else who do you think ungagged you? And I had to stand on tiptoes to do it. I've been keeping an eye on Sydia since she showed up in Bense. Yes, you can thank me profusely for my foresight later. Now shut up and don't make me regret freeing your mouth first."

Magnilmir smiled. He knew who his rescuer was. The line about tiptoes was what had done it. "It's good to see you too, Gindri, my friend," he said.

"Well, let's wait and see how good *it* is when I've untied the others," the wandering dwarf handyman replied. "But I'd say *it* has a chance of getting better."

Karn faced the rotting After Walker across the board. He was perched on the edge of a wooden chair he'd dragged over along with the table, while the draug sat reclined upon his throne. Helltoppr's dead face gave nothing away, but the green balefires of his eyes burned low. The chamber was darker, the flickering light casting unnerving shadows. That was the point, Karn knew, to scare him and throw him off his game. Knowing the strategy didn't make it any easier. The scaring part was working.

Worse, Helltoppr was proving to be a challenging opponent. Karn thought he might be the toughest he had ever faced. Of course, he had never played for his life before.

Helltoppr played with confidence. He didn't hesitate when it was his turn. His bony fingers snatched at pieces the instant Karn completed his own moves.

When it was Karn's turn, he could hardly concentrate on his next move.

"Come on, boy. Hurry it up," Helltoppr snapped if Karn wasn't ready instantly. Harassing your opponent like this was bad form. Just what Karn expected from the draug. And it had the desired effect. Karn was on edge, and he made hasty decisions.

One by one, Helltoppr was removing Karn's shield maidens, stripping him of his defenders. Karn felt a bead of cold sweat form on his temple and slowly run down his cheek. Every attempt Karn made to leave the board was blocked.

Helltoppr played to box Karn's Jarl in. The attacker's side had nearly twice as many draug as Karn had shield maidens. Helltoppr wasn't afraid to sacrifice his own for an advantage. Karn suspected that had been true in life too. You could tell a lot about a Norrønur from his game. Here, Karn was desperate to get his Jarl off the board, to escape. Just as he'd been desperate to leave Korlundr's Farm and the life of a hauld.

Karn wondered how much Helltoppr's game matched his personality. It must be strange being a draug playing Thrones and Bones. Helltoppr was a draug playing a draug.

That's when Karn saw it. Helltoppr was reluctant to move the Black Draug out of the protection of the Barrows. Once or twice his hand strayed above it, only to settle on some other move with one of his minions. It was a revelation. Helltoppr identified with the Black Draug playing piece in a way that Karn did not feel about his own Jarl piece.

"All creatures behave according to their nature," Thianna had taught him. He had been assuming Helltoppr would play logically, like any player worth his salt. He hadn't expected the draug to miss opportunities for sentimental reasons. To win, Karn would have to think like his opponent.

It was his turn. Instead of moving, he leaned back in the chair. He forced himself to sound relaxed.

"Bet you haven't played a game like this in a hundred years," he said. "I can't imagine Snorgil could give you much of a challenge."

"It's your move, boy," the draug growled.

"What's your hurry? So anxious to get back to lurking in the dark? When are you going to play another game like this? Not with Snorgil. And I bet Rifa's even worse. Visgil, now he's a quiet one. Maybe he's a deeper thinker. Visgil give a good game?"

"Hardly," snorted Helltoppr. "Fools, all of them, but they have their uses."

"Really? That's odd. Snorgil was saying something different to me. You see, while they were chasing me all over Norrøngard, seeing the sights, enjoying the hunt, you were just hiding away in here. Sitting in your chair, alone in the dark, rotting. Snorgil doesn't seem so dumb to me."

"They do my bidding. They always have. Why should I exhaust myself when I have followers?"

"Oh, no reason. Especially if you're afraid to go out—"

"Afraid?" the dead dragonship captain roared. "Watch your tongue, boy, or you might lose it."

"I guess you still have nerves," Karn taunted, "because I just hit one. So that's it, is it? Snorgil and friends get to have all the fun, while you hide under the ground."

"Nonsense." Helltoppr's hand strayed from the board, hovered over the handle of his ax. Karn wondered if he'd pushed too far. He made a show of studying the board.

Karn moved a shield maiden away from a barrow mound, clearing a path to Karn's Jarl right in front of Helltoppr's Black Draug. Karn waved at the obvious play.

"They say you can tell a lot about a person by the way they game. I say you're as afraid to leave your barrow as you are to bring your Black Draug into the game."

The balefires in Helltoppr's eyes flared. Then Helltoppr's hand snatched the Black Draug and slid it out of its protective barrow and across the board.

"What does that tell you now, boy?" the draug said.

It tells me I'm right, Karn thought.

However, Karn might have bitten off more than he could chew. Helltoppr wielded the Black Draug expertly. He used its special abilities to carve through Karn's defenders, capturing them turn by turn. Karn was losing, and fast. Helltoppr barked out an exaggerated laugh.

"You've woken a sleeping dragon, boy."

It was an unfortunate choice of words on the draug's part.

Karn put his hands on either side of the board and stood up. He forced himself to lean across the table, right into Helltoppr's face.

"So what?" he said. "I've already woken one dragon earlier this week."

Karn moved a shield maiden across the board, capturing one of Helltoppr's draug and threatening the black one too.

Karn sat down. He was counting on Helltoppr buying his bluff.

Sure enough, the After Walker's moves began coming even faster and faster. Karn's side was whittled away. But his strategy was working. The draug was going for the immediate takedowns, not playing the long game.

Then it was almost over. Karn saw how Helltoppr could win in two more turns. But if he were angry enough, if he were short-sighted . . .

Karn switched his strategy. He had been playing as though escape was all that mattered. Now he knew that some things mattered more. Escape wasn't the only way to win. He deliberately placed a shield maiden in harm's way. It was bait. The draug snatched the maiden from the board in triumph. Misguided triumph. In doing so he exposed the Black Draug.

Karn slid his Jarl across the table, pinning the Black Draug between two pieces. He plucked it from the board. It was done. He had won.

"Game over," he said.

"What?" roared Helltoppr.

Karn showed him the Black Draug in his palm.

"I won. I beat you."

Helltoppr snatched the piece from his palm. The dragonship captain just stared at it as if he couldn't believe what Karn had done.

"Now let my father go," Karn said. Green flames

turned his way. "That's the prize I choose. Just like the rules say. Let my father go. Let them all go."

But the draug did no such thing. Instead, he reached out and grabbed his ax. He hefted it up, held it suspended over the board. Then he sat in his chair. He set his ax down wearily, leaning it against the cold stone seat.

"Fine. It's done," he said, waving his hand dismissively. "Go now."

"Done?" asked Karn, uncertain.

"Yes, done. Done and done. Go now and see."

Karn nodded. Without turning his back to the creature, he made his way to the exit.

"Karn," the draug called to him as he entered the tunnel. His voice sounded plaintive. "You're right. What you said. It has been a while since I've faced a worthy opponent. I may not like the sting of defeat, but a barrow grave can be a dull place, and even a sting has the thrill of life and challenge about it. A good game is perhaps better than a sure outcome. And by my oath, you played a good game."

Karn nodded at the draug. Then he walked out the door and into the world above.

CHAPTER EIGHTEEN

The Battle

There was no sign of Ori or the others. Karn realized that a Thrones and Bones game took considerably longer than a sword fight. Maybe they had assumed he lost and had left. But he hadn't lost. He climbed up the ramp from the barrow and looked around.

The runestones stood unmoving in the night air. They hadn't changed. His father was still stone.

He had really believed he could bring Korlundr back. Had Helltoppr broken his word? Had Karn misunderstood the curse?

Eyes shut, Karn leaned forward and rested his forehead against the cold stone. Only, the stone wasn't cold. It was heating up, right under his forehead. He pulled his head away and opened his eyes.

Colors were forming on the carvings in the gray stone surface. Then the larger runestone began to crack. The image of his father grew more realistic, the crude representation gaining depth and color.

Suddenly, the runestone burst into grains of dust. A wind blew up from nowhere, whipping the dust away. When it dispersed, Korlundr stood blinking in the moonslight.

"Father!" shouted Karn, throwing himself at Korlundr.

"Karn!" Kornlundr hugged his son to his chest. "What happened? Where is Helltoppr?"

"You were turned to stone. You were turned to stone, and I thought you were dead. But I beat Helltoppr, Father. I beat him and made him give you back."

"Stone? You beat him?" said his father, incredulous.

"A runestone," said Karn. "Like them."

He pointed to the other stones of the longship, but they were also bursting apart and crumbling. The strange wind blew again, and a group of some dozen or so men and women found themselves released from their standing stones.

"What is going on?" demanded a burly Norrønur who could easily have been one of Helltoppr's raiders over a century ago.

"That is going to take some explaining," Karn began.

"My son has rescued you," his father interrupted them. "He faced down Helltoppr and freed you all." Korlundr leaned over and whispered in Karn's ear. "When we get

273

home, you're going to have to tell me how you managed that."

Karn nodded, still tingling with relief at having rescued his father. Then thoughts of home triggered a new worry.

"Father, it was Uncle Ori. He tricked us so he could have the farm."

"Ori," said Korlundr, his eyes narrowing.

"There's no time. He has help. And they have Nyra."

"Nyra?"

"And Thianna. I owe her my life. We have to help her."

Karn turned to the newly freed souls, who were clustering around them.

"We are in your debt," said the burly man who had picked up on the tail end of their conversation. "You say you need help now?"

Karn smiled.

"I have a friend in trouble," he said, raising his voice. "She needs rescuing. As does her family. And I have a traitorous uncle that needs catching, and some other villains as well."

"I don't understand," said a woman who held a mean-looking ax.

"What's to understand?" said the burly man. "There's fighting to be done and payback to dish out." He spoke to Karn again. "Lead on, boy. We'll follow." There were grunts of assent all around. They were Norrønir, every one. They understood obligation, they understood payback, and after decades frozen in stone, they were eager for some righteous action.

"Come on," Karn said, leading them down the barrow and toward the woods. "I'll explain on the way."

Thianna stood atop Dragon's Dance with her head bowed. Karn had gone into the barrow, and he hadn't come out. She couldn't bear to admit it, but he wouldn't ever come out again. He had told her that it would be all right, that the game wasn't over. It clearly was.

Karn was gone, and Sydia had the horn. Ori had ordered Rifa to hand it over once he saw that his nephew had been "dealt with." Even so, the leader and her remaining soldier, furious when they discovered their third member had fallen, planned to drag Thianna back with them to face "justice."

The two women packed up their camp quickly. Karn's treacherous uncle Ori stood waiting, clearly expecting something. Thianna was disgusted, but not surprised, when she saw a bag of coins change hands.

Thrudgelmir stood by gloating the whole time. She thought the giant was even worse than Ori. Ori betrayed his own kind for money. Thrudgelmir received no reward for his betrayal, except to fan the fires of his hatred.

Sydia addressed Thianna.

"We are ready to go," she said. "Any trouble, and we'll drop you off halfway."

"That means from way up high," said her companion, stating the obvious.

They shoved Thianna toward a wyvern. This time she'd be tied down across it, the beast led by a rope tied to one of the other mounts. They were taking no chances.

"Hold out your wrists," Sydia said, preparing to bind Thianna's hands.

Thianna hesitated. It galled her, to have come so far.

"Do as you are ordered," the other woman said, bringing her flame lance to bear.

"Never been much good at that," Thianna said, refusing to show fear.

Just then, the hair-raising shouts of Norrønir war cries broke from the forest. A band of strange men and women burst from the shadows. They waved swords, spears, axes. They were racing up the hill.

"Who in the world?" exclaimed Sydia's soldier.

"No matter," her leader replied. She aimed her lance at the newcomers. "They'll burn easily enough with all that hair."

Thianna kicked with the sole of her boot, knocking the lance from Sydia's grasp. The other woman snarled and drew her sword. Thianna raised bare fists.

Magnilmir and Eggthoda leapt out from behind the standing stones. They swung huge clubs—the dragon-headed tent gables they had snapped apart.

One stone club cracked the soldier on the head, and she went down. Sydia fared better, but she was being driven back by swings of the giants' clubs. Thianna took the opportunity to bend down and relieve the fallen soldier of her sword. She was delighted to see that in addition to her newer blade, she also carried the ancient spatha Thianna had found beneath the coliseum. Thianna straightened up, gripping a sword in each hand. It felt very right.

Ori and his thugs charged her, but then a second group burst from behind the wattle-and-daub hut.

"Karn!" Thianna yelled in relief. Beside him she saw his father and a group of Norrønir she didn't recognize.

She pointed a sword at the first group of strangers.

"These with you too?" she asked.

"They insisted on coming when I told them about all the fun." He smiled back.

Karn had split the Norrønir into two groups. The first had provided the noisy distraction, allowing the second group to scale the hill in secret from the opposite direction. It was a good strategy, reflected Thianna, but then she expected nothing less from a skilled Thrones and Bones player.

Then Ori's thugs met Karn's warriors and the fighting was all around them. Swords and axes and spears and lances swung to and fro. Shouts and battle cries rang in the night.

A club whistled in the air over Thianna's head. She ducked and spun, and found Thrudgelmir towering over her.

"I was a fool to think humans could fix my problems," he said. "Now I'm going to get rid of you myself."

Beside him, the two other traitorous giants moved to surround her, but Magnilmir and Eggthoda charged them. It was three against three.

Thrudgelmir came at her fast, his great club swinging, chasing her back. One blow from it would end her.

She never gave it time. Instead, she dove between his legs. Then she flipped around and kicked with both feet to the backs of his knees. Over he went.

"How many times, Thrudgey, will you fall for that trick?"

He never got a chance to answer. Gindri brought down his hammer on Thrudgelmir's head with all the force of an arm used to pounding metals on dwarven anvils. Thrudgey's eyes rolled up in his head and he was out cold.

"Thanks," Thianna told the dwarf.

"My pleasure," Gindri replied.

Then it was back into the fray. She knocked aside a few of Ori's men and raced to help her father and Eggthoda. They didn't need it. The younger giants were hard-pressed to hold their own against the more experienced adults, and Gindri ran among all their legs, smashing his hammer mercilessly into their feet. Karn's sister lobbed rocks at their opponents with wild abandon.

Elsewhere, Karn saw that Korlundr had found a weapon. Even without a magic blade, he was more than a match for the thugs facing him. They didn't last long.

Karn still hadn't found a weapon, but now his uncle ran at him, drawing Korlundr's own sword and howling.

"You should have stayed away! I told you, Karn!" he yelled. "I don't like to lose. You've made me lose, boy. But I won't go alone."

He swung Whitestorm wildly, driving Karn down the hill. The sword missed Karn and took a chunk from a tent gable. Karn stumbled past stone dragons as he sought to avoid Ori's blows.

Karn knew in moments he'd be pinned against the low stone wall, a bad position when facing an uphill attacker. But Ori's anger was making his uncle move too fast, swing too wild. Ori was off-balance. It turned his uphill advantage into a disadvantage. Karn waited for a particularly wild swing, then stepped in close, grabbed Ori's shirt, and then deliberately fell back.

Karn hit the hill and rolled, a move he'd learned from the giantess. They went over, and over again.

He came up on top.

He planted his fist hard in his uncle's nose.

Ori yelped and dropped Whitestorm.

Karn snatched the sword and jumped clear of his uncle's grasping arms.

Ori looked around desperately for his hired muscle. His face fell as he realized he was alone.

"Karn," he said, his voice taking on a pleading edge. "My dear nephew."

"Don't 'dear nephew' me," Karn replied.

"Come now, surely you understand? All that talk of the unfairness of my birth on the road to Bense. Mere seconds kept me from being firstborn instead of my twin. You know I had no choice. I couldn't be expected to strike out on my own without all the workers I've become accustomed to. Just me and a few hirelings. Why, I'd have to actually . . . farm."

"You tried to murder my father. To murder me."

"But I didn't, did I? Here you are. And look at you. How much more resourceful and responsible you are. All's well that ends well, isn't it? Couldn't you just look the other way while I nip off? You couldn't hurt your uncle, could you?"

Karn hesitated. He felt the weight of Whitestorm in his hand. He wanted to swing it now, but how could he take vengeance against an unarmed man kneeling on the ground at his feet?

"I'm no farmer, Karn, we both know that. I really couldn't stand all that . . . dirt."

Suddenly Ori's hand came up as he flung a clump of ice-encrusted mud in Karn's face. Momentarily blinded, Karn raised his free hand to wipe his eyes. Ori shot to his feet and raced down the hill. Gripping Whitestorm's hilt firmly, Karn plunged into the woods after his traitorous uncle.

Thianna was taller than the largest of Ori's men. Her time facing hardship and danger on the run had toughened her. She knocked them aside like snowmen as she sought out Sydia in the chaos.

The foreign soldier saw Thianna coming for her, and her eyes narrowed. Everywhere, Sydia's falling allies were being beaten back. Thianna could see her appraising the situation. The battle here was lost. But it had never really been her battle.

Thianna watched the woman grip Talaria's horn where it lay on a sling at her side. She had what she had come for. Sydia turned and fled the battle, racing to her mount where it waited beside the cabin.

Thianna charged after her. If Sydia took the horn, it had all been for nothing.

Sydia leapt into the saddle. The wyvern beat its wings once. The sudden gust of swirling snow and the rush of air drove Thianna back. When she dropped her hand from her eyes, she saw that the wyvern had taken to the sky. Her heart sank.

Standing a little way off and pawing impatiently at the frozen earth stood the beast Thianna had ridden. It cocked its head at her expectantly.

My orders going forward are a little unclear, it spoke into her mind.

"Speak your meaning," Thianna asked aloud. The wyvern twitched its wings, obviously irritated.

She has the horn. She means to flee this country. I was told to bring you here, but I wasn't told what to do next.

"You mean that I can order you to follow her? She hasn't given you any instructions that would prevent you from helping me?"

Praise the day! She's not too thick-skulled to understand.

"No need to be sarcastic," replied Thianna, approaching the creature and reaching for the saddle. She hauled herself onto its back, hooked her feet into the stirrups. "No time for it either. Let's go."

My thoughts exactly.

With a triumphant screech, the wyvern burst into the sky.

 CHAPTER NINETEEN

Checkmate

Ori led Karn on a swift chase. It was hard to see his uncle in the dark woods, but it wasn't hard to follow him. Ori made as much noise as a bear, if a bear were panting and whimpering. Plus, Karn thought he knew exactly where Ori was headed. He stayed on his uncle's trail, holding Whitestorm out in front of him.

Karn feared letting Ori reach the barrow, but he was having difficulty closing the distance. He had already exerted himself considerably that day, whereas Ori had largely been watching others fight. Karn could get close to him, but not close enough to catch him.

They broke from the woods into the moonslit glade. As he had guessed, Ori was heading straight for Helltoppr's

Barrow. Karn's feet pounded the ground as he put everything he had into gaining on his uncle.

Karn jumped for Ori, his fingers brushing his uncle's coat just as they reached the entrance to the barrow.

In desperation, Ori pounded on the door.

"Helltoppr, get out here!" he shouted. He cast a panicked look at his nephew. Karn steeled himself and tightened his grip on Whitestorm.

"Come away, uncle," said Karn, lowering the tip of the sword to point at Ori.

"For Neth's sake, Helltoppr," his uncle pleaded. "Pry your bones off of that chair and come help me." He looked at Karn with eyes that gleamed with fear and anger both. "I've brought Karn to you. Come and get the meddlesome boy."

From inside the barrow chamber, the green glow of the balefire swelled. Karn heard the rustle of old bones and rusted armor. Helltoppr was coming.

He backed up a step, only to feel a bony hand close on his shoulder.

"Oh, I think you'll want to be here for this," Snorgil said in Karn's ear. He looked at the draug, surprised to see Snorgil's attention focused on Ori, even as his hand held Karn firmly in place.

Rifa appeared on his other side, a wide grin under his perpetually shattered nose. He too was staring at Ori with anticipation. A rustle behind him let Karn know that Visgil had completed the triangle that pinned him in.

From the barrow, Helltoppr emerged, his great ax in his hand.

"It's about time," Ori snapped. "The boy almost had me. If your incompetent After Walkers had done their jobs properly, I wouldn't have had to lead him all the way here myself. *Twice.*"

Helltoppr said nothing. Karn noticed that just like his minions, the undead dragonship captain's gaze fell on his uncle, not on him.

"What are you waiting for?" Ori demanded. "Get him! He's disturbed your rest, so challenge him to another fight."

"Is that true?" Helltoppr asked, finally acknowledging Karn. "Have you come to challenge me again?"

"Nothing doing," said Karn, "It was Uncle Ori who did the knocking."

"What?" exclaimed Ori, a look of alarm breaking out on his face. "No! I led Karn here. I brought him to you. I only knocked to get you to come out, I . . ." Ori stopped, realizing he had just admitted to knocking himself.

"I think it was three times, too," Karn added helpfully.

"Dear me, is that right?" said Helltoppr, a cruel smirk on his face. "Three times, was it?"

"What are you s-saying?" stammered Ori. "You can't mean—surely you don't? Helltoppr, we go way back. We're friends. Snorgil, Rifa, Visgil, tell him. Aren't we all friends?"

"Friends," sneered Snorgil. "What was it he just called us?"

"'Incontinent,' I think," said Rifa.

"He said, 'incompetent,' you idiot," corrected Visgil.

"Right, right," said Rifa. "Not very nice either way, though, is it?"

"What? Did I say that? I didn't mean—Look, Karn is right here. Get him."

"The boy won his battle with me tonight," Helltoppr said. "But he never would have done so if you hadn't dragged me from my grave into your sordid plans for trifling power. I fought all the jarls of Norrøngard in my day, but you can't see any farther than one measly farm. And now your petty little plots have cost me all the stones of my longship."

"This isn't how it is supposed to go," said Ori, genuinely terrified now. "I didn't know. I didn't understand."

"Oh, it's all right," said Helltoppr, laying a skeletal hand on Ori's head in something like affection. "I'm just going to have to start a new collection." His fingers tightened, gripping Ori's head like a melon. "Beginning, I think, with you."

The After Walker looked up at Karn.

"You probably won't want to stay for this next bit, boy," he said. The three draug closed in on Ori. Ori tried to shrink back, but they jostled him roughly toward the corpse door and the tunnel beyond.

"It's been fun, kid," said Snorgil. "See you around."

"I—I don't have a weapon," said Ori, looking for any excuse. "He took my sword. I can't fight you without a sword."

"Not to worry," replied Helltoppr. "I'm sure we can find you one inside. Now come along. I'm anxious to get on with positioning your runestone while the moons are still up."

Ori cried out then and tried to run, but the three draug clamped bony hands on him and shoved him below the earth.

Karn shuddered. It was a horrible fate, even if it was one that was utterly deserved. He left the barrow quickly, heading back toward Dragon's Dance. His own fate awaited him there, along with his father.

In the skies between one place and another, Thianna drove her mount in pursuit of Sydia. She knew that the woman could not be allowed to escape. Not at any cost.

What Sydia carried was a clue to Thianna's own past, a past she cared fiercely about now, after having avoided it for so long. The world was a far larger place than she had ever suspected. Gunnlod's Plateau might be the top of the world, but the top was only a tiny corner. Ignorance of her roots had cost her her home. It had almost cost the lives of her dearest family. She knew now that who she wanted to be could not be separated from who she was.

The Horn of Osius was a powerful tool of oppression.

That made Sydia and her kind bullies. Worse than bullies. Thianna had no patience for bullies of any size, from any land. She wasn't sure how Sydia's people used this horn, but if her mother had abandoned her life to free it from their clutches, that was reason enough to prevent its return.

The cold air whipped around her. Beneath, a landscape of snow gave way to alpine trees as mountains dwindled to foothills and canyon walls.

They were heading south and east, flying in mere moments over land that had taken Thianna and Karn many days to cross. Heading along roughly the same course.

One thing struck Thianna as odd.

"Why doesn't she use the horn herself?" she asked. "Couldn't she use it to stop us?"

Not without hurting her own mount, the wyvern replied. *Also, she lacks the skill.*

"There's a skill? But how did I—?"

You are your mother's child. Not that your inane pipings were in any way harmonious.

"Again with the insults. Are all wyvern as obnoxious as you?"

I'm one of the nicer ones.

"I admit, I've tangled with reptiles worse than you."

The wyvern sent back a wave of indignation, but even as she chuckled at it, Thianna thought about a particularly nasty reptile and the direction they were currently headed.

She looked at the beast under her, saw its life of sub-jugation.

"I don't like bullies," she said through clenched teeth.

What's that?

"I have an idea. Head that way." Thianna indicated a direction at a tangent to Sydia's course.

She's not heading that way, the beast complained.

"Trust me. We're cutting her off. I need to drive her just a touch north."

Thianna found she could think of a direction and the wyvern understood. There was no need to point or speak. Working together, they began to harry Sydia and her mount, forcing tiny course corrections in their flight path. By staying just south of Sydia's position, they drove the soldier north.

Thianna smiled when the ruins of Sardeth came into sight.

"Orm!" she called, yelling with her mind as well as her voice. Hopefully the magic of the horn was still in effect. "Orm, I've kept my promise."

The piles of crumbled stone stretched beneath them, still and dead as they had lain these thousand years and more. Something stirred.

Orm Hinn Langi rose from the ruins of the coli-seum. Even prepared for it, Thianna gasped at the great linnorm's enormous size. She wished she could have seen Sydia's face, but from the suddenly convulsive flapping of her mount's wings, she could imagine it.

Sydia's wyvern hung in the air, uncertain where to turn. The hesitation was the opportunity Thianna needed.

"Quickly. Pour it on."

You want me to go closer? To that thing? The consternation in her wyvern's mind was tangible. As was the fear.

"Trust me."

It's huge.

"Just get us closer to Sydia. Quickly."

To its credit, the wyvern beat its wings furiously, closing the distance.

You return, rumbled Orm in a voice like thunder in the sky. *And you bring the hateful thing.*

"Got your sword too," said Thianna. "Just give me a minute."

She pulled her feet from the stirrups, stood on the saddle.

You can't be serious, her mount said.

"Watch me."

Die well, it replied with a note of cold approval.

Thianna leapt, launching herself through the air.

For an instant, she hung in the sky.

Then she crashed into Sydia, almost knocking the woman from her perch.

The soldier recovered quickly. She shoved her elbow back, connecting painfully with Thianna's jaw.

Thianna butted her forehead into Sydia's skull in response.

The wyvern bucked, still terrified of the dragon.

Sydia tried to draw her sword, but Thianna clamped a hand on the hilt. The soldier drove her elbow back again and again, savage blows slamming into Thianna's jaw and torso.

Thianna laughed in her ear.

"Even Thrudgey hits harder than that," she said.

Thianna grabbed at the horn, yanking it so hard its strap broke. At the feel of the horn coming loose, Sydia gave up her efforts to draw her sword and twisted in the saddle. She grabbed the horn with both hands.

They fought over it in a tug-of-war while struggling to remain on the wyvern. Before them, the furious visage of Orm took up half the sky. Thianna felt the great dragon's eyes upon her. She hoped it would wait one more moment. She could feel Orm's hot breath cutting through the cold air, didn't dare risk a glance at his huge mouth, his spear-sized teeth.

Get ready, she thought, to both Orm and her mount.

"Skapa kaldr skapa kaldr skapa kaldr," she chanted. The horn in her hands suddenly crackled with hoarfrost. Sydia screamed and let it go. Burning cold was hard for the foreigner to take, but nothing to the frost giant's daughter.

With a shriek of triumph, Thianna threw the horn as hard as she could. Sydia screamed, her eyes riveted on the instrument as it tumbled in the air.

Thianna leapt from the back of the wyvern even as Sydia directed the creature into a dive.

For a third time in her life, she tumbled in open air. She watched as Sydia drove her mount after the horn, snatching it in triumph. Then the soldier's expression turned to horror as the dragon's teeth closed around her. Soldier and mount disappeared inside of Orm's mouth.

The wyvern's claws caught Thianna under the armpits and hauled her up from her deadly plunge. She hung suspended in the air, dangling before Orm's great head as the dragon chewed and swallowed. It ran an immense tongue over its lips, considering her.

"I got your sword here too, if you want it back," Thianna said, drawing the blade from its sheath. "You remember it was a loaner, right?"

Orm opened his mouth again, but not to eat. To laugh.

"Keep it," the dragon rumbled. "A gift in return for destroying the hateful thing. And for providing the best diversion I've had in centuries. Go, Thianna, as few have, with your life and my gratitude. But I will sleep now and digest this unexpected meal. So go."

Dangling in the air, Thianna chuckled. Did the dragon actually think she wanted to hang around?

 **CHAPTER TWENTY**

The Parting of the Ways

Her room seemed strangely small to her. Everything on the plateau felt small. It was odd, for a village of giants to feel small.

Thianna gazed at her bed of ice. A cold bed in a small room. Or so it seemed after so many days under the open skies, so many nights sleeping under the canopy of stars.

The giants' world, she realized, was bound in by more than the cliff and the rocks, buried by more than snow and ice.

She sighed deeply. Today was as good a day for it as any other.

Softly, she made her way into the hall and to her father's workshop. She tiptoed, without shame that she could, and paused in the doorway. She watched him at work without interrupting. His large hands could be so gentle, so clever. He was the best father in the world, not just at the top of it. Finally, she cleared her throat and spoke.

"I'm going out."

"When will you be back?" her father said.

"I don't know." She was speaking truthfully.

Magnilmir paused in his carving and set down his tools. Finally, he spoke.

"From the first time I laid eyes on you. From the moment you were born. Always, always I knew this day would come."

"I need answers," Thianna said simply.

"Beyond the ones that I can give," her father said. It was a statement, not a question. She nodded.

He stood, head bowed. Thianna heard a small noise, like the sound of fragile glass cracking. It came from the floor at Magnilmir's feet. She averted her eyes as the next tiny icicle crashed to the stone floor of the cavern and burst. She would not embarrass her father by watching as his frozen tears broke upon the ground. But she did go to him and hug him. They stayed like that awhile, father and daughter.

In the frozen caverns of the Hall of the Fallen, she said a wordless goodbye to her mother. Then she left the halls beneath the mountain and stood in the wind upon the plateau.

Eggthoda was there, waiting for her. The gruff giantess passed her a newly outfitted pack.

"I've stowed some things you may need," Eggthoda said. "Supplies, gear, and such. There are coins in there for you as well."

"Thank you," Thianna said, because saying more was painful. And then, because Eggthoda was studying her strangely, she added, "What?"

"It's nothing. Only that you seem taller."

Thianna laughed at that. Eggthoda ran a finger down Thianna's arm.

"Goose bumps," the giant marveled. "Don't tell me you feel cold?"

Thianna didn't answer, but she surprised Eggthoda by throwing herself into the giantess's arms.

Then she walked away to where the wyvern pawed at the snow. It had hung around after bringing her home. She thought maybe because it sensed she had wanted it to.

"One last ride?" she asked. The reptile inclined its head.

She climbed into its saddle and took to the sky.

They met Karn atop an insignificant hill between places that had real names. He stood apart while Thianna said goodbye to the wyvern. She felt the urge to pet its muzzle like she might a horse. She resisted. The wyvern was too intelligent and too haughty for such treatment.

"Thank you," she said. "What happens now?"

The spell that binds my kind grows weaker every year. Without the horn, we will soon throw off our yokes.

"I mean, to you?"

I have had enough of humans and their struggles. I will go away, somewhere I cannot be found or followed.

"Well, thank you."

And my thanks to you. As a parting gift, I will share this information with you, though I urge you not to make use of it. Your mother's land. It is called Thica.

Thianna gasped. Thica. She had never heard of such a place, but then, she knew little beyond Ymiria. Still, it was a start.

The wyvern flexed its wings, forcing her to step back. Then it rose into the sky.

Thianna watched as it rose into the skies, then turned to join Karn.

After the battle, they had swapped stories, so she knew what had become of Karn's uncle and he had learned of Sydia's fate. But he wanted news of the plateau, and she of the farm.

"Thrudgelmir has been banished," she said. "Gunnlod kicked him and his friends out. Thrudgelmir says they want to start their own village farther north. Keep to the old ways, rebuild the lost glory of the giants and all that nonsense."

"Good luck with that." Karn snickered. "I can't imagine Thrudgelmir being much good as a village leader."

"How about you? What about all those people released from the runestones?"

"Some of them have gone back to their families. But others, well, they were stone for a long time. A really long time. Korlundr is finding work on the farm for those who want it. He's also freed the new slaves that Ori bought."

"He seems like a good man, your father."

"Yours too."

"Oh, speaking of," said Thianna, pulling a package from her satchel. "He made you this." She passed Karn the bundle. "Open it."

Karn's eyes lit up when the contents were revealed.

"It's a new Thrones and Bones set!" he exclaimed.

"Magnilmir carved it himself. To replace the one you lost. I hope it's all right. The bone is mastodon tusk, not whalebone, and there's no silver inlay."

"It's magnificent," said Karn. "Thank him for me. Though I'll thank him myself at Dragon's Dance next spring."

"About that," said Thianna, eyes downcast. She hunched her shoulders for the first time in Karn's experience. "I won't be there."

Karn nodded. He had suspected as much.

"Come with me?" she asked.

Karn smiled sadly.

"You always wanted to see the world," she reminded him.

"And you never did."

"Yeah, well, things change."

"They do," said Karn. "I never realized how much strategy and planning goes into running the farm. It's like a great game that never ends. And it's important. My father needs me. More than I realized. And I need him."

Karn lowered his eyes after his display of emotion. "Anyway, Ori had just about run the farm into the ground. I don't want to be like him. Ever. And my folks and I, my sisters—it'll take a lot of work to straighten it out. But we can do it. I can do it. Now I know that this is where I want to be."

"Look at you," she said. "You'll make a great hauld one day."

Karn didn't answer, because he knew it was true.

"I wish you weren't leaving," he said instead.

"I know. But it's time I made a name for myself."

"Hmmm," said Karn.

"What?"

"Well, I remember Magnilmir said giants don't have last names the way we do. You'll need a last name if you're to travel among us humans. You need to pick something."

"What sort of name?"

"Something to hint at the great deeds you've done. Like Thianna Dragon's Bane or Thianna Worm Rider or something. Thianna Hornblower."

"Those are dreadful." She laughed.

"Well, how about something so you'll remember? Where you come from, I mean."

"Like what?"

Karn stared at the strange girl who had become his best friend.

"I know," he said with a smile. "Frostborn. That way, no matter how far you go, you'll always remember your first home."

"Frostborn," she repeated, rolling the word around in her mouth. "I like it."

She embraced him, a long tight hug that said more than words.

"Be healthy, Karn Korlundsson," she said at last.

"Be healthy, Thianna Frostborn, giant of a friend. I'll never forget you."

They walked away from each other then, parting for good.

Or so they thought.

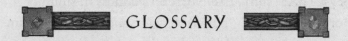

GLOSSARY

Araland (AR-uh-lund): A neighboring country to Norrøngard. Once upon a time the Norrønir raided the Aralish heavily, but now they are strong trading partners. Most Aralish have distinctive orange hair. Their men often wear dresses that they call kilts but Norrønir call dresses.

Argandfjord (AR-gand-fee-yord): The greatest of fjords, the Argandfjord marks the easternmost border of Norrøngard and separates Norrøngard and its neighbor Ymiria from the vast and inhospitable Plains of the Mastodons, where big, furry creatures dwell. And a good thing too.

Bandulfr (BEHN-dull-fur): A fisherman in the city of Bense. Despite the way he looks—and smells—he's always good for a game of Thrones and Bones.

barrow: A mound of earth over a stone burial chamber. Barrows are often full of treasure and sealed with a "corpse door" to make sure the dead stay dead. Don't go in, and hope nothing comes out.

Bense (BEN-suh): A coastal city that has become one of the main centers of trade between Norrøngard and its neighboring countries. Rowdy, smelly, dangerous, and dirty, Bense is a fine example of the best of Norrønir culture. Wearing a helmet to the dinner table is advised.

Beysa (BAY-suh): The Norrønir goddess of summer.

Bork (rhymes with "pork"): A giant, and Thianna's teammate in games of Knattleikr.

drakkar (DRACK-car): Meaning "dragonship" in the Norrønian language, drakkar are long, narrow wooden longboats. They have a shallow draft hull and can be rowed or sailed. Dragonships are built for speed, not comfort. The raiding captain of a dragonship is called a seawolf, but Norrønir don't raid anymore. Honest.

draug (drowg; the "au" sound is pronounced as in the word "sauerkraut"): An undead grave dweller who guards the wealth he or she amassed in life. Draug are vindictive and dangerous. They like nothing better than making life miserable for the living. Avoid at all costs.

Dvergrian (deh-VER-gree-un) **Mountains**: A mountain range in northern Araland. Many dwarves live there now. They say it's nice.

Eggthoda (egg-THOH-duh): A gruff giantess who helps Magnilmir and Thianna. Her hard exterior covers a hard interior. But there's a soft spot in there.

fjord (fee-yord): A long, narrow inlet of the sea formed long ago by glacial erosion. Fjords typically have steep slopes or cliffs on either side.

Franna (FRAH-nuh): Karn's mother, a strong Norrønur woman. Korlundr's Farm would fall apart without her. And don't you forget it.

freeman: A former slave who has been freed by his owner. Many freemen find work on farms.

Gindri (GHIN-dree): A dwarf, a traveling tinker and tradesman. Everybody knows him. He seems to get around. He's probably up to something.

Gordion (GOR-dee-un) **Empire**: A fallen empire that once ruled much of the continent. Gordions enjoyed gladiatorial games, worshiped strange gods, and wore funny hats, and there are still a great many Gordion ruins scattered across the lands. Many modern cities began as Gordion settlements. Reportedly, the Gordion soldiers didn't get along very well with dragons.

Gunnlod (GUN-lod): A giantess, chieftain of Gunnlod's Plateau.

Gunnlod's Plateau: A frost giant village high in the Ymirian Mountains.

hauld (howled): A farmer whose family has possessed a farm for six generations or more. This is the highest rank a person can attain in Norrøngard other than being a jarl or High King.

Helltoppr (HELL-top-per): A draug, a dragonship captain who was too greedy for treasures and revenge to stay properly dead when he was buried.

Jarl (yarl): A local chieftain.

Karn Korlundsson (karn KOHR-lund-sun): Our hero. Karn is a boy growing up on a large farm in Norrøngard but dreaming of even bigger things.

Knattleikr (nat-LIKE-er): A game played with a hard ball in which every player is equipped with a bat. It is a very rough sport and injuries are common. Play at your own risk.

Korlundr hauld Kolason (KOHR-lund-urr howled KOHL-uh-sun): Karn's father. Also called Korlundr or Korlundr Kolason. He swings a mean sword, runs a tight farm, and makes excellent cheese.

Korlundr's Farm: Karn's family farm, home to about one hundred people.

Kvir (kveer): God of luck. Sometimes pictured holding board games and acorns. Like luck itself, Kvir can be fickle. Pray you stay on his good side.

linnorm (LIN-norm): A monstrous snakelike creature, the Norrøngard equivalent of a dragon or sea serpent. Talking to them is ill-advised, but it beats being eaten by them.

Magnilmir (MAHG-neel-meer): Thianna's father, a giant. Tends to be long-winded but is gentle and kind. Also good at crafting things.

Manna (MAH-nuh): The Norrønir goddess of the moon.

mugl (MOO-gull): The term for a mound of snow, or mogul. Means "little heap" in Norrønian.

Neth (rhymes with Beth): Goddess of the underworld. All Norrønir revere her as their benefactor. Neth gave intelligence to humankind and was slain by the other gods for this offense. Her spirit was banished to a deep cavern under the earth, where all Norrønir go when they die, to be with their foster mother.

Norrøngard (NOR-ruhn-gard; the "rr" rolls a little bit; the "ø" is pronounced like the "u" sound in "further"; the "d" is soft but not quite silent): The land inhabited by humans known as Norrønir (plural) or Norrønur (singular). The people farm in the summer months and hunt and trap in the winter. At one time in their history, they were also fierce raiders of foreign lands. They've put that behind them now. Mostly.

Nyra (NEE-ray): One of Karn's older sisters. Pretty tough, but also a good sister.

Ori (OR-ee): Karn's uncle. Sarcastic and a little lazy. He is Korlundr's twin brother.

Orm Hinn Langi (orm hin LAHN-gee): Usually called Orm for short, but there's nothing short about him. This is a very large dragon, one of the most fearsome creatures in all of Norrøngard. Stay as far away as possible.

Pofnir (POFF-neer): A freeman on Korlundr's Farm who has risen to a position of some responsibility and authority. Pofnir likes to hear himself talk, and he *really* likes to tell Karn what to do. Karn enjoys their talks somewhat less.

Rifa (REEF-uh): A draug lackey who works for Helltoppr. He can transform into a horse.

Saisland (SAYZ-lund): A country near Norrøngard. A land of knights, lords, and ladies.

Sardeth (SAR-death): A ruined city, home to the dragon Orm. Once a Gordion outpost.

Serpent's Gulf: A body of water. Bense sits on its coast.

skyr (sheer): A Norrøngard treat made from milk and similar to yogurt. It has the consistency of cream cheese and is often eaten with honey and lingonberries.

Snorgil (SNORE-gill): The leader of three draug who work for Helltoppr. He can transform into a cat.

spatha (SPAH-tah): A type of sword once common in the Gordion Empire. Later Norrønir swords were modeled on this style of weapon. Norrønir know a good thing when they see it.

Stolki (STOLE-key): Proprietor of Stolki's Hall and a prominent figure in Bense.

Stolki's Hall: A tavern in Bense. Rough and rowdy but very popular. The food is fine if taste and smell aren't important to you.

Sydia (SID-ee-uh): A foreign soldier, accompanied by two unnamed soldiers in her command. She's bad news.

Talaria (tuh-LAHR-ee-uh): Thianna's mother, now deceased. She came from a faraway land, but where that is, she wouldn't say.

Thianna (thee-AH-nuh): Our heroine. Thianna is half frost giant, half human.

Thrudgelmir: (THROOD-gull-meer) A giant who bullies Thianna. Bad Thrudgey.

Trollheim (TROLL-hime): Built on ruins of an ancient

dwarven civilization, Trollheim is a city of trolls deep in the Ymirian Mountains. Few people have seen the city and returned to tell of it, as humans typically only enter as slaves or food. Trolls regard Trollheim as the greatest city in the world. It is uncertain what they base this opinion on, as they are unlikely to have much experience anywhere else.

Ungland (UNG-lund): A country near Norrøngard. Not a very friendly place.

Visgil (VISS-gill): A draug lackey who works for Helltoppr. He can transform into a bull.

Whitestorm: The sword of Korlundr hauld Kolason, later carried by Karn. Whitestorm was once a famous blade, though most of its legendary history has been forgotten.

wyvern: A winged reptile slightly larger than a horse. It has a snakelike head, a long neck, two wings, two legs, and a barbed tail. Neither proper dragons nor linnorms and not native to Norrøngard, wyverns have been known to serve as mounts, though they are surly and unpredictable creatures who have a tendency to toss their riders off while flying hundreds of feet in the air.

Ymiria (eye-MEER-ee-uh): The land north of Norrøngard, defined by the enormous mountain range known as the Ymirian Mountains. Ymiria is home to frost giants, trolls, and maybe even a few lingering goblins. The city of Trollheim and the frost giant village of Gunnlod's Plateau are among its few settlements, though ruins of older civilizations may lie buried in its snowy wastes.

Ymirian Mountains (eye-MEER-ee-un): An enormous mountain range to the north of Norrøngard, believed to be formed from the colossal body of the giant Ymir when he was struck down by the first of the Norrønir gods.

THE SONG OF HELLTOPPR
(WITH JONATHAN ANDERS)

Helltoppr his bold warriors heed:
Ship-ruler, man-slayer, he set to sea.
Ocean-proud longship that gleamed with his swords
was his storm-wrath's harbinger to lands manifold.

The lord in his house, the Jarl in his realm,
All shook in death-dread at Helltoppr's name.
For he burst from the whale-paths like Sardeth's fell-worm:
He and his swords did ravage and burn.

Helltoppr conquer'd and great grew his power,
till High King seat alone was it left to devour.
He summoned his swords—and sea-king's storm-wrath
was loosed upon the high-crown and his house.

In triumph the ship-king flashed high his blade;
and lord and Jarl his last command obeyed.
In glory the ship-king raised high his eyes;
and blood they beheld and his dismal demise.

A traitor, a thief, a man spellbound by love;
snatched from the scabbard, the dreadful sword drove.
The blade, storm of white, treacherous dart,
sharp-piercing its thrust through Helltoppr's heart.

Proud ocean-ruler, he now was brought low.
His dominion was scattered; his men were ungathered
Far from his home, the heart of Norrøn,
They earth-covered him in a barrow down.
Then piled the hoard riches upon his tomb,
lest up from death should arise his soul.

Yet night after night, when high climbs the moon,
The undead lord rises from his baleful tomb.
Beware, ye who listen, lest in black midnight,
Helltoppr, dread After Walker, should call you to fight.

Stand you your ground, and stone you may be.
Sword-failing, battle-losing, none then hears your plea.
For if you stand, you'll surely fall;
and if you fall, stand you will for now . . . and all.

RULES OF THE THRONES AND BONES BOARD GAME™

Thrones and Bones is a favorite pastime of the Nor-rønir[1], and no tavern or longhouse is complete without a set. It is a game for two players, played on a board of nine-by-nine squares. One player plays the defenders, called the Jarl's side, which is composed of the Jarl and his eight shield maidens. The other player plays the attackers, called the draug, with fifteen draug minions and a draug leader called the Black Draug.

DEFENDERS

ATTACKERS

JARL

SHIELD MAIDEN

BLACK DRAUG

DRAUG MINION

---

1 Scholars of the multiverse have noted the resemblance between Thrones and Bones and the game Hnefatafl, a board game played by the Viking peoples of the planet Earth. Whether there is some actual connection between the games of these two worlds or whether the similarity is merely a Cosmic Coincidence is a topic of long and furious debate.

The Jarl begins the game on the center square, called the Throne. His eight shield maidens are placed in a cross shape around him (on the two squares above, below, right, and left). The fifteen draug and the Black Draug are placed in the four T-shaped areas along the edges of the board. These areas are called the Barrow Mounds. The Black Draug may initially be placed on any black square in the Barrow Mounds.

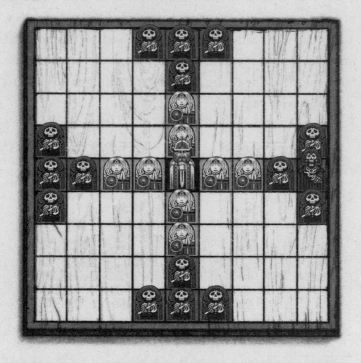

The objective for the Jarl's side is to move the Jarl to any square on the periphery of the board that is not in one of the Barrow Mounds. If this happens, the Jarl has escaped and the Jarl's side wins. The Jarl's side may also win if they capture the Black Draug. If this happens, the Black Draug's minions are "released" and all the attackers are removed from the board. The draug's side wins if they can capture the Jarl before he escapes.

The draug's side always makes the first move. All pieces move like a rook in chess, which is to say they may move any number of unoccupied squares along any straight line. Pieces may not move diagonally, and they may never pass over another piece.

Pieces are captured when they are sandwiched between two enemies along a row or column. A piece can also be captured if it is caught between an enemy piece and a hostile square along a row or a column. (More on hostile squares below.) However, a piece is only captured by the opposing player's move.

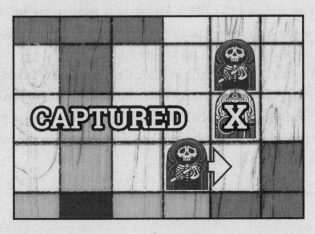

A player moving between two already positioned enemy pieces is not captured. In other words, a player cannot move his own piece into a capture.

❈ ❈ ❈

The Jarl and the Black Draug may participate in captures like any other piece. A captive piece is removed from the board and is no longer in play.

The Jarl is captured just like all other pieces, unless he is in the Throne or one of the four squares surrounding the Throne (above, below, right, and left). In order to capture the Jarl when he is in the Throne, the draug must surround him on all four sides.

In order to capture the Jarl when he is on one of the squares next to the Throne, the draug must surround him on three sides, with the unoccupied Throne on his remaining side.

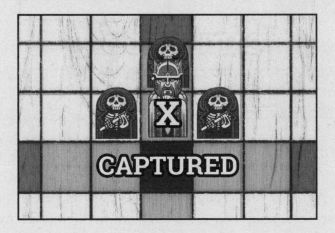

The Throne and the Barrow Mounds are restricted areas, with their own special rules. The Throne may only be occupied by the Jarl and the Black Draug. Once the Jarl has exited the Throne, he may reenter, and all pieces may pass over the Throne when it is empty (but not stop on it). However, the Throne is considered a hostile square, which means that it can stand in for one of the two pieces in a capture. The Throne is always hostile to the draug, but only hostile to the Jarl's side when it is empty. Meanwhile, the Jarl's side can never enter the Barrow Mounds, and the squares of the Barrow Mounds are always hostile to the Jarl's side, but only hostile to the draug when a Barrow Mound is completely empty of all draug.

Although the draug who are initially placed in the Barrow Mounds may move freely within their respective mound, once a draug has left its Barrow Mound it may not return, nor can it enter or pass across another Barrow Mound. The exception to this is the Black Draug. The Black Draug may reenter or pass through any of the squares of any Barrow Mound. The Black Draug may also occupy the Throne. Because of this, the Black Draug is a very special piece, with no restrictions on its movement. But it is also a very vulnerable piece, and therefore the attacking player may choose to leave it safely in the Barrow Mound for the duration of play.

In some quarters of Norrøngard, a further element of risk is introduced to the game. Players bring their own ornately carved pieces. If the Jarl's side wins by the capture of the Black Draug, the losing side forfeits all sixteen of its playing pieces. Likewise, if the Jarl is captured, that player forfeits all nine of his Jarl's-side pieces. No pieces are forfeit if the Jarl's side wins by having the Jarl escape to the edge of the board. The forfeited playing pieces are highly prized trophies in the collections of successful Thrones and Bones players. Guraldr the Gusty, Jarl of Wendholm, has a display table by his throne that is full of the playing pieces of his opponents.

ACKNOWLEDGMENTS

First and foremost, immeasurable thanks to my long-suffering family, whose love and support mean so much to me. Thanks to my former agent, Joe Monti. Joe, I'm lucky to have had you in my corner. Good luck to you in your new endeavor. You are the best! Thanks to my new agent, Barry Goldblatt, of Barry Goldblatt Literary. Thanks to my editor at Crown Books for Young Readers, the incomparable Phoebe Yeh, who has taught me so much, and to Random House Children's Books publisher Barbara Marcus. Thanks to Rachel Weinick, editorial assistant, and Alison Kolani, director of copyediting. Thanks to my amazing artist, Justin Gerard, whose work I am so privileged to have gracing the cover of this book and filling its pages, and for their design thanks also to Isabel Warren-Lynch, executive art director, and Ken Crossland, senior designer. Thanks to my cartographer Robert Lazzaretti for the amazing map of Norrøngard—Lazz, it is such fun to work on maps with you! I cannot wait to get started on the next one. And while his work doesn't appear in this volume, thanks also to my friend, artist Andrew Bosley, who has helped me to visualize more of the denizens of my fantasy world outside of Norrøngard. Enormous gratitude to Trond-Atle Farestveit for help with my Norrønian pronunciation, and to Tina Smith for facilitating same. A special thanks to my Thrones and Bones play-testers, Jonathan Anders and Joshua Anders. And to Jonathan for help with "The Song of Helltoppr." Thanks also due to my first readers: Justin Anders, Louis Anders Jr., Marsha Anders, Judith Anderson, Miles Holmes, Howard Andrew Jones, J. F. Lewis, Janet Lewis, and Max Stehr; and to my readers of earlier things, James Enge, Marjorie M. Liu, Mahesh Raj Mohan, E. C. Myers, Michael Rowley, Rene Sears, Dave Seeley, Cindi Stehr, and Bill Willingham.

Immeasurable thanks are also due to George Mann. George, this thing exists because of you, for commissioning the short story that started me writing again even if it never saw print, for offering such enthusiastic encouragement, and for providing such a great and inspiring example with your own work. I'm also deeply indebted to Mark Hodder, who went above and beyond with my earliest attempts at novel writing, and whose advice and opinions were invaluable. Thank you to my dear friend Amy Plum, whose encouragement, aid, and example are deeply appreciated. A very sincere thanks to Scott H. Andrews, publisher and editor-in-chief of *Beneath Ceaseless Skies,* for additional encouragement in the right direction. Thanks to Mike Resnick, for always-expert advice and friendship. Thanks to John Picacio, for the shoulder and the bond. And to Stephenson Crossley for the same. Thank you all. Your friendship is truly magical.

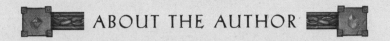

ABOUT THE AUTHOR

Lou Anders is the recipient of a Hugo Award and a Chesley Award. He has published over 500 articles and stories on science fiction and fantasy television and literature. A prolific speaker, Anders regularly attends writing conventions around the country. His research on Norse mythology turned into a love affair with Viking culture, culminating in a first visit to Norway while working on the final draft of *Frostborn,* a novel that he hopes will appeal to boys and girls equally. He and his family reside in Birmingham, Alabama. You can visit Anders online at louanders.com and ThronesandBones.com, on Facebook, on Tumblr at louanders.tumblr.com, and on Twitter at @ThronesandBones.

BONUS CONTENT

A Note from the Author

Origins of the Game

Readers' Guide

Excerpt from *Nightborn*,
Book 2 in the Thrones & Bones Series

A NOTE FROM THE AUTHOR

Frostborn is the first book in the Thrones and Bones series. It's a book for boys and girls. (I have one of each, you see.)

Now, a lot of my own heroes straddle two worlds. I'm the father of biracial children, and it's important to me that they have heroes they can look up to. So the idea of a half frost giant was born.

Enter Thianna, a twelve-year-old who feels too short at seven feet tall. Since I was already dealing with frost giants, I determined I would "go Norse." And by Thor, did I underestimate what I was in for! Those Vikings went everywhere, from North America to the Mediterranean.

As I developed the culture of my land of Norrøngard, I quickly realized that I would also need to know about their faux Celtic neighbors, their clashes with a faux Roman Empire, and how they dealt with their world's version of Slavs, Inuit, English, Germans, and on and on and on. . . . The result was a five-thousand-year history that starts with a mythological past.

Back to Thianna, child of two cultures leaving the only home she knows to step out into the wider world. Obviously she'd need to meet someone there.

How about Karn, a typical Norrønir boy? He lives on a farm, eats yogurt and cheese, dreams of faraway lands, and, like so many kids today, is a total gamer. (In his day, they don't have video games. The favorite Norrønir pastime is playing a board game called Thrones and Bones, which I invented. It is very loosely based on a historical Viking game.)

Meanwhile, my research into Norse culture and mythology has turned into a real love affair with Viking tales. After living and breathing it for over a year, I visited Norway in September 2013. I went to Bergen, Geiranger, Ålesund, and Eidfjord. I ate the Scandinavian yogurt called *skyr*, tried lingonberries, sailed the fjords, stood atop a mountain beside a glacier, and climbed upon an actual Viking burial mound. In fact, I worked on the final draft of this very book while there. It was an amazing experience, and as I gazed out at magnificent mountain peaks and saw waterfalls cascading into deep, green valleys, it was so easy to see Karn and Thianna racing across the landscape, pursued by trolls and warriors and sinister human foes. Theirs is a story about a boy and a girl who don't quite fit in where they find themselves—and how they find themselves by finding each other.

I consider it a great privilege to be able to tell my story. As the Norrønir say, "Only the deeds of heroes live on!"

Lou Anders

ORIGINS
OF THE GAME

Previously published on the Random Acts of Reading *blog*

One of the things that make my novel *Frostborn* unusual, and I hope special, is that it comes with its own set of rules explaining how to play the very same board game that one of its characters plays. Thrones and Bones is the name of the book series that begins with *Frostborn,* but it is also a popular pastime enjoyed by the people of the fictitious Norrøngard, where *Frostborn* is set.

One of the two main characters in *Frostborn* is a boy named Karn Korlundsson. Karn isn't ready for the responsibilities that life has in store for him, so he ducks them by retreating into his favorite board game, Thrones and Bones. Game play is a big part of his personality and also a big part of the plot of the novel.

The idea for Karn's game was inspired by a historical board game played by the people of medieval Scandinavia, called *hnefatafl,* a word that possibly means "board game of the fist" or "king's table." We know of *hnefatafl* from its mention in several medieval sagas, but sadly, no intact version of its rules survives. Various attempts have been made to reconstruct the rules based on moves described in tales, but there's no authoritative version.

When I started writing the book, I thought I could fake it, that a rudimentary understanding of *hnefatafl* would be enough. But I soon realized that I couldn't really write the book, or understand Karn, if I didn't understand the rules and have a working familiarity with game play.

So I set out to create Thrones and Boncs. I looked at multiple reconstructions of *hnefatafl* for inspiration, but no one rule set had what I needed. In fact, the versions are so different that even things like the size of the board aren't set in stone. You can find *hnefatafl* played on a 9 x 9, an 11 x 11, or even a 13 x 13 board of squares. So I chose a 9 x 9 board and fashioned my own rules for Thrones and Bones, which reflected aspects of various *hnefatafl* rules, without truly following any one of them. I polished this for a bit, then added some rules that served the needs of my book and its plot. The result was a game that felt like it could authentically be an alternate world's version of a Scandinavian board game, while still being what I believe is a game in its own right.

Next, I actually built a prototype wooden set so that I could play. It took some time, but the results were worth it. My son and I have played scores of games now, and we really enjoy it. We're about evenly matched too. However, neither of us are master strategy board-game players, so we needed to test my creation in a more demanding crucible. Enter my two oldest nephews, who frequently finish number one and number two in chess tournaments in their division in our home state. I took them to a coffee shop, set the board on the table, and pitted them against each other. Two hours and quite a few games later, they pronounced it sound. In fact, I was late for an appointment and had to pry it away from them. Thrones and Bones had passed its test with flying colors.

The gaming aspect of the narrative is winning a lot of fans, as is the game itself. Charioteers—the board game for *Nightborn,* the next book in the Thrones and Bones series—has already been created, crafted, and play-tested, and I'm starting to explore ideas for a third game for *Skyborn,* book three. In the meantime, why not try your hand at a game of Thrones and Bones? I've set the table. Now it's your move!

READERS' GUIDE

PRE-READING ACTIVITY

Look up information about the Vikings of northern Europe to provide some background for reading this story. Where did the Vikings live? How did they live? There are many misconceptions about Viking culture. Check this website for facts about Vikings:

history.com/news/history-lists/10-things-you-may-not-know-about-the-vikings

Look up stories from Norse mythology. Make a list of Norse gods and goddesses and their characteristics.

Check this website to get started: **viking-mythology.com**

VOCABULARY

Look up meanings for these words in the context of the story: *hauld* (p. 8), *jarl* (p. 8), *nemesis* (p. 11), *barter* (p. 16), *foxfire* (p. 104), *runes* (p. 107), and *fjord* (p. 141).

INTERNET RESOURCES

Information about games of the Norse people:

hurstwic.org/history/articles/daily_living/text/games_and_sports.htm
mnh.si.edu/vikings/learning/boardgame.html

Daily life of the Norse people:

livescience.com/32087-viking-history-facts-myths.html
hurstwic.org/history/articles/daily_living/text/Villages.htm

Weapons of the Norse people:

bbc.co.uk/history/ancient/vikings/weapons_01.shtml
topicpod.com/vikings/what_viking_weapons.html

THIANNA

A twelve-year-old who feels too short at seven feet tall. She is a child of two cultures leaving the only home she knows to step out into the wider world.

KARN

He lives on a farm, eats yogurt and cheese, dreams of faraway lands, and is a total gamer.

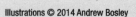

BOOK GROUP DISCUSSION QUESTIONS

❀ Compare Karn's father, Korlundr, and his uncle Ori. How are the two men similar, and how are they different? What does Ori mean when he says, "I play to win" (p. 11)? Why is Korlundr so anxious to teach Karn to barter with other traders and the giants?

❀ What does Karn learn from Gindri, the dwarf, when he plays a game with him at Bense? How does this knowledge help him later on?

❀ What is Thianna's first reaction to meeting humans? What is Karn's first reaction to meeting giants? How do their views change? Discuss Karn's thought: "To think that someone so strange and irritating had become so close to him" (p. 243). Have you had similar experiences with others in your own life?

❀ How does Karn's skill at Thrones and Bones help him when he is facing various opponents—the trader in Bense, the trolls, the draug, the linnorm, Sydia and her soldiers? What life skills does he learn from his understanding of the game?

❀ Compare Karn's skill at playing Thrones and Bones to Thianna's skill at playing Knattleikr. How are these games similar, and how are they different? What games are they similar to in our culture? How does Thianna's skill help them get out of difficult situations?

❀ Why does Thianna reject her human heritage? Why doesn't Karn want to learn about working the farm? How do their feelings early in the story affect the way they interact with others?

❀ What does Eggthoda mean when she says to Thianna: "All creatures behave according to their nature. Find out what their nature is, and you can deal safely with them" (p. 53)? Discuss how this advice helps both Thianna and Karn handle their opponents.

❀ What is the importance of the horn that Thianna's mother brought north with her? Why is Sydia looking for the horn? How does Thianna learn that she can use it for her own purposes? What are some of the unexpected consequences of Thianna's use of the horn?

❀ What does Karn mean when he says, "The playing field was everything" (p. 183)? Describe the times when Karn uses his environment to outwit an opponent.

❀ Discuss this description of Thianna: "She knew now that who she wanted to be could not be separated from who she was" (p. 287). How have Thianna and Karn's adventures throughout the story changed their own ideas about who they are, how they feel about others, and what they want their future to be?

THE COUNTRY OF NORRØNGARD

CAPITAL: Korjengard

NOTABLE SETTLEMENTS: Aarvik, Bense, Herkeby, Nilmgård, Oslendholm, Sindholm, Umsborg, Wendholm

RULER: High King

GOVERNMENT: Regional semi-independent chieftains called jarls, sworn allegiance to a high king

LANGUAGES: Norrønian, Dvergrian, Common

MAJOR RACES: Human (Norrønir), Dwarf, Elf (Svartálfar)

RELIGION: Forn Siðr ("Old Custom")

RESOURCES: Fish, lumber, livestock (cows, sheep, oxen, goats, chickens)

The wyvern and Sydia are from a distant land. Why are they in Norrøngard?

"As I developed the culture of my land of Norrøngard, I quickly realized that I would also need to know about their faux Celtic neighbors, their clashes with a faux Roman Empire, and how they dealt with their world's version of Slavs, Inuit, English, Germans, and on and on and on. . . . The result was a five-thousand-year history that could be traced to a mythological past."

—Lou Anders

YMIRIA

Trollheim

Gunnlod's Plateau

Ruins of Sardeth

Dragon's Dance

Helltoppr's Barrow

Korlundr's Farm

Bense

Plains of the Mastodons

SYDIA

Underheim

Dvergrian Mountains

pent's Gulf

Pil Meck

Doldolford

ARALAND

Widgan - On - Craine

Excerpt from
NIGHTBORN

❊

BOOK 2 IN THE
THRONES & BONES SERIES

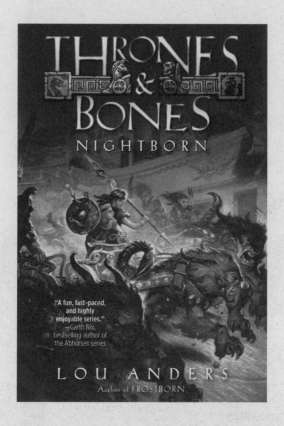

CHAPTER ONE

Dangerous Games

The outside world was the best kind of terrifying.

Small and quick, Desstra darted from shadow to shadow under the light of the moons. Her teammates crept silently through the trees on either side. She felt exposed in the open air. So vulnerable without tons of rock overhead. But the unfamiliar night sky excited her, and the smell of victory kept her focused. They could win this.

Desstra sensed a pressure against her leg and froze. The trip wire was stretched taut across her shin. An ounce more force and it would snap.

She knelt carefully. She caught the thin wire between thumb and forefinger, holding it still as she moved her leg away. Her gaze followed the line to a bent tree limb. A small cluster of spider egg sacs balanced on the branch. The sacs were the size and shape of rotten fruit. No baby spiders here. They would be filled with poison, acid, gas, or something equally nasty. Breaking the wire would send them hurling her way.

It was a crude trap, hastily constructed. The ones she'd set showed more finesse. Hard to detect, harder to disarm.

"What's the delay?" growled a voice to her right—Tanthal. Of all the dark elves who lived in the caverns of Deep Shadow, she liked him the absolute least. Couldn't he see that she had narrowly avoided a trap? Probably saw and didn't care. Tanthal was always critical of her. He was snide and superior. She hated that they were teammates, even if he was one of the two best students in the school.

Tanthal came up to her, a sneer on his pale face. She indicated the trip wire.

"We are in something of a hurry," he said.

"How very helpful of you to point out the obvious."

"If you're done wasting time here—"

"Don't get your tips in a twist," Desstra taunted, but then her own sharp ears twitched. Tanthal noticed and stopped speaking. He was arrogant but far from stupid. The Wyrdwood held worse dangers than rival classmates.

There—a shadow in the tree ahead.

Desstra's right arm whipped forward even as her left shoved Tanthal aside. He rolled gracefully and came to his feet. Then his lips parted in surprise when he saw the dart buried in the ground where he had stood.

A grunt of pain, then a dark elf dropped heavily out of the foliage. Desstra's own slender dart gleamed where it stuck in the elf's neck. He lay facedown.

"Is he—?" Tanthal began.

"Paralysis," Desstra answered. "Diluted hemlock. He'll be okay when it wears off in a few hours."

Tanthal looked as if he might kick the unfortunate elf. She pushed Tanthal aside and rolled her stricken opponent over so he wouldn't suffocate in the last of the winter snow.

"You're too soft," said Tanthal. "Leave him. We have a game to win."

He stepped over their fallen rival. Desstra gritted her teeth and followed. Tanthal was right on both counts. A stronger poison would have been within the rules. And the stakes were too high not to play to win.

Tonight was the final exam, the culmination of two years of training. The classes had been sent into the Wyrdwood and pitted against each other in a contest that would test all their skills—stealth, sabotage, speed, combat, strategy. And an ability to operate on the surface. Only the winning team would graduate and join the elite members of the Underhand, the secret order that protected the people of Deep Shadow and acted as their eyes and ears in the world above. It was the highest honor, not to be cheaply earned.

Desstra, Tanthal, and a female elf named Velsa were all that remained of their team. They slowed as they approached the enemy camp. Desstra flattened herself against the trunk of a tree and peered through its branches. She saw the black banner where it fluttered atop a spear standing alone in a glade. There was no one around. No one she could *see*. Guards would be hidden nearby, and the area would be rigged with snares and other hazards.

She caught Tanthal's eye, then pointed overhead and hoisted herself into the branches. When she was high enough, she climbed slowly out upon a limb. Balancing on her heels, she reached in her satchel for a spool of spider's silk. The thread was amazingly thin but strong as steel. Her specially treated gloves could handle the web without it sticking to her fingers. She let it spool out, dangling the web level with the banner. The wind caught it and carried it toward her target. When the line brushed the banner, it adhered instantly.

Desstra waited while her teammates readied their weapons. Then she gave a quick jerk on the spider silk, yanking the banner, spear and all, from the ground. She caught it in one hand, then leapt from the tree. Around her, three rival elves broke from cover. Time to run.

Tanthal's mace collided with one opponent's skull. The student fell, sprawling, and didn't move. But another elf was directly in front of Desstra, arms spread wide and wicked stilettos in each hand. His smile told her just how easily he expected to subdue her.

Desstra planted the spear in the snow, using it to vault

into the air. As she soared over the surprised elf, she let something fall from her satchel.

The egg sac broke at her opponent's feet, spattering a sticky fungal paste all over him. The paste swelled rapidly, turning into a nasty yellow foam that would hold him tight until it dissolved.

Desstra allowed herself a moment of pride. The object now was to get the stolen banner back to their own base camp. Her classmate Velsa would run interference for her. Desstra would carry the prize. Tanthal had balked at that—he'd wanted that honor for himself—but she was unquestionably the fastest runner in their class.

Unfortunately, the remaining opponent was almost as fast, and he outdistanced Velsa easily. Desstra skipped aside from his slashing knives. Then Velsa was there, grasping but failing to slow the rival elf. Something whipped through the air between them. Tanthal's mace. But it didn't hit anyone. What had he been aiming at?

The trip wire snapped under the force of the projectile. The bent branch hurled its cluster of egg sacs. Enemy and teammate were both showered in an explosion of choking gas. They went down together, clutching their throats and gasping.

It was all Desstra could do not to lob her own egg sac at Tanthal.

"Don't just stand there after I saved you," he said, bending to retrieve his mace. "We need to keep moving."

Desstra hesitated, reaching into her satchel. She might have an antidote for Velsa.

"Leave her," barked Tanthal. "She'd rather bear the pain now than fail to graduate due to your misplaced kindness."

Now they were two. They ran on.

"You sacrificed one of us!" Desstra spat, unable to keep the shock from her voice.

"As long as our team wins, what does it matter?" Tanthal replied. "We'll all graduate. Velsa will thank me when we do. They all will."

Desstra wasn't so sure. While it was true that every member of the winning team would automatically graduate, they would also be evaluated separately. Their individual placement in the Underhand depended on it. It occurred to Desstra that in eliminating one of their own teammates, Tanthal was improving his own chances of being given a higher-ranked position. It was a cold move but not an illegal one. One that benefited the team some but Tanthal more.

They slowed as they drew near their own base camp. Desstra had set all the traps here personally. A complex series of trip wires and hidden spikes made the area nearly impassable to anyone who didn't know the design. For Desstra, sure-footed as she was, dancing across the obstacles was child's play.

But there was a problem. Three rival students had fanned apart to block their approach. Their own guards had been overcome, though Desstra's traps still protected the camp.

"What would you say the chances are you'd let me carry that?" said Tanthal, indicating the banner.

"I'd say, 'not good,'" Desstra replied. She was suspicious of his motives. When the arrogant elf frowned, she said, "Don't ask questions when you think you won't like the answers."

"We need to get past those three. Give me the spear. I'll make sure I have their attention. When they come for me, you can navigate your traps. When you're across, I'll toss the spear to you. Unless you can't catch it."

"I can catch," she growled, though she wasn't ready to agree to his plan.

"Good, then you can run it home."

The strategy made sense. But it seemed unusually selfless of Tanthal. Desstra couldn't see a hole in it, however, so she passed the banner across.

Tanthal broke from cover.

"Looking for this?" he yelled, waving the banner back and forth in the air.

The three rival students converged on him instantly.

Desstra gave them a wide berth, swinging around to head for their base camp. They didn't spare her a glance, all eyes on the banner. If they let it slip by, their chances of graduation were over.

Desstra reached the first trip wire and leapt across.

"Desstra, catch!" came Tanthal's shout.

But that was all wrong. She wasn't anywhere near across.

She turned just in time to see the spear hurtling her

way. She caught it by instinct, not understanding why Tanthal had the plan so wrong.

All three dark elves ran straight at her. Then she saw what Tanthal had done. She had the spear. Only the spear. He had removed the black banner.

But the other team didn't know that. They were heading straight for her. She turned to run, leaping her many trip wires. But the elves in her wake didn't see the traps. They cut right across the wires, each elf snagging several.

Chaos erupted in every direction.

Gas, darts, foam, webbing. They were all engulfed, Desstra included. Her right foot was stuck fast in a vicious glue of her own design, while her left arm was wrapped in a net of spiderwebs that would take some work to untangle.

Fortunately, she had avoided setting any traps with deadly acids or poisons, but the mess she was in now was bad enough. Neither she nor her three rivals were going anywhere soon.

Tanthal chuckled as he strode casually by, nimbly picking his way across the ground. He waved the black banner at them as he passed.

"You—you—the banner—" Desstra couldn't talk. She was choking on her indignation, as well as on an unpleasant purple gas. Her eyes stung and her throat burned.

"Nothing about the rules says the banner has to stay on the spear," he laughed.

"You betrayed me!" she yelled back.

"And we won. Relax, Desstra. I just made sure you graduated."

He gave a short bow, then marched into their camp.

Desstra slumped to the ground, with nothing to do but wait for her traps to dissolve. Her opponents grumbled and cursed, but she was deaf to their complaints. She would graduate, true, but how would her evaluation go? Surely her instructors would see that she had been instrumental in the win—would have won for her team, in fact, had Tanthal not betrayed her. Stuck in the bonds of her own traps, she wasn't sure. Results were what mattered. Not excuses about what could have or should have been. One thing was clear: Tanthal had played both sides expertly, and Tanthal had won.

"I win," said Karn, sliding his Jarl off the edge of the board with a grin. "That's two barrels of fish you owe me for my one ox."

Bandulfr's hairy face loomed over the Thrones and Bones set. His bloodshot eyes studied all the pieces, looking for something to which he could object. Then he spat in defeat and sat back, a wide smile stretching open to show his many missing teeth.

"It's a fine game you play, young Karn Korlundsson," the fisherman said. "But would you make it best two out of three?"

"Wish I could," replied Karn truthfully. "But I've got

to get to the fur market to unload some arctic fox pelts. Pack up the barrels for me, will you? I'll send Pofnir along to collect them later."

Bandulfr's disappointment showed in his face. Then he leaned into Karn's own. Karn could smell the sea all over the man.

"Your father's letting you do all the trading this year, is he? Thinks parading the young hero around gets him a better deal?"

"It's time I learned," said Karn.

"And you have. And well. Too well," said Bandulfr. "But I guess the chance to haggle with a local legend takes the sting out of the hard bargains you drive, eh, boy? Not many Norrønir have done what you've done. Beat old Helltoppr in his barrow and faced down the dragon Orm in his den? Can I see it, then? Just for a moment?"

Karn sighed. Everyone wanted a glimpse.

He withdrew Whitestorm from its sheath and held the sword up. The blade had a red-gold sheen from something unusual mixed in with its steel, and it was lighter than it should be for its size. But it didn't have any fancy engraving. No magic jewels in its oval guard or round pommel; no mystic runes running down its length. It was just an ordinary spatha-style sword, actually a bit too long for him. Better suited for a taller warrior or someone mounted on horseback.

Korlundr had insisted his famous son wear the sword on this trip. Karn had to admit he was enjoying all the attention.

Everywhere he went, folks slapped his back and asked him what it had been like when his uncle had betrayed his father and sent Karn fleeing alone into the northern wastes. They wanted to hear how Karn had stood up to a dragon, how he'd faced an undead draug warrior in his barrow and restored his father to life. But mostly they wanted to hear about Thianna, the half-giant girl from the Ymirian mountain range whom Karn had met in the snows. Thianna, who had been fleeing from her own family problems and who had become his companion in adventure, then his best friend in the world. He wouldn't have survived without her.

"Was she really as big as all that?" asked Bandulfr. "What was she, this big?" He held a hand over his head.

"Bigger," replied Karn, grinning. "In every way."

He left the fisherman's stall and took the street east from the docks, heading to the fur market. Life in Norrøngard was good, but he missed the enormous girl, the excitement of having her in his life. That sort of wild adventuring belonged in the past now.

Lost in thought, Karn didn't notice the shadow falling over him until the beat of wings kicked up dust clouds and people started screaming and pointing and running away.

Sharp-taloned claws caught him under the armpits. Then, the ground falling away fast, Karn was rising into the sky.